Twelve Nights at Rotter House

Twelve Nights at Rotter House

J.W. Ocker

TURNER PUBLISHING COMPANY

Turner Publishing Company
Nashville, Tennessee

www.turnerpublishing.com

Twelve Nights at Rotter House
Copyright © 2019 J.W. Ocker. All rights reserved.

This is a work of fiction. All the characters and events portrayed in this book are either products of the author's imagination or are used fictitiously.

Cover design: M.S. Corley
Book design: Tim Holtz

Library of Congress Cataloging-in-Publication Data Upon Request

9781684423682 Paperback
9781684423699 Hardcover
9781684423705 eBook

Printed in the United States of America
10 9 8 7 6 5 4 3

To Dad

Night
One

Chapter 1

I had to get into the house.

It was towering and dark, asymmetrical and multistoried. It was so dark that it made the starless void behind it look bright, like a flaw in the dark firmament, a ragged black piece excised from the perforated navy of the night sky.

I ran up its concrete steps without pausing to take the edifice in. I knew what it looked like—like a haunted house.

At some point, its exterior had been painted a bright, sunny, annoy-the-neighbors shade of yellow, but over the centuries, where it hadn't completely peeled off in toxic shards of lead, the color that remained had aged to a pale, diseased hue. The green and maroon of its trim had darkened to a dingy black. The exterior of the house was lavishly ornamented with lacy overhangs and pointed dormers in painfully acute angles. The tall, grimy windows of its three floors were stacked atop each other in three columns, crowding the façade like links of bad costume jewelry. It was gaudy even for a Victorian. Of course, it was a Victorian. In its current condition, with plywood filling half of the windows and the lace and siding broken and covered in streaks of mold, it looked like a rotting tier cake. A godawful thing, probably even when brand new and occupied. A large picture window gaped near the top of its single, central tower, the dark square like an eye or a mouth. Atop the flat roof of the tower was the spiky metal crown of a widow's walk, an ornament for decaying royalty.

I had to get in.

3

Four shiny deadbolts marred the edge of the tall door like healed scar tissue from an old break-in. The sweat soaking my hair and the back of my shirt flashed cold as I saw the locks, and I almost dropped the large, sagging cardboard box in my hands. The porch light was off, so I scuffed my boots quickly on the concrete deck to see if there was a mat that could hide a key. Nothing. It made sense. This wasn't the kind of house that would have a welcome mat. I dropped the box onto the porch and raised my fist to knock on the door before realizing how stupid that was, knocking on the door of an abandoned house. I cupped my hands to my eyes as I smudged my nose against the window beside the door. Shreds of yellowing curtain dangled inside—dead jelly fish tentacles in a dark, silty ocean. I couldn't make out anything in there, as if the house stopped at the façade.

I dashed down the steps to the lawn, my bags flapping around me like clunky ostrich wings. I quickly slunk around to the side of the house, knowing that I had just transformed from visitor to trespasser. I sprinted to the side door, which was less ostentatious than the front one but shared with it the existential and physical qualities of being locked firm. The house towered above me—a dark sphinx, oblivious to my plight as I traced my way in a burgeoning panic around its irregular flanks. By the time I completed the entire circuit of the house and jangled three locked doors, I was huffing like an idiot who should've left his bags on the porch.

At either side of the front porch steps were large rhododendron bushes, the kind that grow everywhere but whose thick, waxy leaves and bright blossoms look tropical. These particular specimens looked mostly dead, their leaves shriveled into stiff, brown tubes. I stuck my head and shoulders through the dry, scratchy foliage of each, their sharp, twiggy branches grabbing at my bags as I dug in the dirt looking for large rocks. I found only one, about the size of my fist, so I hefted it. No key beneath, just the dark, soggy wrigglings of a pair of worms.

I stood up too fast and felt woozy, the monster silhouette against the night sky swimming quickly above me before settling back onto its foundation. I shook off the feeling and sprung up the porch steps to the door with new resolve. Everything depended on me getting into this haunted house. I raised up on my toes and stuck my fingers behind the high, ornate lintel of the door. I slid my hand across the top edge in search of a hidden key—and screamed.

I instinctually pulled my hand back in a fist, fixating on the dark gash in the meaty part of my thumb. I shoved it in my mouth, tasting blood and feeling it drip down my chin. I didn't need a porch light to know what had happened. I'd just ripped my hand open on a protruding nail or shard of wood. It hurt bad.

The haunted house got first blood.

I pulled my hand out of my mouth and wiped my chin on my shoulder. As I squeezed my injury in my other hand, I leaned against the door. It felt loose in the jamb.

I reached down and turned the textured surface of the knob with my cradled hand. It stuck firm at first, but after a few moments of slippery grappling, rotated easily. I slowly opened the unlocked door with an ominous, satisfying creak that no Foley artist could have faked.

Forgetting my lacerated hand for a minute, I picked up my box and entered the foyer, stepping from the darkness of the night into the darkness of the house.

It felt like more than a transition from out to in. My ears popped and a sense of vertigo tingled around the base of my skull. It was hard to breathe, like the air was bad. When I did finally draw a deep breath, I detected the mothy scent of dust, old wood, and rotting fabric. A few labored breaths later, I was able to muster enough air to speak through the miasma.

"Hello . . . Rotter House." Silence and darkness in response. Both thick. The kind of silence that hurts your ears. The kind of darkness that strains your eyes.

I closed the door behind me with my hip, throwing my weight against it like it was a heavy airlock hatch. At the ominous sound of the metal latch catching the jamb, I realized that I didn't feel any better now that I was inside the haunted house. And I suddenly regretted what got me here.

Chapter 2

It had taken half a glass of tawny port for me to call Emilia Garza. Not because I was afraid of the woman. She was a stranger to me. But I was calling this stranger to ask a favor—an important one.

I had envisioned myself making this call while leaning back casually in my chair and staring at the ceiling, the way rich people make deals over the phone. Instead, I was hunched over the laptop in my study like I was having trouble ordering a pizza online.

It wasn't really a study. The name it deserved was probably "home office." Sure, I was surrounded by books. But they weren't elegant leather tomes displayed in solid cherry built-ins. They were cheap paper wrapped in gaudy covers designed by a marketing department to attack the eye, and they were sitting on shelves made of Walmart pressboard. And my desk wasn't a solid, dark, polished block of important-work-happens-here. It was a cheap, beige monstrosity with popped screws that I picked up secondhand off Craigslist. I had stolen the desk chair, the one I wasn't casually leaning back in, from the kitchen table downstairs.

The first time I called Garza, I got this weird buzzing sound. It didn't even sound digital. I double-checked my notes to make sure it was the correct number. I'd pulled it off one of those generic-looking people-search websites for $9.99, so there was a good chance it was wrong and that my credit card information had been stolen. But I hadn't mistaken the digits. That left my options as either spending more eye-searing hours online looking for her actual number or trying the number again and hoping that the universe would resolve everything in my favor. Since in an infinite universe everything that could happen does happen, I chose the easy route.

Somebody picked up this time, and the first two words of the conversation went extremely well.

"Hello?" the voice said.

"Hello," I replied. "Is this Emilia Garcia?" I had practiced this conversation about twenty-five times, so naturally I flubbed it right away, misstating her last name, even though I'd written it in four-inch-high black Sharpie letters on a sheet of paper that leaned against my laptop screen in front of me like a cue card.

"This is Emilia *Garza*. Is this a goddamn telemarketer? You having trouble reading your screen?"

"No, I'm not a telemarketer." I paused. I had worse news for her than that.

"Then who are you? Why are you calling me?"

"I'm calling you because you own . . . you're the owner of Rotter House, correct?" Silence on the other end of the line.

Finally: "I own Rotterdam Mansion, yes." Shit, that was a big tell, and she had caught it right away. "Is this a goddamn ghost hunter?"

"No, no. Not at all. Not. At. All. No." I punctuated my vehemence by chopping the air in front of me, hoping, I guess, that she could sense the gesture in my voice. "I don't even believe in ghost hunters." No laugh. At least from her. A weak, weird sound tittered from my lips. I soldiered forward. "My name is Felix Allsey. I'm an author. I want to write a book about Rotter . . . dam Mansion."

"Oh. You want an interview."

"Yes, I do, but it's more than that. I'm a travel writer." It was always a rough confession. "I'm hoping it would be possible to stay at your house and write about the place."

"Travel writer."

"It's an auspicious genre. Goes back thousands of years. *The Odyssey* was travel literature."

"No, it wasn't."

"No, no it wasn't. But everybody from Charles Dickens to John Steinbeck has written travel books." I left off the why: because it was an easy addition to an established writer's bibliography. You go on vacation, you write about it, your name on the cover sells it.

"Shouldn't you be on a top-ten beach somewhere?"

"I wish," I faked a laugh. "I don't get to find the best lobster joints in New England or discover the secret to a well-lived life by island-hopping the South Pacific. My books are more . . . spooky, I guess."

More silence. I wondered what Elsa was doing right now. I'd shut the study door out of embarrassment over this call, but I should still hear her somewhere moving around or watching TV. The house was basically made of paper.

I had finished off the glass of port before Garza spoke again.

"I bought this house as an investment. I haven't even started all the work that the place needs for it to be habitable. When it's finished, I'm turning it into a historical attraction. You can tour it then—with a tour group. I'm so goddamned tired of ghost hunters contacting me. You want to traipse around in an empty house in the dark like bored teenagers? Ghost-hunt your own houses."

"I totally get that. I do. And, again, I'm not a ghost hunter. I write books about the macabre. And Rotter House does have a macabre history. One that's very interesting . . . in an interesting way." I winced. "But you know that. How else did you land a 7,000-square-foot home for $400,000?"

"Because the place is in shambles and needs about a million and a half dollars' worth of work." That was a fair point. "So you're not at all interested in the place's ghosts?"

That weird buzzing sound pierced the earpiece. I pulled the phone away from my head and looked at the screen to make sure we were still connected. "I'm sorry, can you hear me?"

"Yes."

"Uh . . . ghosts. I am interested in them . . . along with the history of the place, though. You have to admit, it's all part of the package with Rotterdam." I sped up. "See, I got this idea. I want to write a book that's never been written before. I want to stay for an extended period of time in a notoriously haunted house without leaving, without any contact with the outside world, without a team of people wandering around with me. I disappear into the house and then write about whatever I experience. You know, if I survive." I forced another laugh. I wasn't telling her the whole story of my plans for the book, but it didn't really matter—to her, at least.

"That's been done before."

"In fiction it has. That's every haunted house book on the shelves. But nobody has tried to do it for real. Not all the way. Not using the haunted house as a sensory deprivation tank and submerging themselves for a long, uninterrupted time in an environment legendary for its violent history and paranormal reputation. The nonfiction books about haunted houses are either based around short visits or they're about people who lived everyday lives in a haunted house, but that's different. They went to work and the grocery store and friends' houses. This kind of total immersion of a stranger in a strange house has never been done."

"I'll take your word for it. Skeptically. Why Rotterdam?"

"Rotterdam isn't a tourist attraction. Not yet, anyway. I couldn't do this project at a famous haunted house, say, the Winchester Mystery House. It has hundreds of people marching through it every day and a staff of like fifty. It wouldn't work. I might as well stay at Epcot. Plus, nobody has lived at Rotterdam for a very long time. What is it, a decade since somebody called Rotterdam home?"

"About that."

"If I chose an inhabited house, say, the Snedeker House. You know that one? That's the house the movie *The Haunting in Connecticut* was based on. People live there, so me moving in wouldn't change the state of the house. There would be no inciting incident. I also like that the story of Rotter House isn't mainstream. It's locally infamous, but nobody else really knows about it. Culture hasn't tamed it.

"Those are the main reasons, anyway. There are a couple minor ones, too. It's not too far from where I live. It was easy to find your number. It's a big house—I can't make tramping around a double-wide interesting. Most ghosts have more refined taste than that, anyway. They stick to mansions."

Garza didn't immediately reply. Then she said, "And when I say 'no' to this idea?"

I was ready for that one. "I'd find a different haunted house. Make that one famous."

"You think you'll make it famous? What would I do with a famous haunted house?"

"Anything you want, really. You're turning this house into a historical attraction? Well, attractions need press—and I mean press beyond the local paranormal websites."

"I'll hire a PR agent when it's ready. Buy a Facebook ad campaign. I've always wanted to commission skywriting."

This woman was kind of a bastard. "You ever hear about the Amityville Horror house?" I asked.

"Maybe."

"Last month, that house sold for $850,000. And it's a relatively small, bland Dutch Colonial. It's worth that sum because it's famous. And it's famous because somebody wrote a spooky book about it." I squinted and held up a fist as I waited for her response, hoping she didn't know the rest of the story, that Jay Anson, the author of the book *The Amityville Horror*, had come out decades later admitting his account of the famous Long Island house was put together based on zero interaction with the family that had experienced the haunting and that it was at least partially fictionalized. In fact, it was probably mostly so. I was also hoping that Garza didn't know that the Amityville Horror house sold for almost a million dollars despite its reputation, not because of it. The place was waterfront property forty minutes from Manhattan. You can put up with both demons and curious onlookers for that.

"You think you can do that for me? Make Rotterdam Mansion the next Amity Horror house?"

"Amityville. Amity was the island in *Jaws*."

"Whatever. You think you can really increase the value of my investment? What else have you written? Anything I've heard of?"

The cocktail party question. The one I hated. My eyes turned to the Walmart pressboard lining two walls. A tiny section of those gaudy A/B-tested covers were mine. I looked at the titles on each spine and chose one at random. "My biggest book was probably *The Town Without a Face*."

"Never heard of it."

"I spent a month in Sleepy Hollow, New York, and wrote about the town's obsession with Washington Irving's *The Legend of Sleepy Hollow*. The author lived there and based the story on the town. Now they can't let it go. There are plaques on all the story landmarks, a statue of the chase scene in the town square. They throw a big Halloween party every year." No response on the other end of the line. Had she not been able to check my story so easily, I would have lied and pretended I had written one of Bill Bryson's books. *"The New York Times* reviewed it. They called me 'Vincent Price with a GPS.'" That was an obfuscation. Possibly a lie. I had been reviewed for that book by *The New York Times*, but only with three sentences that basically stated that my book was out and seemed to have been professionally proofread. *The Parsippany Daily Record* was the one that gave me the nickname, and they misspelled my last name—and GPS.

"Did it sell well?"

I paused for a few seconds, and she hung up. Good for her. If I can't even lie fast in response to that question, then my sales must be miserable indeed.

I vacillated between finding the bottle of port to refill my glass or calling her right back. I really couldn't give up on this project. Couldn't afford to, really. And, honestly, despite her questions—and probably because of the port—I was starting to feel hopeful. Or I was feeling "damn it all," which is the same thing. I decided to call her back right away because the bottle was all the way in the kitchen. But she called me back first.

"Sorry about that. I was trying to look up your books on my phone and hit the wrong button. They don't get a lot of reviews on Amazon. Are you self-published?"

"No. I have a publisher. A Manhattan one. My books have made them enough money that they're always up for another." It was long-tail money, but at least somebody made money off my books. "What you're saying is true, though. I haven't found my audience yet. But listen, *The Amityville Horror* was the first book that author ever wrote. He was a complete unknown before that. It became a *New York Times* Best Seller, translated into fifteen languages, launched a movie series that hit its thirteenth sequel just last month, almost four decades after the original incident. That's a phenomenon. And a repeatable one, I believe."

"So you want to tell your twelve readers that my house is full of ghosts and hope that everybody else will want to read about it, too."

"Exactly. I mean, what do you have to lose? You don't live there, so I won't be in your way. It won't cost you anything." I tried to speak her native language. Her other native language. "That means zero investment for a possibly unlimited return."

"I don't want to attract more stupid ghost hunters."

"They're annoying, sure, but they're also very important to the economy of historic properties these days. Hell, even the White House allows ghost tours."

"That's not true."

"That's not true."

"Aren't you scared of the ghosts?"

"I hope I am. It'll be a boring book, otherwise." I fake-laughed again. "So you know all about the legends surrounding the place?"

"Of course I do. I research every element of an investment before I commit even one dollar to it."

"Do you believe in ghosts?"

"Sure, why not? I mean, not enough to let people in black sweat-shirts stomp through my house, but I'm open-minded. Whether Rotter House itself has any ghosts, I'm not so sure. I've never seen any. I think it's just the most eccentric-looking house in town, so the locals throw stories at it every generation. Some of them stick."

And that's when I knew I'd won. When she called it Rotter House. I took a celebratory sip of the empty glass in my hand and said, "Well then, not to sound like a ghost hunter, but have you ever stayed the night there?"

"No way. I don't know if it's haunted, but that place is defi-nitely goddamned spooky. Besides, my home has electricity—and a hot tub."

"Makes sense . . . wait . . . Rotter House has no electricity?"

"It's wired for it, of course, but it hasn't worked in years. Some local electrician is going to make a lot of money off me here soon. You didn't know that?"

"No. No, I did not know that." I wasn't afraid to live the seventeenth-century life in a nineteenth-century haunted mansion, but I had planned to do a whole chapter on watching haunted house movies in a haunted house. It was pretty much the idea that sparked the concept for the book. I'd already picked the list of movies: *The Legend of Hell House*, *House on Haunted Hill* (both versions), the originals of *Poltergeist* and *The Amityville Horror*, *The Others*, *Crimson Peak*, Disney's *The Haunted Mansion* and/or Universal's *The Ghost and Mr. Chicken* (in case I needed a break), and, of course, Robert Wise's *The Haunting*, the pinnacle of all haunted house cinema. Now, I'd have to do a movie marathon in advance. Binge-watch them, as the kids say. It wouldn't have quite the same impact. "How about water?"

"The water's hooked up. Smells like sulfur, though. And the pipes sound like an earthquake. How long do you want to stay in my house?"

"Thirteen nights. The book will be called *Thirteen Nights at Rotter House*."

Chapter 3

That phone call with Garza felt far away. At the time, I'd wished she'd ended it ominously. I would have been overjoyed at a "be careful in that house" that I could have included in the book. Now, bleeding in the foyer, the darkness so thick I could have been wearing a bag over my head, I'm glad it had ended with mere practical details—one of which, I thought, was that she was going to leave the key in the lock for me. She'd apparently left the door unlocked instead. Maybe she didn't want me to have a key.

No matter. I didn't need a key now that I was inside. After all, I wasn't leaving this place for thirteen straight nights. Two giant duffle bags were strapped across my shoulders, and a camping pack bent my spine forward. The three bags held all the clothes, food, and equipment I needed to get me through two weeks of total immersion.

Although I couldn't make out much of the house in the dark, I knew it decently well. I'd studied its plans. At least, its current plans. The house had undergone a series of significant and confusing renovations in the two centuries since it had been erected. Today, it was three stories, forty rooms. Enough space for at least three suicides, eight murders, two deaths of undetermined cause, four deaths of unbelievable cause, two disappearances, and it was once used as a hideout by a multiple murderer. This was going to be a blast.

I walked into the large drawing room to the left, threw my bags on the floor with the relief of a soul released from sin, and pulled out a first aid kit. Using my phone as a light, I quickly wrapped the base of my hand in gauze without even assessing the damage. The phone's battery icon showed 3 percent, but that was fine. This experience was supposed to be disconnected from the outside world. I wanted nothing that could alleviate any fears over the course of the experience. "Here. Talk in 13 nites. Luv u," I texted to Elsa before adding a heart and two ghost emojis. I waited for the "delivered" notification to pop up, which made it just in time for the screen to go black.

I slipped the dead piece of glass into the side pocket of one of my bags in exchange for a long metal flashlight. I turned it on and returned to the foyer, which ran the depth of the house to a rear mudroom and the back door. The flashlight revealed an old console table displaying years of dust and nothing else. A simple deacon's bench sat against an opposite wall, its upholstery full of holes as if tiny landmines had been set off inside. There was a hall tree missing its mirror and half of its coat hooks. Doorways on either side, most with doors long rotted from their hinges and missing, ran to a kitchen, a dining room, a parlor, a library, and other rooms. The bottom half of the walls were paneled in gray, rotting wood, and the top half was covered in wallpaper lined with small, faint chains of leafy flourishes. "Covered" isn't exactly accurate, though. Great cracks that could have been earthquake damage exposed the thin wooden slats and horsehair plaster of the walls. Large pieces of wallpaper cascaded down, dangling above the floor like the fronds of ferns. On the walls were metal sconces, most hanging by a single screw or completely upside down, and here and there mirrors riddled with shatter lines split my flashlight beam, throwing light around me. Not a bad haunted house. Classic-looking. The place needed more cobwebs, though. I paused, pulled a small blue notebook and pen out of my back pocket, and jotted down on its first page, "What's the difference between a cobweb and a spider web?" A world without Google in your hand is a hard one.

I made my way to the foot of the grand staircase, which started about twenty feet from the front door on the left side and looped up and around a long landing, its bannister a giant mahogany anaconda. The image reminded me of that scene in *Beetlejuice*, where the railing becomes a giant snake/Michael Keaton thing that attacks Catherine O'Hara and that one guy who turned out to be a pervert in real life. I shined the light up past the second-story landing, where it caught glints of polished wood and crystal chandeliers. Dust motes passed across the beam like a cloud of insect souls. I set a foot on the first step. It was wide enough to sleep on.

A board creaked somewhere in an upper story.

I stopped. The few moments of resolve I had mustered since entering this place dissipated.

I backed away from the stairs and walked cautiously among the rooms on the first floor, shining my light into corners and across walls, jumping when the moving light caused a shadow to shift unexpectedly. Half of the furniture on this floor was covered in dingy white sheets, as if somebody wanted the furniture to match the house's ghosts. And the first floor had plenty of furniture, surely bought and left by countless past residents who dared call this behemoth home. When you flee in terror, you rarely stop for the ottomans.

The place seemed uniformly colorless in the sliding circle of my flashlight beam, a combination of the layers of dust, the depth of decay, and the dimness of the night. I felt like I was in an old horror movie. Maybe *The Old Dark House* with Boris Karloff or *The Uninvited* with Ray Milland. I felt another pang of regret at the lack of electricity. An old horror movie would do me pretty good right now. "The first thing I did in this haunted house," I said out loud, composing in the moment, "was watch a hand wipe dust off the title card of Paul Leni's *The Cat and the Canary*." The old house barely echoed my statement back.

I returned to the drawing room at the front of the house. The room looked well past its drawing days. The hardwood floor had rotted into splotchy shapes as if it had contracted tree blight. It was strewn with grayish humps, a dunescape of covered furniture. A large blocky sheet near the exterior wall hid a piano, no doubt. Another must have been a small round table. A massive black marble fireplace crouched defiantly against one wall, daring anybody to light it.

I picked the shape that looked the most like a couch and ripped the sheet off to find an antique specimen, burgundy velvet cushions and gold-painted wood, and then I did the same with a modern coffee table, all tempered glass and brushed steel. I threw my cardboard box on the latter before dropping my ass onto the stiff fabric of the former.

Inside that box was enough research to make a legitimate book, even without my first person experiences. There were architectural plans, copies of newspaper stories, police reports, genealogical records, deeds, photographs, interview transcripts, coupons for Dunkin' Donuts—although I'm not sure how those got in there. All the research I would need during two weeks of no internet.

So far I'd spent more time preparing this library in a box than digging into the research itself, but that was fine. I'd scanned most of it, and I'd have plenty of time in between jump scares over the next thirteen days to really get to know the material. In haunted house stories, there's usually a scene where the new homeowners head to the local library or newspaper office to learn more about the house that they just bought because something strange has stoked their curiosity. Not in my book. Any revelations will have to come from within the house itself.

I stared at the box in the dark for a while. I needed to explore the house, needed to establish the confines of the stunt and the story, needed to know where all the bathrooms were. But something was stopping me. Maybe the same thing that had me retreat from the *Beetlejuice* staircase. I don't know exactly why I couldn't go up those steps. In my defense, stairs are always ominous. They lead into unknown spaces, and you're extremely vulnerable on them. They're often used as murder weapons in stories. It only takes one slight push. Whatever the reason, the upper floors hung heavy above me, pinning me to the first floor.

I was definitely beat. That was for sure. First nights on my trips were a lot like first chapters in the books themselves: hard to start. I would have plenty of time, though. Twelve more nights. Seemed like an eternity. Guess that's how the ghosts of Rotter House feel too. And I needed to pace myself. And right now, pacing equaled sitting on a couch in a drawing room reading about the very house in which I was rattling around inside. I had been itching to really dig into that box for a few days now anyway.

I reached into a bag and pulled out a battery-operated lantern. It looked like an old-fashioned candle-lit one, all black metal and glass, the kind ancient gravediggers use while wandering their workplaces at night or early nineteenth-century cops use at midnight murder scenes in cobblestoned back alleys. Setting it on the coffee table, I found it was marginally more effective than my flashlight.

I reached into the box and grabbed a handful of documents at random, but it took less than an hour to become bored with eye-watering printouts and blurry photos. Fortunately, also in that box were about half a dozen haunted house books, so I exchanged the documents for one of those. It was a massive paperback anthology published in the early 1990s called *The Humongous Book of Haunted Houses*. If I couldn't watch haunted house movies, I could at least read some haunted house stories. Its cover depicted a dark, castle-like edifice in which a single window glowed, revealing a blotchy silhouette of something vaguely sinister. A lone figure approached the house, obviously about to ask for shelter for the night and about to get much more than that. It was the entire reason I had picked this anthology.

I started with an M. R. James story and discovered that it was a lot easier to read a haunted house story in a haunted house than I thought it would be. Sure, part of me imagined the events in the book happening in the rooms around me, but it felt almost too meta to be genuinely scary. I continued through a story by Edith Wharton and then made it halfway through one by Joyce Carol Oates before realizing I was getting sleepy and that I still hadn't done the most important task of the night: my journal entry.

I reached into my bag and pulled out a thick book with a plain mint green cover. It was a cheap journal, from the dollar section at Target, but the pages were lined, and the book was easy enough to write in. I also had half a dozen pocket-sized notebooks, like the blue one currently bending into a curve in my back pocket, that I could carry around to jot notes in whenever I needed to.

I cracked open the journal, and before I knew it, I had filled up three pages, a respectable amount for not having done anything in this house yet. It took me a while to figure out that first line, though. The first words in this virgin journal should be something momentous—and ominous. Something Neil Armstrong-ish. And Zacherle-ish. But I didn't have anything and felt exhausted, so I started the entry with "I'm here. In Rotter House." And ended it with "I have no idea how this book will end." And then I realized that was the first line I was looking for.

As I wrote, it occurred to me that, in this moment, Rotter House felt less like a haunted house and more like a stuffy old house. My only real thought about the place was that I was glad I didn't have to spend the money to get it back into shape. I think Garza's estimate of $1.5 million is probably low if the rest of the floors are similar to the first floor. I wonder if there's asbestos floating around. I should have asked her about that.

Anyway, so far no ghosts. But that's to be expected. This isn't a one-night stand like a ghost-hunting show. My mind is more on the physical elements of the house right now, getting to know its rooms, connecting its history with the architectural spaces. Once that is fully done, I can concentrate on its spectral elements. But that shouldn't be up to me; it should be up to the ghosts. And it seems as if they're willing to let me stay here for at least one night without molesting me. Nice of them, for sure.

That reminded me.

"I've got a surprise for you," I spoke to the darkness that pressed closely around the edges of the lantern glow. I reached into the box, pulled out a severed arm, and placed it on the coffee table beside the lantern. "Recognize that?"

No answer from the house.

After a few more minutes of waiting to see if anything happened, I picked up the haunted house anthology and read until I fell asleep around 4 a.m. on an uncomfortable couch twenty feet from the front door of a three-story fifteen-bedroom mansion.

My last thought as I submerged was that I should have at least checked the upper floors for vagrants.

Night Two

Chapter 4

My sleep was exhausting. It was a deep and fast descent when it happened, but soon enough, I surfaced, submerged, and kept repeating. A couple of hours after I first fell asleep, the sun rose, although the pitch black of the drawing room grew only slightly less murky. Where the windows weren't covered in thick, musty curtains, they were patched with plywood. I kept threading in and out of consciousness. I think it was the silence in the house more than anything. No refrigerators humming or heater kicking on. Without that pulse and thrum, the place was a dead husk. It was also cold. I fell asleep in my clothes, my sleeping bag rolled up inside my camping pack about an arm's length away from where I lay on the couch.

My final surface was a gulping, terrified reflex. I didn't know where I was or what I was doing or why I wasn't in my bed with Elsa beside me. Once awake, it still took me a few moments to figure it all out.

I was in a haunted house. By myself. What the hell.

A weak light suffused the room, and I had a craving for half-cooked bacon and over-easy eggs with Tabasco sauce. I automatically reached for my phone to see exactly what time of the morning it was, before remembering the phone was dead and buried in one of my bags. I had brought an old wristwatch for this exact reason, but it was also somewhere in one my bags and I didn't feel like digging for it. I sat there staring into the dimness of the room and tried to order my thoughts. I didn't have many. Mostly, I tried to piece together the decisions that brought me to waking up in a haunted house. As I sat there in a semi-stupor, the dimness deepened, and I realized that it wasn't morning. The thought motivated me to find my watch and check the time. It was dusk.

I had apparently just crossed the finish line on a marathon of sleep—a badly run one, but a marathon nonetheless. I had slept through the rest of the night and most of the next day. I would have been ashamed at that, but really, it was the perfect way to start this project. To maximize my experiences in this haunted house, I needed to stay awake through the terrifying nights and sleep through the easier days. It was the best way to put me on edge and constantly keep me, and the reader, there. I had thought it would take me a little while to flip my diurnal cycle, but it looked like my biological clock was already adapting to the Twilight Zone.

But that was my only success of the night. I had basically done nothing on my first night in Rotter House except read a few newspaper accounts and some short stories. It was the exact same things I'd do if I'd spent the day at a library. This book would have a slow start.

I could leverage some tricks of fiction, I guess. Like go heavy on the foreshadowing. Maybe dramatize one of the past events that happened in the house. Maybe try to write something from the perspective of the house. All those tricks felt cheesy, though. And manipulative. I needed my account to be as straightforward as possible. If nothing happened or if everything happened, I couldn't have people doubting the veracity of my book. Well, that wasn't true. Doubt was fine, just not widespread enough to rise to the level of ridicule. I needed the book to sell.

I suddenly realized that my head was being a jerk. It hurt bad, like something was pressing in on my temples. I rubbed them hard and opened and closed my jaw, trying to make the pressure dissipate. I reached over to the coffee table and turned on the electric lantern. It took me a few tries.

In the blue glow of the lantern, I could see that my shirt and my hands were covered in dark smears.

I had blood all over me.

Waking up alone in a haunted house is surreal. Waking up alone and bloody in a haunted house is a nightmare.

I didn't know what to do, so I sat there, waiting for everything to dissolve around me or someone to walk out of a corner to explain everything to me.

And then I noticed the rag around my wrist.

I jumped off the couch, grabbed my flashlight and the first aid kit that was still sitting out from last night, and headed fast to the nearest sink.

I set the first aid kit on the kitchen counter and turned on the water in the large metal basin. The moan of a thousand damned souls filled the house, followed by an explosive shake of plumbing before the faucet finally shot out an inconstant stream of water that smelled like bad eggs. At least the water was clear—or clear enough in the beam of my flashlight.

The gauze I had applied the previous night with clumsy fingers had pulled down to my wrist while I slept, and I had bled everywhere. I yanked it off and then shoved both my hands and arms beneath the smelly stream of water. So much blood. I didn't even try to get the stains out of my shirt. I examined the gash I'd gotten from the front door. It was livid and long, dark and barely dry. It had almost split the meat of my thumb into two hemispheres. Borderline project-ending. Certainly a tetanus shot was in order on night fourteen. I stared at it for a few moments before re-mummifying it with gauze.

Once the bandage was wound tight enough that I could feel my heartbeat in my hand, I looked at my surroundings. The kitchen was massive. You could film a three-camera cooking show in here, complete with studio audience. As I trailed the bright disk of the flashlight beam around, the room's features flared briefly to life like I was creating them *ex nihilo*. A large black marble-topped island stood in the middle. Black cabinets the size of coffins lined every wall. A dumbwaiter's door was closed by the counter. If this haunted house was worth its reputation, there'd be a body stuffed in there. Or at least a severed head on a silver serving platter. I gently placed my fingers on the underside of the handle, took a deep breath, and then slammed the door up while simultaneously jumping three feet back. Empty. The dumbwaiter gaped expectantly.

I started to close the tiny elevator but reconsidered and left it open. Otherwise, I'd be opening that thing every time I passed it. I started checking all the cabinets, each door creaking open like its own miniature haunted house. Not much left in them—a sealed tin of peanuts, a nickel from 1955, an old wasp nest, a crushed can of Pepsi Blue. I was halfway through the motion of bringing my phone to my lips to ask Siri what year that marketing stunt happened when I remembered that my phone was a glass paperweight in one of my bags. Sighing, I scribbled the question in my notebook. Figuring I might as well make use of the cabinet space, I retrieved one of my bags from the den and threw it on the marble island with a thud of jostling metal and plastic.

In choosing the menu for my stay, I'd stuck to apocalypse food—anything a survivor could find in a vending machine after the world ended—mostly because that's what I like to eat anyway, even though Elsa hates it. But in this case specifically, it was stuff that didn't need to be refrigerated or warmed. The place had about half a dozen fireplaces, but Garza had warned me that none of them had been inspected or cleaned and were probably wildlife dens at this point. I pulled out cans of soup that I could stomach cold, beef jerky—lots and lots of beef jerky—crackers, trail mix, chocolate, cheese, cured meats, dried fruit, booze. Drunk in a haunted house was good for a whole chapter, I figured. I stuck it all in one of the cabinets except for a cylinder of peppered salami that I left out to gnaw on while I decided what to do next.

The pressure in my head wasn't going away. I was fathoms deep in the ocean. I rubbed my forehead vigorously and popped a couple of Tylenol.

Explore. I needed to explore the house room by room, death by death.

I returned to the drawing room and turned on the lantern. Dusk had dissolved into full night, and I could almost feel the oily darkness of it on my skin. I sat back on the couch and picked up the arm that had been lying on the coffee table all night. The prosthetic clanked and knocked together in my hand. A severed arm that solved a severed arm. It extended from shoulder to fingertip and was an intricate combination of polished steel and brass and burled oak. With its gears and springs and thin, spidery fingers, it looked like a steampunk work of art. But this prosthetic was vintage. I put the arm back on the table and then dove into the box of papers until I found what I was looking for: building plans.

I walked over to the round table in the corner and spread the scroll across its sheet-covered surface. I set the electric lantern on one corner of the plans and my flashlight on the other. I chewed the salami as I gazed down at the pleasantly ordered geometry of the document. At some point, Elsa had scribbled a red line through the rooms and labeled it, "escape route." There were a dozen rooms on the first floor, plus the foyer that ran the depth of the house. On one side of the foyer was the drawing room and kitchen, which had been my entire world in this house so far, then there was the formal dining room, a parlor, and a den. People had a lot of room names back when this house was built, but Rotter House outpaced all of them. My own house had a bedroom, a bathroom, and a kitchen, and then everything else was pretty much a TV room, including the bedroom and, thanks to the wonders of mobile devices, the bathroom.

On the other side of Rotter House's foyer was an equal number of rooms, including a library, a bathroom, a small dining room, and a sitting room. There was a door to the basement under the stairs.

On the second floor was another dozen rooms, this time a double row of bedrooms that lined the hall, plus a couple of bathrooms. The top floor was another warren of rooms—more bedrooms, a game room—from which a set of stairs wended up the tower. I assumed that all the secret passages and hidden rooms mandated by the local building codes for haunted mansions weren't going to be on the blueprints.

I wandered back through the kitchen to the dining room on the opposite side. A large table made from dark wood filled the room like a caged beast. No white sheet protected it, possibly none was large enough to. It was surrounded by thick chairs of the same dark wood, their seats padded in light-colored fabric of the sort susceptible to ass prints. Large, ornate cabinets held down the carpet in three of the corners. The whole arrangement made it look as if judgement was pronounced there, instead of dinners served.

But those chairs. Those stupid chairs.

A. L. Rotterdam became a multimillionaire off those chairs. Chairs, for god's sake. Not stocks. Not real estate. Not software. Chairs. He was a Prussian immigrant who fled the revolutionary uprisings of the mid-nineteenth century because he wanted to chill out somewhere. Like many of his fellow expats in the day, he'd tried to hide his heritage and Americanize his surname by cutting off some of its more Germanic syllables, but that gave him a way worse name—Rotter—although it turned out to be a great name for a haunted house. So he stuck it out as A. L. Rotterdam because he could at least hide the Abelard Leopold part.

While other American entrepreneurs of the nineteenth century were making it big on trade or mining or manufacturing, Rotterdam figured all those traders and miners and manufacturers needed to drop their butts onto something soft and sturdy, so he made chairs. Stupid chairs.

It wasn't his own revelation. The town he found himself in after he immigrated was famous for its furniture. Millions of tables and dressers and cabinets flew out of the city in its heyday, which was a long time ago. On my way to the house, I'd passed the town courthouse. On its lawn towered a twenty-foot-tall bronze wardrobe as a monument to the history and pride in craftsmanship long since beaten into the dust by IKEA and overseas labor.

Rotterdam Furniture Co. started out with Rotterdam, a carving chisel, and a foot-powered lathe. Eventually his business took off and expanded into an empire. It was like nobody had ever even considered building chairs before. Soon enough, Rotterdam's carpenter callouses faded into a pink softness from a new life of handshakes and contract signatures. After enough of those, he was ready for the mansion phase of his wealth. After all, a multimillionaire is only as good as the overwrought palace he builds to keep his toothbrush in.

And Rotterdam Mansion was a beaut of a toothbrush holder.

It doesn't hold a candle to your average Beverly Hills mansion, but in its day, news of its construction brought visitors from all over the country. He imported much of the wood from the Black Forest of his homeland. If it was metal, it probably came from Spain. Marble or glass? Italy. Stone or ceramic? Greece. It was even rumored that he bought old European gravestones to line one of the foyer walls. That sounds creepy, but in my travels, I'd come across the practice many times, always from wealthy people obsessed with Europe for one reason or another. It was often a jerk move. Sometimes it was a romantic gesture. Mostly, it was cheap building materials.

Once Rotterdam had his expensive snail shell, he filled it with art from every country on his home continent. It was as if he was crafting a European confederation of materials to make up for all the unrest he had fled. All of the furniture, of course, was custom-made right there in town, in the good old U. S. of A. We aren't ones for grand gestures of art and architecture, but we could support an ass like nobody's business.

As I said, a beaut of a toothbrush holder, even if it was just a carcass now. And I hadn't even fully explored the first floor, despite being here for almost twenty-four hours. I decided right then to do exactly that. I grabbed my flashlight and flicked off the electric lantern to save its batteries. I wasn't going to carry that thing around, anyway. Walking around lifting a lantern was asking for a spooky encounter. The flashlight, on the other hand, felt solid and modern in my palm.

In the foyer, I looked for the gravestone wall, going so far as to peek between the exposed lathes, but I didn't see it. Many of the original expensive materials had been pulled out at various points in the house's history, but the gravestones were supposed to still be there. I'd probably have to destroy the wall to see them, though. I crossed to one of the first-floor rooms I hadn't looked into yet—the library. I had grand hopes for this room— rolling ladders, metal latticework, velvet reading chairs, maybe something overall Jules Verne-themed, right off the *Nautilus*. I was planning to write a lot of notes in the library, maybe even entire chapters, even if I did have to write them longhand. The library once held one of the best book collections in the region. On Rotterdam's death, it had jumpstarted two different athenaeums.

What my flashlight revealed when I entered, though, was something more like a rural public library after a flood. I mean, I wasn't expecting it to be in good condition or full of books, but I was looking for at least a skeleton of bygone romance. Instead, metal brackets dangled off blank white walls. Wood planks that once held books were now haphazardly stacked piles of lumber in the corner. Mounds of books moldered here and there as if they had been pulped, and the distinct smell of mildew pervaded the place instead of the comforting, earthy scent of decaying leather and paper. Depressing. Nothing was getting written here.

The parlor was next, and it looked similar to the drawing room, although its fireplace was white marble. I didn't know the difference between a drawing room and a parlor, so I wrote another to-be-Googled note in my notebook, using abbreviations that I had no chance of deciphering two weeks into the future.

The other rooms on the first floor were more of the same: furniture, sheets, rot, emptiness, age, dust, memory, history— and no ghosts. As I wandered among the rooms with only a flashlight beam as a companion, I wondered if I had, on only the second night of my stay in this haunted house, cracked the secret of haunted houses. Or at least the epilogue of my book. It wasn't anything about the physical elements of old empty houses that made us feel the need to populate them with ghosts. Not their age nor their decay nor their size nor the lives they once harbored that had long since expired. Not the way they could echo a voice or fill themselves with shadow. It wasn't that they looked spooky that made us put spooks in them. Instead, it was how we felt walking through such an environment, one familiar enough for us to recognize every single element of it but alien enough for us to feel completely untethered from its reality. We feel ghost-like in these houses, so we put ghosts in them. I made it halfway to pulling my notebook out of my pocket again before I thought better of it. Two nights alone in a creepy house and I was turning into a low-rent Socrates.

Anyway, that was the first floor.

According to the blueprints, the second floor was almost all bedrooms. S-and-S rooms, a friend of mine called them, for sex and sleep. And the bedrooms of Rotter House had probably seen equal amounts of both.

And a lot of that first "S" was probably due to A. L. Rotterdam himself.

A lot of haunted house stories involve a bride at some point. For instance, the home is built by a wealthy groom for his bride as a wedding present. Invariably, the bride dies before it's finished or maybe cheats on the husband before the last brick is mortared. The husband then leaves the place to rot out of grief. The former is the story of Boldt Castle out in the Thousand Islands region of New York. The latter is, well, the lyrics to Kris Kristofferson's "Darby's Castle," I guess. But it can go the other way, too, where the husband dies before it's finished, leaving the wife with the burden and guilt of this massive project. None of those stories were even close to the story of Rotter House.

A. L. Rotterdam never married. He was more of a harem guy.

The dozen bedrooms on the second floor weren't for the off chance of a parade's worth of visitors. It was because he was a hedonist, at least sexually. That, many believed, was the real reason he built such a big house—not to hold his toothbrush, not to keep the rain off his head, not even to show off his wealth. It was simply to keep a voracious, imaginative, multiparticipant sex life private, behind walls lined with European gravestones.

The pressure at my temples hadn't really abated despite the tiny white pills I'd tossed down my throat, so I paced back and forth in the foyer a bit. It reminded me of when I'd gotten my wisdom teeth removed as a teenager. The teeth were impacted, and one of them had pinched a nerve. If I sat down for too long, the pain would start to build until it became unbearable, and the only relief came from standing up and walking around, as tiring as it was after a while. I spent the two days before the surgery alternating between exhaustion and nerve pain.

The headache seemed to get worse the closer I got to the base of the stairs.

I went back to the drawing room and tried to distract myself with research from my library in a box, but it didn't work. I headed to the kitchen and tried to chase it away with another two Tylenols and a Snickers. Seemed like dumb attempts at remedies, but I couldn't run out to the pharmacy for something stronger. One of my biggest and more legitimate fears in undertaking this project was getting sick. I always thought of it in terms of catching the flu, something that would make me so miserable that I'd have to cancel the experiment midway. It wasn't the type of experiment you could get a do-over for. Although I was amused by the idea of a ghost trying to scare me when I'm fever-weak, can't breathe through my nose, and am teetering on vomiting every hour. I get bitchy when I'm sick.

Eventually, with nothing else working, I decided to head upstairs and distract myself that way. A headache was a more powerful motivator than mere curiosity any day.

I only made it up three stair steps before I stopped.

Another board creaked somewhere above. I knew that, after more than 150 years, the house was no longer plumb and that "it's just the house settling" could easily explain the noise. But I didn't want to use that excuse. It was a harbinger of bad times, if I'd learned anything from horror movies. The board creaked again.

And then it creaked again.

And that's when I freaked out.

J. W. Ocker

For the past two nights, I had wandered the creepy first floor of this old haunted house like I was a bored security guard sleep-walking rounds, remarking on the state of the wallpaper, examining the condition of the furniture, thinking about the history of this place in the abstract, poking it with a flashlight not because I thought I'd find something interesting but because I really had nothing else to do. So far, this haunted house experience was as mundane as it could get.

And then, born on one of the cold drafts that permanently circulated through the house, something happened.

For the first time, I thought of this haunted house as not a sub-genre of storytelling, separate from the walls and floor and ceiling around me, but as a thing.

A thing I was inside of.

I was staring up into the dark maw of the stairway, knowing that I still had most of the mansion to explore, knowing that I was absolutely alone—except that maybe I wasn't. Hearing innocuous floorboard noises quickly conjured an entire phylum of demons in my head. I felt fear welling up from my stomach, icing my chest and bruising my neck, and the maw seemed as if it were extending to swallow me.

I threw myself into the corner of the foyer by the front door, wrapped my arms around my legs, and buried my head in my knees. I squeezed my eyes shut, but the thin membranes did nothing to protect me. It was like a nightmare where you try to shut out the horrors by closing your eyes, but you find out you can't because your eyes are already closed. The horrors are actually happening inside of you. And then I saw . . .

. . . a floating woman dressed in white wafting in the air above me, her face covered by a veil . . .

. . . a blood-soaked man with an ax in his hand stomping down the stairs, his face a rage of insanity . . .

36

. . . a naked body with no arms and no head dancing under the chandelier in the middle of the foyer . . .

. . . a throng of shadowy things pouring through a doorway at the far end of the house . . .

I tried to banish each image out of my mind as soon as it came, but it was replaced by the next and the next and the next. It was as if my imagination was mutinying. I wanted to flee the house, to open the door and stumble down the steps and drop into the cold, prickly grass, to breathe open air, to get as far away from the foyer and the staircase as I could, to run home to Elsa and hold onto her like a buoy in a storm. I tried to think of her, but her face decayed into gray terror. I tried to think of something innocuous, a field of dandelions in full sun, but it rotted into a corpsescape. My elementary school playground, but it filled with black-eyed children. I could hear myself whimpering as I squeezed my eyelids tight and then loose, tight and then loose, never opening them, trying to wake up from the nightmare.

And then I heard the front door open.

Chapter 5

"This is exactly how I thought I'd find you," said the first voice I'd heard in this house besides my own.

I opened my eyes and saw a figure towering over me in the doorway. I didn't respond at first. I looked around the foyer instead. Dark floor, dark walls, dark doorways, dark furniture, dark chandelier hanging from the dark ceiling. Still. Old. Inanimate. Incapable of touching me even at my most vulnerable and terrified.

"What happened?" the figure asked, extending his hand to me.

I took it and stood up slowly, feeling weak and cold and kind of euphoric, like I'd emptied my stomach after hours of gut pain. I shined my flashlight around. No ghosts. Just a perfect setting for them.

"I think I spooked myself a little." I shined my flashlight at his face. He squinted in annoyance and tried to flick the light away with one of his hands. "Welcome to Rotter House. I thought you weren't coming until tomorrow."

He shrugged.

And that's when the strangeness of the situation settled on me, enough to push my little moment of panic right out of my head. Thomas. Right here. Talking to me. Like what had happened between us never occurred, like the past year of avoiding each other was a dream from which I had just awoken.

And from the way he was standing silently there in the dark, Thomas was feeling it, too.

When I called Thomas Ruth a couple of weeks ago after a year of not talking to him, I wasn't sure how he would react—to a call from me in general but also about this project specifically. I mean, Thomas dug this kind of stuff. We'd grown up watching horror movies together. But the phone conversation had been uncomfortable at first, neither of us certain what to say, what should be said, or what to avoid saying. Finally, I broached the subject. His first comment: "Sounds like *1408*."

As we talked about the idea, Thomas seemed genuinely excited about it—until I asked him to join me. Turned out he loved the idea of a haunted house more than the reality of one. By the end of the conversation, it had become an argument, one that we never really resolved, which was why we were still having it in the foyer of an actual haunted house.

"Where are your bags?"

"In the car."

"This place doesn't have any bellhops. You should probably get them."

"I don't think I'm staying."

"But you're here already. You're a part of it now. You, me, and Rotter House." I waved my flashlight around the foyer like I was painting it into existence.

"I'm here because you're not answering your phone."

"Battery's dead. Plus that's one of the rules. I told you about those."

"I remember. *Ten Rules for Not Surviving a Haunted House* by Felix Allsey."

"Me and you in a haunted house, man. We were made for this project. We almost wrote this screenplay in college." The joking nature of our conversation was disconcerting. Despite what I was arguing for, part of me wished that Thomas would turn around and leave the house.

"Don't try nostalgia on me. I'm here. I'm tentatively thinking about joining you. Although, now that I'm here, I'm really leaning in the direction of leaving your carcass for the ghosts." He looked around, although what he was looking at without a flashlight, I had no clue.

"I really need you to do this with me." *Do I? Do I really?*

He looked at me as if I'd changed the subject on him. "Which one of these rooms is the Exposition Room?"

I led him into the drawing room. I sat on the couch and shined my flashlight on a chair-shaped hump of sheet. Thomas lowered himself delicately onto the edge of the seat without removing the white shroud. His eyes flicked toward the front door, like he wanted to make sure he didn't get too far away from it. I stuck my flashlight under my chin as if I were about to tell a scary story. "I've got two reasons why I need you here. First, a book full of dialogue will be way more interesting to read than a book full of interior monologue."

"Not to me," said Thomas, still looking at the front door. "Dialogue always sounds fake in books. It's always people either overexplaining or underexplaining. Give me solid paragraphs of description and exposition any day."

"That's very nineteenth century of you. I need to sell this to twenty-first century readers."

"No such thing." In the darkness, I could barely sense him shifting uncomfortably around in the seat. "There are no lights at all in this place? I have to listen to you by flashlight?"

"Hold on." I got up and walked over to the table in the corner and turned on the electric lantern before carrying it to the coffee table. "Better?"

"You've got blood all over you."

I looked down at my shirt, patterned with blood. It was like I was wearing camouflage for a shooting spree. I guess I hadn't changed clothes since I'd arrived. "Oh yeah, that's from this." I held up my bandaged hand so that he could see it clearly in the light. "The house bit me when I tried to get in. I think I snagged it on a nail in the door. Looks worse than it is."

"It looks like you need a transfusion."

"Nah. I'm good at making blood." I settled back into the couch and turned off my flashlight.

"Next question. Why is there an arm on the table?"

"Oh, you're going to like this." I picked up the arm and shook it so that its hand waved at Thomas, the metal and wood clanking together at the joints. "This is the arm of A. L. Rotterdam himself." I had told him the story of Rotterdam over the phone, most of it anyway. I left the more interesting parts for when we were face-to-face in the house.

"Rotterdam was a wooden robot?"

"A one-armed carpenter."

I explained to Thomas that before Rotterdam's empire took off, he had fallen against an ax blade in his workshop, suffering a deep gash in the bicep of his right arm. The wound festered, and per medical protocols at the time, the arm was amputated. Back then, it was a fifty-fifty chance of surviving the operation. But he did. And once armed, he got back on the sawhorse. He also designed his own prosthetics over the years, one of which was lying on the coffee table in front of us at that very moment.

"Rotterdam was rich enough and skilled enough to take advantage of the best in nineteenth-century engineering to make some pretty advanced prosthetics. Check this out." I grabbed a section of the bicep and twisted it a few times with the same motion I'd use to remove the cap on a gas tank. I put the arm back on the glass table, where it started jumping slowly and laboriously, like it was trying to take off into the air but was too heavy—and was an arm.

"Why does it do that?" asked Thomas.

"Well, it does *that* because it's like 150 years old and is past its warranty. What it did when it was new was a much faster, more precise version of that. It vibrated."

"Vibrated."

"For the ladies—and sometimes the men."

"A. L. Rotterdam's arm was a vibrator?"

"I told you this guy prioritized his pleasure." The arm gave one last slow hump on the glass before the counterweight stilled and the arm was once more a mere prosthetic.

"How'd you get it?"

"Borrowed it from the local historical society."

"They let you walk out with an antique?"

I shrugged. "They don't know I borrowed it. I found it in the historical society basement while I was there researching the house. It was stuck in a box on a top shelf, all dusty and forgotten. I didn't even know what it was myself until I read the paperwork it was packed with. After our haunted house adventure is over, I'll return it on the pretense of more research and they'll never know it was missing."

"Until they read the book."

"Yup."

"And why did you *borrow* it?"

"I don't know. Just felt right to have it here. A talisman, maybe. Or a visual aid." I leaned forward and lowered my voice. "Maybe to use for provoking the ghost of A. L. Rotterdam himself." I settled back into the couch. "Which brings me to the most important reason I need you on this project."

"You don't believe in ghosts," said Thomas.

It was weird to hear it spoken, like Thomas had tipped my hand to the house. I could imagine a quick camera cut from him saying those words to something, I don't know, maybe in the tower, maybe in one of the bedrooms, pulsing and alive, biding its time, waiting for those exact words to be spoken. Thomas didn't seem to feel the import. He had rolled his eyes as he said it.

"Nobody wants to read a skeptic's take on a haunted house," I said. "It would be thirteen chapters of commentary on loose plumbing and chimney drafts and pareidolia and the vagaries of the human mind."

"You don't want to come off as an asshole." Thomas wagged his finger at me as if he'd nailed my entire character motivation. "But they *will* read a haunted house book by a skeptic if that skeptic believes by the end of his stay. That's every ghost story. We love seeing a person's entire conception of the universe balled up and thrown in their face."

"Well, yeah, if the book was a novel and it was plotted out that way, sure. But this isn't fiction. There is zero chance that the next two weeks are going to change the way I fundamentally view the world. Aside from general skepticism, I've been through too many macabre situations in my work to believe otherwise. So I need somebody with me that honestly, sincerely, deeply, believes in ghosts. And that's you, my gullible, gullible friend."

Thomas laughed loudly, throwing his head back so I could see the entire white arc of his upper teeth and that one silver filling in the back. It was probably the first real laugh this house had known in a long time. I missed that laugh. "Only you could be in a situation like this," he said. And then the lingering smile died. He was still uncertain. I decided to keep talking.

"I know. I make my living doing spooky things, but I don't believe in spooky things. I'm a contradiction."

"We're all contradictions."

Because of the macabre subject matter of my books, I was sometimes asked to give talks to ghost-hunting groups or do interviews on paranormal podcasts. I'd always tell the organizer of the event or the host of the show about where I stood on the paranormal, but that usually didn't matter to them. I'd reveal it the audience right up front, too. I'd tell them that I love ghost stories and exploring abandoned buildings and cemeteries at night, that I love researching old history. Basically, I love everything about ghost-hunting . . . except for the ghost-hunting part. And then I would wholeheartedly join the inevitably scheduled ghost-hunt after the talk.

"Staying at a haunted house appeals to me on a level that has nothing to do with finding evidence of the paranormal. It's mostly an aesthetic thing. I dig spooky," I said.

"Yeah."

"More importantly, I think this book will sell well."

"I've never heard you say that about any of your books."

"And I've been right every single time. But this one, it has, I don't know, something. There's something classic about the setup, so it'll appeal to a more mainstream audience. At least I hope." I paused and then looked right at him in the blue-white nimbus of the electric lantern. "But only if you stay here with me. That's the only way this book works."

"Because you hope I'll see ghosts where you can't."

"Or what you think are ghosts, sure. You're already here, man. And you know Yvette is cool with getting a two-week break from you. We'll be like a paranormal *Odd Couple*."

Thomas sat there, looking around at the dark house beyond the edges of the lantern glow, but I knew what he was thinking. He wasn't trying to decide whether or not to stay. He'd already decided to stay, despite giving me a hard time about it. That's why he was sitting on that sheet-covered chair right now in the middle of the night instead of being in his own home in his own bed with his own wife. And it wasn't about the house—or the ghosts. He wasn't really trying to help out with the book, either. He was going to stay for me, for the friendship, to try to repair it. Thomas was a good guy.

"My name's already Felix," I coaxed.

Thomas sighed. "Yeah, I'd watch the hell out of that show."

I squeezed my uninjured hand into a fist and pumped it in the air before extending it toward him. After a pause, he knocked my knuckles solidly with his own. "All right, man," I said. "This is going to be fun." I was almost surprised at the genuine enthusiasm I was feeling. "Let me give you a tour . . . of a haunted house."

Chapter 6

Neither of us stood up right away, as if despite our decision, we were both reticent to leave the lantern's sphere of light.

"This is your second night here, right?" asked Thomas.

"Yeah."

"Anything happen so far?"

"No. I've just done a lot of walking around in the dark."

"So, seriously, what happened over there," he jerked his head toward the foyer.

"Why was I crumbled in the corner? I don't know. I guess I let my imagination take over. I didn't see anything, just panicked in the dark and closed my eyes and tried to make it all go away." I didn't mention the creaking floorboards. It felt silly.

"Hmm." Thomas looked down at the arm on the table, as if waiting for it to thump back to life. "How'd you find this place?"

"Saw it in a movie."

"A documentary?"

"No, a feature. It was filmed here."

"You're kidding. What was it called?"

"*Blackest House*. It was an indie. A real obscure one. I don't even know if there's an IMDb entry for it."

"Never heard of it."

"I don't remember how exactly I learned about it. Probably one of those late-night, random picks from Netflix. The movie was filmed here like two years ago. The set was so creepy that it was obvious the production value came from a real location. I paused the movie fifteen minutes in to find out where it was filmed. When

I saw that it was filmed in a real house and that the house was nearby, I dug deeper and learned about its history. Then I drove by it a few times, and the outside passed the spooky-in-real-life test."

Thomas looked around and finally stood up. "The inside passes the spooky-in-real-life test, too," he said. "Do you have another flashlight?"

I rifled through my bags at the foot of the couch, retrieving a pair of smooth, pale cylinders and a lighter wrapped in a dragon decal.

"That's not a flashlight."

I set the two cylinders on the coffee table and flicked the lighter a few times. A small yellow flame lit up its end. I touched it to the wick of each candle until they flared weakly in the electronic light. The smell of warming wax was pleasant.

"Are those things scented?"

"Pumpkin spice. They were on sale," I said. "These will do for now, but we really need to find a candelabra in here some-where. They must have one. A nice brassy thing that we can carry around like Vincent Price in a Roger Corman movie. What kind of haunted house wouldn't have a candelabra lying around?"

He took one of the candles off the table and held it up at eye level. "I'm going to give this ambiance shit of yours another ten minutes before it gets annoying." We got up and walked into the foyer, gingerly holding our candles. Shadows flickered around us as if they'd been suddenly freed by the fresh candlelight.

I gave Thomas a quick tour of the first floor before we found ourselves at the base of the stairs. "Wait a sec." I rushed back to the drawing room and grabbed one of my bags. As I returned to the foyer, I could hear Thomas muttering.

"Talking to yourself?" I asked. "You getting creeped out already?"

Thomas looked at me as if he were surprised I had returned. "Nah. It's hard to be too creeped out when I'm hanging with a skeptic. Makes me root for the ghosts." A board creaked upstairs. I looked at Thomas immediately to see if he heard it. Judging by the way he looked up, he had. "Give it some time, though. I'm sure I'll be creeped out soon."

"Let's go." I started boldly up the stairs for the first time. My headache seemed to have gone away, and I felt lighter than I had since first opening the front door. It suddenly felt good exploring the old mansion. I was glad Thomas was here.

"This place looks like the *Psycho* house," said Thomas.

At the top of the stairs, the landing curved around to a long section of hallway, interspersed with about a dozen doors. The black-and-white effect of the house was accentuated here. Each door was jet black, almost as if they were newly painted, but large pale splotches of faint white mold grew on most of them.

"I guess it could be worse," said Thomas. "There could be portraits on the walls with holes in the eyes."

"Those are inside the rooms," I said. I dropped my bag on the floor and, clumsily holding the candle in my bandaged hand, rummaged around inside the bag with the other until I pulled out a spiral notebook, a Sharpie, and a small tape dispenser. I stood back up. "Welcome to the Hall of Death."

"Watch your drama."

"I'm almost understating it. According to the stories, there's been a lot of death in these rooms. Murders, suicides, murder-suicides, suicide-suicides, murder-murders. Here, hold my candle."

Thomas took it and stood there with a candle in each hand, awkwardly, like an overage altar boy. I knew this hallway better than any area of the house, story-wise at least. And this is where almost all of the stories were. The real story of Rotter House wasn't that once upon a time these bedrooms had been filled with Rotterdam's mistresses sweating up a storm doing whatever passed for sexual adventure before latex and batteries and silicon.

It was what happened in these rooms after his death that were the real stories of Rotter House.

After Rotterdam died, his three sons and two daughters fought over what was left of the inheritance. There wasn't a lot. You live by the chair, you die by the chair. Rotterdam's descendants ended up selling the mansion. Eventually it was turned into a rooming house. And then into a disreputable rooming house. And then into a *really* disreputable rooming house. Sometimes a hideout for criminals, sometimes a speakeasy, at all times a brothel. A lot of people had slept in these bedrooms. Some of them didn't wake up. Some of them wished they hadn't.

I opened the first door in the hallway. The candlelight illuminated a four-poster bed in the center. Everything still looked black and white in the gloom, but I was able to pick up a vague tint here and there that told me the sunlight would probably reveal the room as a faded blue. What the night couldn't hide is that the ratty wallpaper looked like one giant water stain, as if the room had flooded at some point to a foot below the ceiling.

"In this room, a man hanged himself from . . . hold the candles up a bit . . . yeah, that chandelier." It was a thorny-looking thing made of interlaced deer antlers, their tips capped in brass. "He left no suicide note, had no identification. Nobody came to claim the body. Ten years later, another man hung himself in this same room under the exact same circumstances. Both men had written the same name in the register: Joseph Dunlevy."

I opened the brand new spiralbound notebook and scribbled with Sharpie on the first page. I ripped the page out, and after snagging a section of tape from the dispenser, stuck the notebook page to the door. SUICIDE ROOM, it read.

"You couldn't just call it the Blue Room?" asked Thomas.

I shut the door and walked across the hall to the next room. In it, a jumble of wooden furniture was smashed in the middle like someone was starting a bonfire. The tint here seemed green, although that might have come from the mildew stains everywhere. Empty picture frames hung on all four walls. I wrote down another phrase in my notebook, ripped out the page, and taped it to the door: AUTOEROTIC ASPHYXIATION ROOM. Thomas stared at me with his head cocked to the side. I let it ride for about fifteen seconds before I ripped it down. "Kidding. A prostitute by the name of Ellen Markson was found in this room, long, livid bruises around her neck, her face frozen in a smile." I paused. "That's the whole story." I hastily scratched another pair of words, ripped out the page roughly—leaving a corner of it stuck in the spirals of the notebook spine—and taped it to the door: STRAN-GULATION ROOM.

"Is the owner of the place going to let you write the marketing copy for the website?" asked Thomas.

"Pay attention because at some point tonight, you'll need to pick which of these rooms will be *your* bedroom." I wasn't looking at him when I said that, but I could tell by the way the shadows jostled that he'd almost dropped the candles.

The next room I dubbed the Familicide Room, although I'm pretty sure I didn't spell it right. Cuckolded husband, unabashed wife, two unlucky kids, shiny handgun. That's all the relevant details.

"Man," said Thomas. "I feel like every time you open the door a scream should come out."

We progressed from there to the Shotgun Room, the Unknown Causes Room, the Stabbing Room, the Head Trauma Room, the Suffocation Room, and a few others, eventually ending at the Spontaneous Combustion Room. Some of the stories were mysterious, others not, but they all had violence and death in common. The only room left on the floor was the one at the end of the hall.

I stopped at the door, my hand on the brass knob, and faced Thomas. "This room, it's a special room. This is where I'm sleeping . . . the master bedroom."

Thomas's face stilled in the candlelight.

"What?" I asked. Standing there at the door of the main bedroom of this mansion, I suddenly realized where this conversation might go, and I wasn't sure I wanted it to go there yet.

Thomas pulled one of the candles close to his face so that the light reflected off his dark skin. "Am I getting the slave quarters?"

"What are you talking about?" I thought about it a few beats longer. "Oh." And then another couple of beats. "Oh." I felt both relieved and confused. "I have honestly never, ever thought about that phrase like that. Is that really what it means?"

Thomas stared at me with one eyebrow raised. Then he tilted his head back and smiled. "I have no idea. I'm just playing around with you. You should have seen me do that to my realtor. Really twisted him up. He must have apologized to me and Yvette like thirty times."

"I bet. That house you bought was worth quite the commission for him."

"It's a nice house—with a great master bedroom."

A weight dropped into my stomach when he said that, but I didn't want him to know, so I said, "Honestly, man, you can have this bedroom if you want. Besides, for the rest of our stay, I'll be calling it . . . "—I quickly made another sign and taped it to the door—"the Murder-Suicide Room. Now. All those death stories I just told you. Every single one of them? I have zero proof that they happened."

Thomas turned his head to look behind us. The hallway stretched back into darkness, each doorway bearing its new pale rectangle of paper. "That's dumb," he said.

"Don't get me wrong, most of these stories are legitimate legends. Some of them date back more than a hundred years. Many

J. W. Ocker

of them use names of actual people who actually stayed here. I just can't find any hard sources for those death stories—not a newspaper account, not an autopsy report. And remember, I've been to the top shelves of the basement of the town's historical society. I've found lots of spooky stories about it online and in books published by niche presses. Lots of copypasta. But that's usually the way with haunted houses. A single name on a deed can spin off into a seven-part horror miniseries. And then all you need is one psychic medium to pull the first letter of that name out of the air, and it's enough confirmation to keep that legend going. However, before you get too comfortable—"

"I am not at all comfortable."

"What happened behind this door is the most documented event in the history of this entire house. Every grisly detail of it can be dug up if you poke around enough. The newspaper accounts are lurid, the TV news programs even more so. I've seen the autopsy reports. I've been to the victims' graves. Of all the stories in this place, this is the one that interests me the most. It's the most disturbing story in this entire house—and not only because it's absolutely true."

I opened the door.

Chapter 7

The room looked like it belonged to a seven-year-old grandmother.

It was lacy—very lacy. And, were my eyes able to adjust to the dark and see through the dust that covered it all, probably pink. The bedspread had lace fringes, and the curtains matched exactly. The wallpaper was covered in a lace pattern, and doilies were spread out on every surface as if they were extruded there. That was the grandmother part. The seven-year-old part sat atop all of those doilies and was much worse: antique dolls. Good old custom-made for a horror movie dolls, with old-fashioned dresses, porcelain faces. Lifeless eyes. Black eyes. Like a shark's eyes. About a dozen in all, counting the half dozen or so strewn about the floor, on their backs, looking blankly at the ceiling, or facedown, obviously thrown there in horror. Relative to the other rooms, this one looked almost untouched by the ravages of time. Or, more accurately, that time had ravaged it in a different way.

"Elsa would love this room, man," said Thomas.

"Don't talk about my wife, jerk," I said playfully, but the statement felt weird and flat, as if it had been sucked down the dark hallway stretching behind us. But he was right. Elsa was a sucker for frills and antique dolls. The spare bedroom in our boring split-level looked like it belonged in a haunted house, thanks to her.

I entered, stepping gingerly across the dolls until I got to the bed. I hopped up onto the high mattress, my feet dangling over the edge and above the dolls like crocodile-infested waters were below. Thomas followed but chose to sit on a couch against the wall. It was velvet with a carved oak frame, similar to the couch in the drawing room. He placed both of the candles on a table next to him and then nudged at a couple of the dolls on the floor with his foot, like he was testing to see if they would jump up and dash across the room.

"The year was 1984," I said, slipping into the cadence of one of my book talks. "*Ghostbusters* and *Gremlins* are in theaters. Bruce Springsteen's *Born in the U.S.A.* is giving everybody blue ring around the collar, and the AIDS virus starts taking most of the fun out of sex. At that time, Rotter House was privately owned, but not lived in by its owner. It was mainly rented out to vacationers, like Chris and Monica Wynder. Shit."

"What?" asked Thomas, looking quickly around the room at all of the dolls.

"I'm supposed to be showing you a picture of them when I say that. All my materials are downstairs in my box." I debated internally for a few seconds. "Hand me a candle and give me two minutes to go grab it. You really need to see the before and after photos of these kids."

Thomas shook his head. "Nope. You can pretend you showed them to me in the book."

"It's fascinating stuff."

"Show it to me later."

"Okay. Feels less cinematic this way, though." I leaned against the edge of the bed. "Chris and Monica were in their mid-twenties. Honeymooners. Both fans of stonewash and neon based on the photos I've seen of them. The property manager met them in the morning with the key, showed them around, and then left after they fronted half the rental fee. A week later, he returned to see them off and collect the second payment. He hadn't heard anything from them in the interim, but that wasn't unusual. He typically only heard from tenants if something went wrong with the house.

"The Wynders' car was in the driveway, but there was no answer at the door. The manager used his key and entered, calling their names while he waited in the foyer. Nothing. He went into the kitchen. There were no groceries on the counter, no trash in the wastebasket, not even an unwashed spoon in the sink. He called their names a few more times and went upstairs. He walked straight to the master—biggest bedroom in the house. And that's where he found them."

"Happily sitting on the floor playing Connect Four?"

"Both on the bed, dead. Their bodies were naked and covered in burns, scrapes, punctures, and gashes. Around them in the bed and on the floor were minor implements of torture—lighters and plyers, a curling iron, sewing needles. At first, the coroner hesitated to hypothesize the cause of death but would later go on to write a scientific paper on their wounds, a morbid mishmash of both inflicted and self-inflected injuries, like they were characters in some self-obsessed indie movie. It seemed like they had spent their entire honeymoon taking turns harming themselves and each other."

"Kinky."

"You'd think that, and it would make the story a lot more easy to dismiss, but that same coroner would also rule that zero sex had occurred between the couple. They simply disassembled each other until they bled to death, lying beside each other on the bed."

"Was it a Satanic ritual? I've heard news stories about stuff like that. Always out of Europe, I think."

"It was investigated as a working theory, but they eventually ruled it out. No ritual iconography was present. Which, I guess, just means no pentagrams."

"Could still have been ritualistic, even if it wasn't an officially recognized ritual—" He stopped suddenly. "Wait. Is this the same bed?"

"I . . . think so."

"Fuck. Fuck. Fuck. You can have this room. I don't care what you call it."

"I'm sure they changed the bedding."

"This is the last one, right? We're done with spooky S-and-S rooms?"

"We're done with this floor."

A stairway at the end of the hall took us up and into another hallway. Here were more spooky bedrooms, as well as other rooms of indeterminate use. Some of the bedrooms got signs: the Crucifixion Room, which was self-explanatory. The Vanishing Room, after a woman who had mysteriously disappeared. "The most popular theory," I said, "was that she was murdered, cut into pieces, and taken out in her attacker's suitcase."

"Shouldn't it be the Dismemberment Room then?"

"That would be over here." I walked across the hall and opened another door. "A man was cut into half a dozen pieces, his body parts arranged on the floor in the shape of a swastika."

"No verification of these stories either?"

"None."

Eventually, we found ourselves in a single large room. At one time, it had been divided into three rooms, but a past owner had turned it into a massive game room—in both senses of the word. An uneven pool table with rips in the felt sagged in the middle of the room. An early twentieth-century foosball table in which half the wooden players were decapitated and the other half amputated below the waist sat off to one side. A giant dartboard, big enough for someone to throw javelins into it, took up one wall, and a shuffleboard court had been built into the floor. And then there were all the dead animals.

"Oh, this is where the taxidermy went," I said, just to be oddball. Thomas didn't acknowledge the joke. Instead, he noted the color of the walls.

"Very *Masque of the Red Death*."

"Are the walls red?" I asked. "I think I must have terrible night vision. They just look dark to me. More importantly, are you going to make movie references all night? There's only so much italicizing I want to do in this book."

"Makes it easier for me to be here if I think of it like a movie. And this seems like a movie. You can't argue that this room is total Norman Bates."

He was right. If the Bates Motel were located in Zimbabwe. The room was an African safari, frozen in time. A tiger posed aggressively mid-prowl, its fiery orange coat dimmed by dust and age. An elephant head adorned a wall, its trunk lifted in an "S" shape, looking ecstatic to be rid of its bulky body. A rhinoceros in the corner dwarfed the pool table in the center. "How'd they even get that thing up the stairs?" asked Thomas. Extravagantly horned prey filled much of the room. I remembered reading one of the real estate listings for the place: "Taxidermy comes with house." That was a real amenity, up there with stainless steel appliances and a good school district.

"How many horror movies do you know off the top of your head where taxidermy comes to life?" I asked Thomas.

"Four. Wait . . . *Evil Dead II*. That's five."

"That was my count too."

"What's next, a game of pool?"

"Eventually. But we've still got to level-up one more time." In the corner of the room, right by the rhinoceros rump, was a door. It opened onto a flight of stairs that we ascended into what at first seemed like a small, empty attic space with a rough wooden floor—and then we saw the massive picture window. The eye, or mouth, of the house. We were in the tower.

Outside the window, a bank of fog almost completely covered the house's surroundings. Vague glimmers of light here and there showed that the world around us still existed, that we hadn't been yanked into another dimension.

"Don't do that!" I whisper-yelled at Thomas. He was standing at the window holding his candle up like he was manning a lighthouse.

"What?"

"Get the candle away from the window. I don't want people to see light coming from this house."

"Why not? You've got permission to be here."

"But not everybody knows that. Last thing I need is for somebody to see a light in the house, call the cops, and then I have to go to the station until things are cleared up. Would totally destroy my project."

"All right, all right." He moved away from the window. "That goes to the widow's walk?" In the corner was a small wrought-iron staircase that wound upward to a trapdoor in the ceiling.

"It does. You up for some fresh air?"

"I think I'd rather have the fresh air outside the front door, but this'll do."

Thomas went up the stairs first, twisting his body around the turns more than walking up the steps. I watched him push at the trapdoor, but it didn't budge.

"You're kidding me. We're not going to be able to get out on the widow's walk?" I asked.

"Hold on." Thomas maneuvered his body until his shoulder was wedged tightly against the trapdoor and then threw his weight at it. The door shuddered but didn't budge. "Shit. I guess that's the end of the tour."

"Bummer. I've never walked a widow's walk. But the tour isn't quite over," I said. Thomas looked down at me, his body ridiculously scrunched up against the ceiling. "We still have the basement."

As soon as I said it, I flashed back to my earlier moment of panic. Had Thomas not been there, I might have curled myself in the corner again. The idea of heading down three flights of stairs, crossing all the planes of this haunted house in one go, suddenly seemed like an impossible feat. Moving that purposefully through a house that demanded tiptoes and furtive peeks around corners felt wrong. I reached into my back pocket to retrieve my notepad and scribbled "demanded tiptoes and furtive peeks around corners."

"What's in the basement?" Thomas asked as he detangled himself from the wrought-iron staircase.

"Nothing really. It's more like a cellar than a basement."

"Let's save it for later, then. I don't feel like getting dirtier than I am." He wiped dust from the staircase off his shirt.

"I'm glad you're staying, man. I really do appreciate it."

"Yeah." Thomas looked at the floor for a few seconds and seemed to reset himself. "But don't think you don't owe me big. You're going to need to make me sound pretty awesome in the book."

"You'll be an era-defining character, I promise you. Like Holden Caulfield or Gollum."

Thomas looked out the window. "There's one thing missing from your haunted house tour."

"What's that?"

"Ghost stories. You haven't told me a single one since I've been here."

I laughed. "Man, I guess I haven't. Honestly? It's because the ghost stories aren't that great."

"You picked a bad haunted house?"

"No, not all. It's just that this house has every single ghost story. Strange lights and voices and smells and sounds. Shadow figures, floaty things, women in white, women in black, moving furniture, oozing walls, levitating objects."

"That sounds pretty intense."

"That sounds like every single haunted house in the country. Every single one with some age in its studs, at least. In the entire history of haunted houses, there are only twelve things that ghosts can do—and they do it all here. That's how you know a place isn't really haunted, when it accrues every single ghost story just because it's a spooky-looking place. One made-up story in a high school cafeteria catches on and Rotter House becomes incrementally more haunted. Haunted houses don't give us the stories. We give the stories to them. And sometimes we suck at stories."

"You're coming off as that asshole. You want me to tell you every time that happens?"

I ignored the comment.

"Tell me some ghost stories," he insisted.

"I'm serious. You've heard them all before. And even if you weren't a horror movie fan, you'd still have heard them all before." I shrugged my shoulders. "I've got a bunch of stuff I printed off the local ghost forums in my box downstairs. I'll show them to you. Right now, we've got to figure out where you're going to sleep."

After a lot of deliberation that had me wondering if we were both going to end up on the couch in the drawing room, Thomas finally settled on the Spontaneous Combustion Room for two reasons. One, it was right next to mine. Two, while he believed in ghosts, he didn't believe in spontaneous combustion. I tried to explain to him that it didn't matter how the victim in that room caught on fire, falling asleep with a cigarette in their mouth or supernaturally hitting the temperature at which adipose burns, a burn-scarred ghost is far more terrifying than, say, a hanged ghost. He walked away from me in the middle of my explanation and slammed the door loud enough that every dust mote in the hallway leaped into the air.

The Murder-Suicide Room was too large for me—far too large. In another house, in another place, the size would have felt luxurious. But here, in Rotter House, it gave my imagination too much space to populate it with barely seen forms and looming shadows and, worse, two figures in both love and death with each other, lolling about the room, embracing, coaxing streams of red from each other's bodies—and all of those terrors waiting for me to close my eyes so that they could rush at me.

And then there were those stupid dolls. Why were we so afraid of children's toys that there was an entire horror movie sub-genre based on them: *Child's Play*, *Annabelle*, *The Boy*, *Dolls*, all the *Puppet Master* movies? What kind of psychological inference could we make from these strange stories? That what draws us as children, terrifies us as adults? It was an inversion of sorts. Kids are terrified of the dark, of closets, of the space under the bed, stuff that adults don't even notice. But with toys, children could finally turn the tables on adults. It was the ultimate emancipation—and a strain of philosophizing that I wasn't at all ready for. Creaky floorboards? I'll deal. Dead-eyed dolls? That's all, folks. I gathered them all up like I was picking up something disgusting off the side of the road and dumped them into drawers, knowing full well that when I woke up they would be back in their places, their glass eyes staring at me coldly and their porcelain lips laughing without moving.

I knew one thing for sure, though. I could never have slept in this room with nobody else in the house, regardless of my stance on ghosts.

I was glad Thomas had stayed, not for helping me face my fears of second-floor bedrooms, but because I knew he was there to help us get back to where we were. That's the only reason he came, the only reason Yvette would let him come, the only reason he was sleeping in a haunted house tonight. We'd known each other since

high school, got married the same year. We were each other's
Best Man. Elsa and Yvette had become close friends. Thomas and
I had built amazing lives—until that night happened. We'd tried
to get through it, sewn it all up like a battlefield wound, badly
and without knowing if it would be successful. The rents in our
friendship had widened over the year as we maintained distance,
and they were on the verge of completely ripping open. When I'd
asked Thomas to help me with my book, he had read between the
lines. Thomas was a good guy.

But it felt weird, as if that night a year ago never happened.
I kind of liked that and I kind of hated it. I shouldn't have to pretend that it never happened. I shouldn't be the one reaching out
first to try to mend the wounds. I should be the passive one in
this situation. He should be the one doing his utmost to fix things.
I mean, I'm staying at a haunted house, pulling him into a book
project, making him a part of my work. And all he has to do is
show up, act like nothing happened, argue about ghosts with me.
Seems unfair. It could be the only way for us to fix things, though.

I do know that the book will be better with him here. I really
believe that. It has to be. It absolutely has to be.

As I laid in bed wrapped in a sleeping bag atop the musty,
pale bedspread, I tried not to think about what had gone on here
that one week in 1984. I must have tried too hard, though, as my
headache started up again. I tried to literally write it off, filling up
my journal with pages of notes from the day and a few sketches
of doll faces. I don't know if it worked, but as the room started
to lighten a bit, I eventually fell asleep—in an actual bedroom,
where two mysterious deaths had occurred, in a house notorious
for its ghosts.

As unimaginative as those ghosts were.

Night
Three

Chapter 8

"What the hell is that?" Thomas asked.

"The name's right on the box. Look, the letters glow."

We were hanging out in the game room that Thomas insisted was red and which I still considered dark. I had set up a couple of electric lanterns that lit most of the room decently enough. The "ambiance shit" that Thomas had called me out on had started to wear thin for me, too. It turns out that candles are annoying things to carry around. Despite the glass eyes staring at us from all directions and the bared teeth reflecting that electric light, I had to admit, the game room was the least spooky room in the house. After all, how could a room with a foosball table and a giant dartboard ever be spooky?

Thomas's question was in reference to a long, thin box that I showed him. The letters on the box were indeed glowing, not spectrally but in that green chemical way that gimmicky toys and T-shirts do.

The box was purple and also adorned with a chemically glowing moon and sun. The name on the box read: OUIJA.

"I know what it is. I want to know why you're pulling it out of your bag," said Thomas.

"Because we're going to play it. This is a game room, you know."

"No. No, we're not going to play that. I don't mess with that stuff."

"What do you mean 'that stuff'? Board games?" I asked.

"Yes, if by board games you mean portals to bad places."

"You know I bought this at a toy store, right? Pulled it off the shelf from right between Jenga and Candy Land." I shrugged. "The section wasn't alphabetized." I extended the box to him. "Look, the thing's a registered trademark of Hasbro. They own Mr. Potato Head."

"That doesn't mean it's not dangerous. Ted Bundy killed thirty-six people with a kitchen knife he bought from the housewares aisle of a Walmart."

"Not true."

"The idea of it is."

"Listen, man. It's a kid's toy. Does Yahtzee make you queasy?"

"It is not a kid's toy. It's based on old hoodoo. You don't want to be opening yourself up to that. And certainly not in a place like this."

"Because I'll see ghosts?"

"If you're lucky that's all that'll happen. Who knows what you'll unleash."

"Then we should definitely do it. Settle this argument between us about ghosts forever. I don't know why we haven't tried the Ouija together yet, actually."

"I know exactly why. It's because I don't do that stuff."

"The Consumer Product Safety Commission won't even let a company release a toy if there's a one in a million chance of a choking hazard. You remember the rocket-firing Boba Fett action figure debacle from the '80s? Old-school Kinder Eggs? Lawn darts? Are you telling me that they're completely okay with companies selling games that will unleash demons? And that's not even counting the legal ramifications for Hasbro. Because that's a class-action lawsuit waiting to happen. No way the corporate lawyers would let them do it, even if those lawyers do have gold-plated Furbies sitting on their desks. Corporate liability is our biggest evidence against the existence of the paranormal."

"I don't know what to tell you. I don't do that kind of stuff. And if you have any ideas about us sitting in a pentagram and slicing our palms, you can count me out on that, too. Quote me on that in your book."

"Yup. Will do." I whipped out my notebook and pantomimed writing. "Wet blanket. Utter cowardice. Complete ignorance." Thomas snorted. I put the notebook away and tried a different tactic. "All right. History lesson time. The Ouija board was invented in 1890 in Baltimore by a guy named Elijah Bond. A simple, money-grubbing businessman. His gravestone even has a Ouija board etched onto it. True story. Seen it myself."

"Great."

"The *game* eventually became so popular that Parker Brothers bought it. Parker Brothers is owned by Hasbro these days. But in 1967, the year after Parker Brothers bought the patent, Ouija boards outsold the perennially popular Monopoly to the tune of like two million . . . one of the few board games to ever do so in the history of board games. And you know what happened in 1967?"

"What?"

"The Summer of Love. The exact opposite of a mass influx of demons into the world."

"Don't care. I don't mess with it. Besides, why would you want to do something so cliché as use a Ouija board in your book? This is supposed to be a different kind of haunted house book, right? That's your whole thing."

"Fair point. Which is, honestly, surprising coming from you. If I were writing this as a novel, as complete fiction, then this thing," I knocked on the top of the box, "wouldn't come anywhere near its pages. However, I need my readers to know that I gave it my all. That my time in this haunted house wasn't spent avoiding spirits or cutting corners around traditional spiritualist beliefs. So as conventional as it is, I need to try to talk to ghosts. And since neither you nor I are mediums, we need the help of the manufacturer of Nerf."

"I think you're tempting fate just by being in this house, and with this spirit board, you're outright seducing it. Still a pass for me."

"What if we Film Fight for it? Movies with Ouija boards in them."

"No."

"Come on, when was the last time we played Film Fight for anything?" We had invented this game in college and had obsessively played it ever since, usually after booze. We hadn't kept a lifetime score, but if I had to guess, we were probably about half and half. But Thomas still fancied himself way more of a human horror movie encyclopedia than I did. He couldn't say "no" and save face. Not when I was being so blatant with my challenge. And I knew it had been over a year since he played—because who else could he have played with? It was our game. Thomas looked at the board nervously, so I showed him the back of the box. On it were four blonde, suburban-looking fourteen-year-old girls gathered around the spirit board and having the time of their lives in a room decorated with rainbow-colored unicorns.

Eventually, he relented. Probably after he thought up enough movies with Ouija boards in them to believe he had the edge. I should have held off on picking the topic. "Okay, but only because there's no way I lose Film Fight on this one," he said. "You picked the topic, I pick the rules: only one movie in a series can be used—and that includes remakes—only English-language movies, and you don't have to include the year." He rattled off the items like he was choosing which cards were wild in a poker game.

"Okay. I mean, way to hamstring me by cutting out all of my J-horror knowledge, but okay. I'll let you choose who goes first." I mimicked the voice of an ancient and weary Knight Templar. "But choose wisely."

"I'll start," he said.

"Doesn't matter to me either way."

"*The Exorcist*," said Thomas.

"*Witchboard*," I returned, pantomiming a tennis racket shot with my arm.

"I'll say it. *Ouija*. So no *Ouija: Origin of Evil* for you."

"Don't need it. *Paranormal Activity*."

"*A Haunted House*."

"Already resorting to parodies? *Repossessed*, then," I said.

"*The Pact*."

"Technically not a Ouija *board*, since she just drew letters on the floorboards, but style points for the choice. I'll let it slide. *Tales from the Crypt*. The 1972 Amicus anthology."

"Of course, you're going to let it slide. And, of course, the 1972 Amicus anthology. *Thirteen Ghosts*."

"Ah. I wanted *Thirteen Ghosts*. How about *What Lies Beneath*."

"*Sorority House Massacre . . .*" He drew out the last syllable for a few seconds and squeezed one of his eyes shut. ". . . *II*?"

"You got lucky on that numeral. *Only You*."

"What do you mean, only you?"

"No, no. The movie *Only You*. The one with Marisa Tomei and Robert Downey Jr."

"Oh. Well, fuck you for that one."

"You didn't say only horror movies."

"What's the one from the 1940s? The one with Ray Milland?" Thomas was starting to struggle.

"I'm helping you out with this?"

"Shut up. The one that drove Gail Russell to alcoholism? *Invite . . .*"

"Careful . . ."

"*The Uninvited*."

"Nice landing. *Spookies*, jerk."

"*Grim*, asshole."

"*The Unleashed*."

Thomas stopped, straining to come up with a title. Finally, he said, "*Séance on a Wet Afternoon?*"

I made that annoying wrong-answer noise. "Nope. No Ouija boards in that one, just your classic hand-holding séance. You started, so I need one more movie to win." I honestly didn't have one on the tip of my tongue, other than a couple of Asian movies that didn't count. I gazed at an elk-like beast with horns so impressively twisty that he must have gotten laid by his entire herd. And then it hit me. "*Amityville* . . ." I waited long enough for Thomas to start jumping out of his skin. "*3-D*. Winner."

"Son of a bitch. I'm sitting in a haunted house, and I didn't come up with *Amityville 3-D*." He looked at me suspiciously. "You prepped in advance for exactly this situation."

"Highly possible, although you threw me a curveball with the no foreign films caveat. Where do you want to lose your soul?"

"Let's not do this man. You won the game, great. But for real, let's not do this."

"I need to do it, man. For the book. And now you need to do it—for the game. You've never backed out on Film Fights."

"I know." He looked down at the floor. I felt a twinge of guilt over forcing him to do this with me, but I ignored it, and it quickly went away. I really did need to do this for the book.

"One of the bedrooms maybe?" I asked.

"No way. Definitely some spirits we don't want to encounter there."

"I slept well enough in mine. How about right here, then?"

Thomas looked around, gauging the eeriness of the surroundings. The animals seemed to stare hopefully at him, like they really wanted to be chosen. "Nah. Let's get away from these beasts. The lantern light in their eyes makes them look alive."

He stood up. "I vote tower. A nice, empty space. Let's get this over with."

"You want me to go make us some drinks? Could make this whole thing a lot of fun and a lot easier for you to get through."

Thomas looked away from me and paused for a few seconds before saying, "No. No, I don't."

"Okay. To the tower then."

We climbed up the stairs and into the darkness of the room at the top of the tower. Well, semi-darkness. The night flowing through the window was tinged with moonlight reflecting off the fog that still enveloped the town. I grabbed a couple of candles from my bag and set them up in opposite corners of the small room before lighting them, not only because ambiance shit seemed to be actually called for here but because I didn't want to blast electric light out of the window for anybody to see. Nobody would notice two measly candles if we kept them on the floor, but they cast just enough light to help us contact spirits through a piece of creased cardboard.

Thomas sat down and crossed his legs without the least bit of self-consciousness. We used to be avid board-gamers back in the day. While everyone else in the dorm played video games or hit up the basketball courts, we and a few friends of ours spent our time trash-talking each other over cardboard and plastic—Risk, Clue, Scrabble. It was a holdover from our high school years when my parents wouldn't let me get me a video game system and we needed something to do when Thomas hung out at my house.

I ripped off the plastic seal from the purple box, opened it up, and unhinged the board inside. It glowed a green so bright in the dimness that it was almost white. The entire alphabet spread across the board in black, Old English letters, plus some basic numerals and one-word answers like "yes" and "no" and "maybe." The heart-shaped planchette was cheap plastic and also glowed

in the dark. It came in two pieces that I had to snap together. I
dropped the planchette into a neutral position on the board. For
a second, I had an image in my mind of traveling back in time
to the nineteenth century, the golden age of spiritualism, and
showing them my glow-in-the-dark spirit board. I'd have really
wowed them.

"First, I want to apologize that this board is so cheesy-looking.
It's all I could find on short notice. I wanted an ancient-looking
one, one that looked like burned wood or old parchment, ideally
with blood stains."

"Forgiven."

"Second, let's get a photo of us with the board."

"Unforgiven. What do you need that . . . oh, the book."

"This is the first photo-worthy thing we've done so far." I
pulled a tripod and my point-and-shoot out of the bag and set it
up so that it looked slightly down at us and the board at an unflat-
tering angle. "Now stay as still as you can. It's going to be hard
enough to take pictures in this candlelight. I don't want to risk the
flash." I hit the timer and jumped back into place.

"How much time do I have?" said Thomas as the camera
clicked. "Shit. Don't put that one in the book."

"Keep smiling. It's on scattershot. Will take a photo every—"
Click. "Shit. Three seconds."

"Shouldn't we pretend to play the board?" he asked. Click.

"That's a good idea." We put our hands on the board, straightened our backs, and closed our eyes. We stayed still for three
more clicks. I was half tempted to let it keep taking pictures as we
played, but the digital shutter sound was annoying. I got up and
turned the timer off, right after it took one more shot, a close-up
of my abdomen. I cycled through the photos before putting the
camera and the tripod back in my bag.

"Any good ones?"

"Hard to tell on a two-inch screen." I settled back into place, crossing my legs. "Now. Should I read the rules so that we can do this thing for real?"

Thomas held up his two hands loosely in front of him, their backs toward me, like a surgeon readying to get his hands bloody and then, after shooting me a look of disdain, dropped them down so that two fingers from each hand rested lightly on the planchette. I did the same.

"For the record," he said, "this is a mistake."

"For the record, that's exactly what you're not supposed to say before something like this. Do you want to go first? You can ask the spirits whether it's a mistake or not."

"It's your book."

I took a deep breath. It wasn't the first time I'd messed with a Ouija board. For one of my books, *Deadsville*, I'd spent a month in Lily Dale, New York, a village about ten miles from the shores of Lake Erie. A group of mediums had established the village back in the late 1800s, and today, they still completely populate the tiny village. Walking through the quaint streets of the place, I saw neat, tidy, colorful little houses like they were made out of gingerbread, each one bearing on its door a hand-painted placard announcing the name of the psychic and his or her business hours. It was usually a her, and the her was usually over sixty-five years old. One night, I'd sat in on a Ouija board session with a group of residents squarely in that demographic. They called it High Tea. We drank margaritas, and those grandmotherly mediums seemed to be competing with each other over who could bring in the most dead people. It was surreal.

"Greetings, spirits of this house. We have many questions to ask you. We hope you will listen to us and answer." I paused. "How much longer are Ouija boards going to be horror movie clichés?"

Thomas huffed. "Careful, man. If we're going to do this, let's take it seriously. We're messing with powers here."

"Okay, okay." The rebuke was well-taken. I did want to give this a legitimate try. I spoke again, "Are there any ghosts in this house?"

Thomas huffed again. "Don't use the G word."

"What? The 'G' word?"

"You should have done a lot more research into the paranormal before you started this project. You don't want to upset the spirits. They might not even know that they're ghosts. Or worse, they might not even be ghosts. Here. Let me show you. I'm going to ask a question—respectfully—and don't you make a noise for at least three minutes." He settled back and closed his eyes. When he was sure I wasn't going to say anything, he intoned, "Is there anyone out there, anyone at all, who wants to talk to us right now?"

I lowered my head and stared at the planchette on the board, our fingers lightly touching the plastic like we were trying to coax life into it, which I guess we were. The circular window in its center showed the bottom part of an F and the top part of a T. For some reason, I couldn't look at Thomas while we waited for whatever it was we were waiting for. It felt weird. Not so much silly as too intimate. When I had played with the Ouija board in Lily Dale, there were enough people in the room to fill the silence with breathing and shuffling feet, creaking furniture. Just Thomas and I in this tower was suffocating. And nothing was happening on the board. A watched planchette never moves, I guess.

After an eternity without so much as an indecisive twitch of the planchette, I spoke up. "My turn." I lifted my chin and spoke into the air, again without looking at Thomas. "Are you okay with us staying in this house?"

Silence and stillness were the only replies. I felt as if my eardrums were being pressed on by unseen fingers. I couldn't even hear Thomas's breathing. I flexed my back and shoulders without removing my fingers from the planchette. The glowing board played with my eyes a bit so that if I stared at it too long without blinking, the letters and numbers seemed to leak together like they were fresh ink.

Again, an eternity. Again, no response on the board.

Thomas's turn. "Did anybody ever die in this house?"

This ritual or game or whatever it was felt like Russian roulette. The only thing I wanted more right now than to see the planchette move was for the planchette not to move. It was a completely irrational response, but, I don't know. Maybe this house was getting to me. At the very least, the position of my body was. My back and arms were starting to ache, and my fingers were tingling.

"Does this house hold any secrets?" I asked. It wasn't a great question, but I didn't really know what questions I should be asking. The game should have come with a list of officially validated sample questions, the ones that the spirits most often responded to. Instead, on the inside of the box lid, where the instructions were printed, a marketing copywriter suggested that I ask the spirits if I would break a hundred subs on my YouTube channel or if I would have a boyfriend by the end of the school year. I don't know. Maybe ghosts were gossipy.

"I think we're missing something," I said to Thomas and any ghosts who might be hanging around us with their hands mischievously clasped over their boo-holes. "It's okay if I get up, right? I'm not breaking the circle or anything like that?"

Thomas opened his eyes. "That's for séances."

"I know, man. I'm just screwing around with you." I rose creakily to my feet and walked over to my bag. "And speaking of screwing around . . ." I reached into the bag and held up Rotterdam's arm.

"I don't know if this planchette is big enough for another hand," said Thomas.

"If you want a ghost to talk, you should set out a conversation piece." I placed the arm by the board with a soft jangle of metal and wood and then resumed my Ouija position. "Whose turn is it to ask a question?"

"My turn." Thomas closed his eyes and let the silence stretch until the mood had reset. "Is A. L. Rotterdam here?"

We let the question waft in the room until I felt my head getting light. I gave it a try.

"Is this the arm of A. L. Rotterdam?"

Again, nothing. Or the same things: darkness, stillness, silence.

I finally glanced at Thomas and was surprised to find him intently concentrating. His eyes were still closed, his head uplifted, and his fingers resting lightly on the planchette as if we were drawing sustenance from it. Any second he would be levitating to the widow's walk. He was so entranced that when it was his turn to ask a question, he didn't. He just kept examining the back of his eyelids like he was getting YouTube in there.

I decided to skip his turn. Except I didn't know what to ask next, really. It's hard to carry on a one-sided conversation. I decided to push things.

"Do you know that you are a . . . ghost?"

The sound was loud, painfully loud. A crack. Like wood splintering. And it seemed to emanate from right in front of my face. I instinctively threw my hands up to protect myself.

Chapter 9

The crack struck again, and I heard Thomas moan. I lowered my hands and saw him crouched over his knees with his arms clasped behind his head. "Are you okay?" I asked loudly.

It hit again.

"What is that?" he screamed from under his arms.

"I don't know," I yelled back, as the crack seemed to vibrate the room again. I looked around, but nothing *looked* wrong. The candles barely flickered. The prosthetic arm was limp and motionless.

The crack happened again and again and again, so loud, so chaotic, like the world was breaking in two. We dived into separate corners of the room, covering our ears and our heads and knocking over the candles, which sputtered in their molten wax. My head started to throb to the beat of the noise, but my heart felt as if its rhythm was being disrupted. "Stop! Stop! Stop! Stop!" yelled Thomas. I joined his chorus.

It did stop. Like all we had to do was ask. We looked at each other warily as if we had missed death by a fraction of an inch and weren't sure if it would come around for a gimme.

And then it happened again, sudden enough to make us jump but not as loud. It wasn't in the room anymore. It wasn't inside of us. It was below, in the game room.

I came to my senses. "We need to follow it." I grabbed a flashlight from my bag, almost more for the confidence of a sturdy weapon than a light. As I stood up, I could see through the window that the fog was still a thick, dark, twinkling mass, a spectral tide almost washing up against the sill.

"No, man. No," said Thomas, still in the corner, his eyes squeezed shut as if in pain. The sound happened again in the game room below us.

"You're staying here by yourself then." I ran to the door, the cheap plastic planchette crunching to shards beneath my boot. I yanked the door open and ran down the stairs. The sound of footsteps and a wildly careening beam of light matching my own told me that Thomas was at my back, despite what he had said. We made it into the game room, which was still lit by our electric lanterns, and we stopped abruptly at the pool table in the center.

Silence.

Nothing moved.

We held our breaths.

The frozen animals surrounding us looked like they were trying not to attract the attention of . . . whatever it was.

We heard it again.

It was below us, somewhere on the second floor. We raced down the steps to the Hall of Death.

The hallway extended in front of us, swallowing our light beams, which only touched here and there, illuminating the paper signs taped to the doors. All the signs were still. All the doors were shut. No dust motes wafted through the air. Nothing had passed through here.

The sound cracked below us, on the first floor.

"This thing is leading us, man," said Thomas, so close behind me that his voice near my ear actually made me shiver.

"I know." We took off down the hall.

When we arrived at the bottom of the stairs, all was quiet. I shined my flashlight in one direction, and Thomas followed suit in another. The two circles of light danced like large glowing insects across the walls of the foyer and into open rooms as we walked its length. Nothing.

"What was that?" asked Thomas.

"I don't know. I really don't know."

"It wanted us to come down here. Now what?"

"I don't know, man. Maybe we should——"

Crack! The noise exploded right in my ear, driving me to my knees and causing me to drop my flashlight. Thomas dropped, too, letting out a wail that sounded deep and terrifying.

My hands over my ears, I turned to see where the sound had come from. A closed wooden door loomed above me, scratched and pitted but practically the only interior door still intact on the first floor.

I slowly dropped my hands from my ears. "The cellar," I said. "It wants us to go down into the cellar." I winced at my own words.

Thomas didn't say anything. He crouched there on the floor like he had been beaten and wasn't sure it was over. I rose slowly to my feet and squared myself with the door. By the time I had gathered the courage to place my hand on the knob, I felt Thomas standing behind me. I opened the door, which swung out without a sound—no creak of hinges, no scrape against the floor, as if it were kindly leading us to our doom.

I looked down into the darkness, almost afraid to shine my light into it, fully content to let whatever was down there stay hidden. When no sound came, I lifted my flashlight. It illuminated the stairs, rough wooden planks that were almost afterthoughts, as if the builders were surprised anybody would want to go into the cellar.

My beam traveled quickly down the boards like it was running away from me before jumping to the darkness beyond. But it never made it to the darkness beyond. As it flashed past the bottom of the stairs, it caught the edge of something solid and dark and tall at the foot of the stairs. Somebody was standing there, not moving, like it was waiting for me to see it before it ran up the stairs to attack me. My breath thickened in my throat and my ribs felt like they were tightening in my chest as I moved the light to the top of the figure, hoping whatever was down there would move away before I saw its face. I didn't want to see its face. I almost closed my eyes as the light touched it.

Its face was monstrous.

I almost ran through Thomas in my efforts to dive back into the foyer and slam the door shut behind me. "There's something down there!" I screamed at him.

Thomas didn't need elaboration. He led the way as we ran like children, right across the foyer to the front door. Thomas fiddled with the locks and then yanked the door open. He made it to the bottom of the steps in about three leaps. I stopped suddenly in the doorway.

Thomas seemed to sense my hesitation immediately and spun around. "Why'd you stop?" He was grimacing and yelled the question through great gasps of breath, like he had just surfaced from holding his breath too long underwater.

"Why did everything stop?" I had just realized it in that second. Nothing was happening. No more ear-splitting cracks, no steps on the cellar stairs. No fiends bursting through the cellar door after us. Only agitated dust particles from our retreat floating though the beam of my flashlight. I looked down at the corner where I'd had my panic attack. Maybe that panic attack had inoculated myself against the spooks. I suddenly felt no reason to flee the house.

"What did you see downstairs?" asked Thomas.

"A monster."

Thomas planted his hands on his hips, dropped his head, and laughed. "Oh, I get it, man. It'll make for some funny interludes in your book if you fuck with me. You're an asshole."

"No, man. I swear I saw something down there. It was at the base of the stairs looking up at me like it was waiting for us. It was holding its arms out like this . . ." As I lifted my arms, it hit me. "Oh. I think I get it. I don't understand it, but I think I get it. Come back inside."

Thomas didn't accede, but when he saw that I wasn't coming outside, he finally ascended the stairs and stepped past me, just inside the doorway. "You're taking this 'not leaving the house' thing a little too literally, aren't you?"

"I'm already planning my TV interviews, 'No, Mr. Fallon, I didn't set a single foot outside the door for thirteen whole nights. Not so much as a big toe.' But, just for you, man . . ." I jumped across the threshold, stood there for a second, and then stepped back inside. I immediately regretted it. It felt like I had ruined the project.

I led the way back to the cellar door. Even though I thought I knew what was down there, a part of me still wasn't totally sure. And all of me still had no idea how it connected with that sound. "You're with me, right?" I asked Thomas.

"I'm indecisive."

"How are you going to sleep tonight if you don't know what's down here?"

"Sleep? I thought it was a foregone conclusion that we weren't staying another night here now." Thomas threw his head back and sighed deeply. "This book of yours better sell a million copies."

"What do you care? You're not getting a cut."

I opened the door quickly. Nothing leaped out at us from the darkness. Shining my light down to the bottom, there was the monster, a humanoid figure, decaying and goopy, like a Lucio Fulci version of a zombie. In fact, it reminded me of Dr. Freudstein in *The House by the Cemetery*. That zombie mad-man of a monster had hidden in the cellar, too. Our monster hadn't moved a single muscle, though. It was still looking up at me through the dark, its arms outstretched in a classic "boo" pose—too classic.

"What the—" Thomas saw the thing at the bottom of the stairs and jumped back into the foyer. He slowly returned when he realized that I remained staunchly in the doorway. After giving the thing a second look, he said, "That's a wax figure."

"Yeah, although I doubt it's wax. They use polyresin these days. More durable."

"What do you mean *they*?"

"Haunters. Monster-makers. Those types. See?" I shined the light past the creature into the rest of the cellar. It revealed a humanoid pig in chains, a witch with bright yellow eyes and a bumpy nose, a werewolf with a mohawk. All in that same "boo" pose.

"Holy shit," said Thomas.

We descended into the cellar of monsters to find full-sized creatures of every fantastical species sporting real clothes and glass eyes and authentic hair. Many of them were the quality of Hollywood special effects. They were all generic, though. None of them were IP. No Stan Winston Pumpkinhead or Millicent Patrick Gill-man. Just a nonspecific demon clown and alien invader and caped vampire. And there were more than monsters. There were giant, furry spiders piled in a stack in the corner and white-sheeted ghosts dangling from the ceiling, coffins in stacks, skeletons on hooks, old mirrors, cans of black-light paint. I almost tripped over half of a zombie set up to appear as if it were rising from the floor. And, since it was a dirt floor, the special effect was especially effective. Thomas and I walked carefully among the Halloween props and figures like we were checking on flowers in a garden.

"That bastard. Historical attraction, my ass," I said.

"Who are you talking about?"

"Garza. The owner of this place. She gave me hell when I asked her for permission to stay here. Wasn't too keen on my spooky bibliography. And the entire time she was planning on turning this place into a haunt attraction. She was probably ecstatic when I used the 'Vincent Price with a GPS' line."

"Is there ever a day you don't bring that up?"

"She probably wanted this book from the start. Hell, she probably would have paid me ten times my advance from the publisher to write it. I should have known. Who else buys a place with the reputation that Rotter House has and doesn't live in it? Somebody who's about to capitalize on that reputation, that's who."

"Also Nicolas Cage," said Thomas.

"Nicolas Cage bought Rotter House?" I asked before I realized what a ridiculous question it was.

"No, he bought the LaLaurie Mansion in New Orleans, the one where Delphine LaLaurie tortured and mutilated all those slaves. It's one of the most infamous haunted houses in the country."

"I know the LaLaurie Mansion. I didn't know about Cage, though. Did he live in it? Turn it into a haunt?"

"Nah. I think he let it go into foreclosure. Probably a drunk purchase. I accidentally order Slaughter's greatest hits on CD when I drink too much; he buys an infamous mansion."

That'd be a good place for a book, I thought. *Got to finish this one first, though.*

"Oh, no," said Thomas.

"What's the matter?"

"You know what's worse than monsters in the cellar of a haunted house in the middle of the night?"

"No."

"A cellar with a dirt floor. Walls keep people out, roofs keep the weather out, and the foundation keeps the dead out. We're basically exposed to the dead."

"This ain't a cemetery."

"Oh, somebody is definitely buried down here. This house is 200 years old. And from what you've told me, it has a pretty sketchy history. That's too long a time with too many opportunities for somebody to *not* have been buried in this cellar."

As we meandered through the haunted house innards, I almost forgot that we had been chasing a sound, distracted by this haunted house within a haunted house.

One ghoul in particular drew my attention. It was a female figure in a lacy, flowing teal robe with large red rose blossoms atop a black bustier and panties. She was wearing red heels. Although I only judged the figure as female based on her body shape and clothing. Her face was split open, eyes dangling to the side like a chameleon's. Inside, the split wasn't a mess of blood and muscle and bone and brain, though. Each half was sealed with a membrane of skin that was smooth and pink, almost vaginal. In the center, where the two halves met, was a thin strip of bone. The moisture effect on the membranes was so real, I reached out to touch the skin before I realized what I was doing.

"Sexy," said Thomas right behind me, startling me. "What kind of monster wears lingerie?"

I looked away from the split-faced woman and turned to Thomas. "One of Dracula's brides, I think."

In a corner of the cellar was a massive stone cistern, one of its walls crumbling to reveal an open space full of dirt and debris. "This is where your buried body probably really is. Want to jump in there and look around for it?" I asked.

"No way." Thomas flashed his light around the cellar. "So what made that sound? And why was it leading us down here?"

"I don't know."

"It definitely led us down here."

"Yeah, it seemed to."

"But why? To show us some Halloween decorations? We'd eventually have found this stuff on our own."

"The whole thing is strange and suspicious." I gave a nearby reptile-man the side-eye, like I was ready to pull its mask off. Thomas was squinting into the oversized monocle of a mad scientist.

Eventually, after combing every inch of that cellar looking for the source of that sound, we let the monsters be and headed back upstairs to our rooms. I had a lot of notes to take from this night.

I hadn't been in there for ten minutes, though, when I heard a knock on the door. "Here's Johnny?" came a muffled voice on the other side.

"Come in, man."

Thomas opened the door. "I, uh, kind of don't want to sleep alone tonight. Not after that noise."

"I'm down with that. You want the bed? I can take the couch over there."

"No, the couch is good for me." Thomas laid down while I continued to shine a light on the journal I was writing in. "Where are all the dolls?"

"Kicked 'em out. They kept running across the floor while I tried to sleep. Really annoying." I opened a drawer next to me and drew one out at random. It had the usual dark eyes and pale, shiny skin and was dressed for fox-chasing. I threw it at Thomas. "Here you go."

"Yuck. Feels wet," he said and tossed it on the ground.

"Probably mildew. Or the blood of past victims. Will it bother you if I keep my flashlight on while I finish writing my notes?"

"Go for it," said Thomas, settling into the hard couch. I was in my sleeping bag, so I pulled one of the blankets off the bed and threw it at him. He caught the blanket and then disappeared under it.

I wrote for another twenty minutes and then shut off my flashlight and put the notebook away. I slid the flashlight under my pillow.

"Shit," I heard Thomas say in the darkness. "We didn't close the Ouija board."

"We don't have to be that neat while we're staying here. We can clean up after ourselves when we leave."

"No, I mean *close* it. Move the planchette to the 'Goodbye' spot on the board."

"I kind of stomped the planchette to pieces when we ran out. What does it matter?"

"That means we left the portal to the other side open."

"Dude. C'mon. Ideomotor effect."

"Fuck you."

I thought some more about the Ouija board as I lay in the darkness waiting for Thomas to start snoring. I couldn't decide whether I could classify that experiment as a bust or a success. Actually, experiment is probably the wrong word to use. Prop is more accurate to my intentions. Sure, something weird happened while we were using it, but that could have been a coincidence. I mean, we didn't get a single "Boo!" out of the letters on that board—just that terrible sound.

As much as I tried, I couldn't come up with a reasonable explanation for that sound. It didn't immediately strike me as spectral, although Thomas is obviously assuming it is. He also thinks it led us to the cellar. That's possible. Or maybe it led us to the farthest point away in the house. Or maybe it didn't lead us at all. Maybe it was trying to get away from us. And maybe it was all a bit more random than that. After all, like Thomas said, it only led us to a bunch of fake monsters that we would have found on our own once we got around to exploring the cellar. And those fake monsters made the origin of that sound even more suspect to me.

But, in the end, it was just a sound. It didn't do anything to us, other than hurt our ears for a second and then shut up. Definitely fits the ghost story template. Vague, pointless, and harmless interactions that stop as mysteriously as they start, just like every single story in a haunted house anthology, every single scene on a ghost-hunting show.

However, I was glad—for the moment, at least—that Thomas was ten feet away from me.

Night
Four

Chapter 10

"The fact that we're still here after our experience last night and not twenty miles away in the safety of a Taco Bell drive-through with an order of Cheesy Gordita Crunches warming our laps makes me rethink every single haunted house movie that I've ever seen." Thomas was telescoping a camera tripod to its full length in the foyer.

The strange sound that we had followed the previous night had dominated our conversation since we had gotten up, wondering if it would happen again, what was causing it, why it was happening, but those threads ended in dead ends pretty fast. We even hung out in the tower room among the shards of broken planchette and tipped over candles and the antique prosthetic arm slash sex aid we had forgotten up there waiting to see if it would happen again. It didn't. That left really only one thing to explore—our reactions to it.

"I could totally go for some Cheesy Gordita Crunches right now. I never thought I'd get tired of beef jerky, but that's what this house has driven me to. Not madness, jerky apathy." I was only a few feet away, holding a flashlight between my chin and chest and angrily fiddling with the settings on a small device. "But it kind of makes sense when you think about it. I mean, the unknown of it was frightening in the moment—and maybe still is. But, in the end, it was just a sound. A stupid sound. And not even a growl or a scream or something freaky and distorted like you hear on EVPs. It wasn't even really, I don't know, otherworldly sounding. It was like somebody was karate-chopping boards over and over again.

Feels kind of silly that we reacted to it the way we did. And I'll for sure never be able to write it up in the book in a convincing way. I guess that might be decent evidence of how fundamentally *not* scary it should have been to us in the moment."

"Shirley Jackson did it."

"Shirley Jackson is Shirley Jackson. I can't pull off a pair of horn-rims, either. And that was fiction. She didn't have to convince us the sound happened in real life or that two grown men cowered in a corner because of it. A sound, man. Afraid of a sound. You more than me, of course."

"If by that you mean I value my well-being a little bit more than you, I'm okay with that. I have a little bit more to value than you do." Thomas dropped the fully extended tripod upright on the ground like he'd performed a magic trick. "Whatever that sound was last night, it seems more strange than scary now. Maybe it was those stupid Halloween props. They make everything about this house seem fake. If it happened right now, this minute, I think I'd hit the ceiling with a broom and tell the kids upstairs to knock it off."

We both paused instinctively, waiting for the devil that Thomas had named. Nothing, though. Not so much as a soft thump in the night.

"Whatever doesn't scare you to death makes you braver? I also want to say that it all feels fine in the cold light of day, but I haven't seen that in about a week."

"I can't believe you've finally had your own paranormal experience. After all these years. I think I feel . . . proud of you."

"Stop it. Something happened, but I'm not comfortable pinning it on see-through dead people yet. It could be mental. It could be faked. It could be a lot of things."

"Occam's razor can't cut ectoplasm. Besides, it doesn't have to be dead people. It could be a lot of things: energy abnormalities, interdimensional beings, malfunctions in the hologram. I had a pastor one time who told me that ghosts were reflections of souls in hell. That's why they were always moaning and screaming—because they were being burned alive."

"What did you say to him?

"I told him to pitch that script to someone with cash ASAP."

"Aha!" I shouted, holding the device up in the darkness as if I'd just discovered it. "Got it working."

"What kind of a camera is that, anyway?" It was about six inches tall and rectangular. It had three rows of tiny lightbulbs, a lens, and one or two other less identifiable mechanisms on its surface. It looked like the type of child's toy that could transform into a robot after five minutes of twisting and pulling.

"This is a Bearstalker 7507," I said in my best Patrick Bateman voice, "a highly durable, motion-activated, infrared camera that will prove to the entire world the existence of ghosts. Or it will spend the next seven days photographing stray insects and you and I running from sounds."

"So we're officially ghost hunters now." Thomas started whistling the theme from *The Odd Couple*, slow and spooky-like.

"Not exactly. I actually wasn't planning to do this at all."

"You've got a lot of equipment there for somebody who wasn't planning on setting it all up." He flashed his light at my hiker's backpack, which had collapsed and was spewing metal- and glass-wrapped circuitry all over the tattered rugs and hardwood of the foyer floor.

"I'm not staying at this place to prove or disprove the existence of ghosts. That's not what this book is about. I'm here to tell people what it's like to live in what is generally considered a haunted house, both from my perspective as an unbeliever and your perspective as a believer. To see how we react to this physical and psychological space and then to delve into those reactions.

This is going to be a very profound book, sir." I held my flashlight to my chin and showed him my serious face.

Thomas ignored it. "But more my reactions, right? Because you don't believe in ghosts. Although so far our reactions have been the same."

"That's part of my point. Just because I don't believe doesn't mean I won't react. I mean, I freak myself out all the time. You caught the tail end of a freak-out over there, you know." I pointed my flashlight at the front of the foyer. Thomas nodded. "You know what I do. A lot of spooky stuff—midnights in asylum cemeteries, overnights at murder scenes and abandoned prisons, one time even an afternoon at the house of Beatrix Potter. I love to do that kind of stuff, but it can get to you. Hell, it doesn't even have to be a particularly spooky place. It can be worse when it's not a spooky place. When I'm in a cemetery at night, I kind of expect that my brain will start interpreting shadows and noises in the scariest way possible. I'm prepared for that. And I want something interesting to happen. Helps the story. My worst freak-outs have always been at home. When Elsa's gone for a week on a business trip and I'm all alone and not expecting a disembodied pair of eyeballs to float out of my garbage disposal. So that's naturally when my imagination torments me with the idea of a pair of eyeballs floating out of my garbage disposal. It's the violation of my home space that's really terrifying and can have me sleeping with all the lights on and *Gilmore Girls* turned up at full volume until morning."

Thomas squeezed an eye shut and swung his head from side to side. "But does that take you anywhere interesting? Like last night. We heard a strange sound. It panicked us. We followed it. It stopped. We went to bed. Not a fascinating set of reactions."

"I don't know. But that's what the prolonged immersion and being cut off from the outside world is for. I usually only do book stunts for a night or so, and I'm usually live-tweeting it. This time, I need to give the freak-out a chance."

"That's a very long explanation for why you weren't planning on setting up this equipment." Thomas laid a hand on the top of the tripod as if he were showing off Exhibit A at a trial.

"I didn't think anything bizarre was going to happen at all over the course of our stay. Anything tangible, at least. I was sure I'd get spooked, that I'd have to investigate some of the more mundane sounds that you'll always encounter in old, decrepit houses, that you would go completely nutzoid at some—and possibly multiple—points. But this was supposed to be more of a book about us in a haunted house than it was about the haunted house itself. I think that's changed now. And I prepared for that possibility, more out of hope than anything else. Whatever that sound was, I need to see if I can figure it out. These cameras are part of that. I don't think I'm going to see a ghost. But if I do? This book becomes a testimonial. Crap." The camera in my hands had gone into sleep mode, and I didn't know how to wake it up. As I fiddled with its buttons, I continued, "But, even so, I still want to treat this haunted house differently than ghost hunters treat haunted houses."

"What do you mean?"

"What do you think of when you hear the term 'ghost hunter'?"

Thomas looked silently around the foyer, as if he were imagining a team trudging back and forth through the dark rooms on either side. "Infrared-tinged people in black hoodies and jeans talking to the air and waving EMF detectors."

"Right. Exactly. And even aside from the extremely dubitable ideas behind the efficacy of today's ghost-hunting methods, all that imagery and terminology has slipped into cliché these days. So I don't want to document this house that way—no EVPs, no EMF detectors. I want to document the house like a biologist documents animals in the forest. Check it." I tossed the camera, which was finally working, to Thomas. He caught it so smoothly despite holding a flashlight and it being dark that it must have been a complete accident.

"It's painted camouflage."

"Yup. A trail cam. Unfortunately, they don't sell these in haunted house paint schemes. You put a trail cam up in the forest and wait for critters to trip it. It's that simple. I'm putting trail cams up in a haunted house to see if anything passes by and pisses on a chair. It's probably something I should have done already, honestly. For the same reason that we did the Ouija board."

"Where did you get trail cams?"

"I bought them secondhand a couple years back. Remember when I did that book on the Pine Barrens of New Jersey?"

"The Jersey Devil book? The one with the dumb title?"

"*New Jersey, Old Devil*. The publisher came up with the title. But, yeah, I had to stay a couple nights in the forest for it, so I spent most of my advance on equipment. It's also the only reason I own a tent, a camping stove, a survival hatchet, and this here camping pack." I gave the neoprene and aluminum thing on the floor a soft kick. Its contents clanked in response.

"So if you're treating the ghosts in this place like animals, where's your bait?"

I started whistling the theme from *The Odd Couple*. I didn't stop until it got awkward. "We are. You and me. Shaggy and Scooby."

"So we walk around in the hopes that the Creeper jumps out at us?"

"Basically. Think about it. It's like the whole question about whether a tree falling in the forest makes a sound. If there is no living person inside the house to experience the haunting, is the house really haunted?"

Thomas thought for a second. "Schrödinger's ghost? I mean, I assume it is still haunted, right? Maybe they're not shooting down the hall menacingly, but they're probably still wandering, caught in whatever loop it is that has them stuck in this world in the first place."

"If they're that regular, then why's it so hard to get that activity caught on crystal-clear 4K video? I think if it exists, it must be more like a chemical reaction. You have some substance that's completely inert—and when I use this example in the book, I'll Google something scholarly so that I can be more specific about the substance since I suck at chemistry. But when a second substance is added to that inert substance . . . "

"Mentos and Coke."

"Mentos and Coke. Good. Maybe that's the secret of all hauntings. It's not a repeating phenomenon that you have to be in the right place to witness. It's a set of very specific variables that have to be met. The right person, the right haunt, the right time, the right ghost. See? I'm a narrator that both believers and nonbelievers can identify with."

"So in this weird mishmash of analogy and metaphor and pseudoscience that you're spewing, you have to realize that there's a chance that we're not the right bait."

"If last night was any indication, we are exactly the right bait," I said.

Thomas turned the camera over in his hand. "Does it record sound?"

"It does."

He scraped the camera across the top of the tripod and then shined his flashlight at the bottom edge of the camouflaged box. "There's no screw hole."

"It's an older trail cam. You're supposed to just strap it to a tree." I took a Velcro strap from my bag, grabbed the camera from

Thomas, and affixed it haphazardly to the top aluminum shaft of the tripod. "You can also smear it in animal musk, but we can skip that step. I only have two of these tripods, though, so we'll have to be creative with the others."

"How many cameras do you have? One for every room?"

"Hell, no. These guys are like seventy dollars per."

"Oh, okay, so that's the real reason you're recycling your old trail cams. You just couldn't afford a set of new, state-of-the-art cameras for this project."

"That is potentially an accurate statement. Anyway, I have six cams. We'll have to place them strategically. I figure here, in the hallway upstairs, in the game room, the cellar, my room, and that leaves one that we can shift among the other rooms."

"Uck. You're going to film yourself sleeping?"

"I'll turn that one off when I'm in there. Otherwise, they're all motion-activated, so they're going to record anytime we're in the room. Or when the stray rat is. Or, hopefully, whenever whatever is behind those sounds does its thing. That'll also help save memory cards and batteries."

"Will this even work on ghosts? I mean, do they move in a sense that motion-activation technology will recognize?"

"I have no idea. But it's the best I got, and we need something to do to pass the hours anyway. Our Ouija board is broken." When we had gone to the tower earlier in the evening, we'd discovered that not only had I decimated the planchette, each glow-in-the-dark piece landing on a letter like miniature planchettes, but I'd also bent the board pretty badly. We tried to Boggle the letters that all the pieces landed on but could come up with no message from the beyond. Thomas closed the Ouija board by sprinkling all the pieces on the Goodbye spot, and then we grabbed up the board and A. L. Rotterdam's arm and left the tower to rig up my cameras.

All told, that took about an hour to do. The only flaw in using these trail cams was that they had no screen for playback. But I honestly didn't think there would be anything to see either way, regardless of those strange sounds from last night.

I really needed to figure those noises out. Not for the book— books about ghosts are always vague and inconclusive. Readers would sort of expect that, so I was safe there. But I, personally, wouldn't be able to leave this house without an explanation for that sound.

The hardest camera to place was the one in the cellar. There wasn't a good angle for getting the whole space. We tried shoving it in the chest cavity of a skeleton, but that skewed the camera badly and one of the ribs partially blocked the lens. We also tried strapping it to a ghost pirate like a parrot, but it was too loose. We ended up placing it on the top of the cistern wall, even though that meant only a portion of the cellar was in its view. I could only imagine how unnerving infrared footage of frozen cellar monsters would be whenever I watched it—if it ever got set off by anything other than us, that is.

We were back in the foyer tripping our first camera setup when we heard another loud cracking noise.

We bolted again.

Chapter 11

The cracking sound this time was different. Still spooky, but different. We rushed in absolute delight to the nearest window that wasn't boarded up.

Nothing happened at first.

Then, in an instant, rain began pelting hard against the glass, dissolving the outside world into blurry rivulets. A flash of lightning made the blur merely bright before the thunder hit us again.

"Did you plan this?" asked Thomas, a big grin on his face.

"I'm not going to say I didn't check the ten-day forecast, but it was only a hope." My smile was just as broad.

We both loved thunderstorms for the same, silly reason.

"Man, I wish we could watch a horror movie right now. I don't care if this is a haunted house."

Back home, one crack of thunder and we'd dive for our shelves to grab a remote control. Scary movies are predominantly about atmosphere. The same creep show watched at 11 a.m. during the summer in a house with no central AC is a much different experience than the same one watched in October on a dark and stormy night hunkered under an afghan.

"I've got some haunted house books in my bag," I said.

"I'd really kill for the Blu-ray of *Identity* right now. It rains the entire movie."

"*Clue*. I want *Clue*. And then we can pretend we're Tim Curry awaiting a board game's worth of visitors, all coming in soggy out of the rain."

I snapped my fingers. "We should at least head up to the tower and watch this thing from above. Hold on." I walked into the kitchen and shoved a bottle, a jar, and two plastic cups into my bag. When I returned, Thomas was jumping in and out of the trail cam's frame, causing it to blink on and off.

"Poor thing," said Thomas. "It really wants to capture a ghost so badly."

Upstairs in the tower room, it felt like being in an aquarium or inside an old tube TV, where the screen was all staticky. The square shape of the room really made that impression vivid. The large window was liquid with rain, a porthole during an ocean storm. It was easy to imagine that the entire force of the storm was being hurtled at us in our isolated tower above a house full of ghosts.

Thomas leaned his forehead against the cool glass. "So. Really. What do you think that noise yesterday was?"

I settled back into a corner, holding up the flashlight like a lightsaber, flowing the beam across the ceiling and the square outline of the door to the widow's walk. "I have no idea, man."

"But are you open to the idea that it may have been paranormal?"

"No. I mean, I'm open, I guess. But I'm on my fourth night here, and the only thing that's happened is a sound? Feels like a haunted place would be more consistently haunted."

"Well, not if we're the wrong Mentos for its Coke."

"It wasn't that clever, man."

"Seriously, though. Maybe it takes some time to warm up." Thomas turned around and took up station at the foot of the wrought-iron staircase, his own lightsaber aimed squarely at the trapdoor. "You only have three categories of explanation, you know."

"I know."

"So if you don't think it was paranormal, it was either natural or man-made. Which are you leaning toward?"

I looked down at the yellow rubber toggle switch of my flashlight. "I can't believe it was natural. Just don't know what would have made those noises for that duration and spread across the house. "Man-made, well, that would put us in a real *The Private Eyes* situation."

"All right, Don Knotts, who are your suspects?"

"Well, Emilia Garza, the house's owner, would be suspect number one. After all, she has complete access to the entire house. Could have easily prepped something. And now that we know about her haunted house aspirations, that also gives her the means of pulling off a trick like that. Who knows what special effects she's got wired into this house already. And then there's the motive. It's in her interests for me to find this place haunted and publicize it to my twelve readers."

"Twelve readers?"

"A joke she made when I first talked to her. She was kind of a bastard. So it could either be her or someone she's hired."

"Is that it?"

"No. There could be some randos. Pranksters, kids who saw us come in. A squatter who was here before us." I listened to the sound of the rain on the window for a few seconds. "You know who it could also be? Elsa and Yvette."

"The girls. Yeah, I'd thought of that. I didn't tell anybody but Yvette that I'd be here. They could have whipped up something. They're devious enough together for that."

"Oh yeah, that's not a bad plot twist. I told one other person than Elsa, though."

"Your editor?"

"No. I'm keeping the location secret even from him." I flashed the light in Thomas's face. "I'm talking about you."

Thomas let out a loud laugh, a big one, showing off the undersides of his upper teeth and his silver filling again. "And I guess you'd be my number one suspect."

"Told you I wish I had a copy of *Clue* here."

"Felix Allsey in the tower room with a flashlight."

"Thomas Ruth in the cellar with a ceramic skull."

The rain continued to lull us. Thomas was leaning back on the iron stairs like they were the most comfortable furniture in the whole place. I was sitting on the floor against the wall opposite the picture window so that I could stare into the pleasing wet-static pattern. After a few minutes wandering the spooky corridors of our own minds, Thomas spoke up.

"You know what the noise kind of reminded me of? Algernon Blackwood's *The Willows*. You ever read it?"

"Yeah. Don't remember much about it, though. Just that it was pages and pages of description. Right up your alley."

"It's about these two guys who are canoeing somewhere in Europe. They stop at this island full of willow trees and weird things start happening. Makes them think they might be at a dimensional crossroads, intersecting with terrible beings that they can't fully sense. One of those weird things is a gong sound without a source that repeats itself—like our sound."

"I'll have to reread it."

"One of my favorite lines in all literature is in that story, 'Our insignificance perhaps may save us.'"

"I like it. Could be better reversed, though: our salvation might make us insignificant."

Thomas crossed his arms and rubbed his biceps. "I should have brought a sweater with me."

"Wouldn't be a haunted house if it weren't cold," I said.

Thomas gave up on warming himself and tapped his flashlight barrel against one of the wrought-iron balusters. "What would you have done last night if I hadn't been here?"

I thought about it for a long time. Thomas didn't rush me. Finally, I said, "I honestly don't know. Now that something has happened, I do kind of wish I had taken on this project alone. Me versus the ghosties. No offense. Of course, if that's the only thing that happens during the entire stay, you'll still have your uses."

"Good to know. And I hope that's the only thing that happens the entire stay. No offense."

"Scaredy-cat."

Thomas looked like he was pondering the epithet for a few moments. Then he asked, "What are the scariest things you can think of? Not scared-for-your-life type of things. Not huddled in a bathroom during a hurricane, but like, scared in a heebie-jeebies kind of way?"

"Oh, I've got a list." I rummaged in my bags and pulled out the items I'd grabbed from the kitchen. "But want a drink first? I've got the fixin's for a lazy martini." It was a drink I had invented years ago. Elsa was good at making cocktails. No, great. And she enjoyed it. I could go months without once picking up a shaker and still drink enough cocktails to embalm myself. As a result, my cocktail game had atrophied over the years. Often, I'd want to keep drinking after she was done, but by that time, I was so buzzed I didn't care how good the cocktail was. While she dozed on the couch, I'd take my glass, head over to the kitchen counter, where she had all the hardware and software laid out for a five-star-restaurant cocktail, and splash some gin into a glass. I'd follow it with some olive brine because I loved them dirty, skip the vermouth because who needs that stuff, throw in a few olives sans skewer, and then stick it under the ice maker to let gravity and ice cubes mix it up nice and sloppy-like. It was the drink any drunk could make. I didn't have an ice maker here, but I could at least make a terrible martini.

Thomas looked at me, his eyes half squinted and his mouth pursed. After a few beats, "no" was all he said.

I didn't try to convince him. I just took the plastic cup, bottle of gin, and olives—stuffed with blue cheese and with skin so thick and firm they could break toothpicks—and laid them out like I was about to perform a religious rite. "Pipkin can do it to me."

"Your ghost cat?"

Thomas called him that because he was never around. Slept all day at the corner of mine and Elsa's bed, hardly moved, hated to be petted, never came out when guests were over. The orange tabby was barely a pet. "Since he's only really active at night, I hear him when I'm writing late or lying in bed trying to sleep. He climbs walls, runs from invisible pursuers, and vocalizes these weird syllables that never even come close to a meow. Every once in a while, he gets to doing that, and I break into cold sweats at the 0.1 percent chance that I'm hearing those thumps and footsteps and noises in the house while the cat is still sleeping on the corner of my bed. I refuse to look at the spot on the bedspread, just in case." Thomas laughed. I took a drink of my lazy martini. It was room temperature and the ratio of olive brine to gin was off. It was terrible—or would have been had it not been my first drink in four days. So it was delicious. "But I've had worse freak-outs. Like with the outside motion lights on my house. Some nights, those lights turn on for no apparent reason."

"The wind."

"I know, I know. That's nothing I haven't told myself in the moment. But that's also what future victims in horror movies say. It could also be one of the too many skunks that wander my neighborhood. I swear my neighbor is feeding them under her porch. But walking by my window at night and seeing those motion lights awake tells the caveman part of my brain: someone or something just walked across my yard. One time, the lights refused to shut off. And you know what my brain turned that into?"

"What set them off . . . was still there," said Thomas, like he was performing the punchline of a campfire story.

"Exactly. As soon as I thought that, I went right to bed. None of the windows in my bedroom face the motion lights."

"I got one," said Thomas, leaning forward. "My windows." He threw his flashlight beam at the dark, blurry glass of the tower window, but pulled it back quickly when I started to curse him out. "They're the Jekyll and Hyde of residential construction. During the day, they're awesome. At night, they're the worst things ever invented. And mostly I'm talking about ground-level windows. The ones somebody could walk up to and stare straight into my house whenever they want. You know where I live. It's never pitch black out there because of the lights from downtown, so there's always something vaguely visible in the darkness. I've done double takes so many times because of those stupid windows. Like that urban legend about the person who sees a man who fits the description of an escaped serial killer staring into his window and it turns out to be the murderer's reflection . . ." Thomas changed back to his campfire voice. "Because he's already inside the house!"

"It's even worse when there's fresh snow outside."

"Snow?"

"I'm always afraid I'll look out my window at night after a fresh snowfall and see footprints. Like somebody just walked across my yard. You ever hear of the Hinterkaifeck murders?"

"Hinter-what?

"Hinterkaifeck."

"No. Do I want to hear about it while I'm living in a haunted house?"

"You don't read my books, do you?"

"Which one was that in?"

"*Murder Mystery Sites of the World.*"

"That the one where your advance was too small to travel to all the sites?"

"Yeah, I had to write most of it from pure research. Bothers me to this day." I took a large swig of gin and brine. "The Hinterkaifeck murders took place during the winter of 1922 on a

Bavarian farmstead called Hinterkaifeck. A man named Hans Gruber came home one day to see tracks in the snow leading from the forest to his house but none returning. He didn't pay them much mind and thought they might have been from his wife or one of his daughters. They were definitely too big for his grandchildren to have made. But after that, according to what Gruber told his neighbors, the family starting hearing footsteps in the attic. They found items that didn't belong in the house. Things that did belong went missing. And their maid left for fear the house was haunted." I drained the rest of my martini.

"Eventually, the Grubers stopped coming into town, and when the neighbors went to investigate, they found the entire family dead, bludgeoned with a pickax. The murders were never solved, but people realized that whoever had done them had probably been hiding in that house with the family the entire time."

"Holy shit," said Thomas, casting a glance behind him at the tower window and looking relieved to see only rain. Judging by his face, he was beginning to regret the conversation. I, on the other hand, was having a blast, reunited with my best friend, trading spooky tales in a haunted house during a rainstorm, drinking martinis. At least one of us was.

"Let's have the ghost debate," I said, and started working on another, even lazier lazy martini.

"Only one martini in, and you already want to have that argument?"

"We need to have this conversation. For the book. And to see if your arguments have evolved much over the past . . ." I let the sentence die and concentrated hard on the olives I was dropping into the drink. Thomas came to the rescue.

"Nothing's changed. Plus I thought we settled this long ago. It's not an argument anymore. You don't believe in ghosts because you've never had an experience with ghosts. Simple as that."

"No, not that simple."

"Basically that simple."

"I've never had an experience with a Vijayan's night frog, and I still believe in them."

Thomas laughed in the darkness. "You've changed that analogy, huh? No more tiny spiders living on the underside of underpasses?"

"The Braken Bat Cave meshweaver?" I laughed this time. "Yeah, I've updated my reference. Same principle, though. The Vijayan's night frog was discovered in 2017 in the jungles of India. Full grown, it's smaller than an M&M. And it's already an endangered species. So it's very rare, very tiny, and hidden in a jungle. Scientists found it, took photos of it, balanced it on coins and fingertips to emphasize its size. Even more relevant, I automatically believed in it as soon as I heard about the discovery."

"Yawn, dude. There are hundreds of credible photos of ghosts." Thomas flicked his flashlight on and off a few times like he was trying to figure out what he should say when he reviewed it on Amazon.

"Hardly. And we live in a millennium where camera and video equipment are omnipresent, and it still hasn't yielded evidence that even shifts the conversation on ghosts, much less overturns it. We have multiple high-res videos of rare oarfish swimming in the vast ocean and enough one-in-a-million occurrence videos to fuel thirty seasons of *America's Funniest Home Videos*—but not a single clear shot of my dead great-great-great-grandmother."

"I've always wondered how *AFV* is even still around in the YouTube era."

"But it's not about the photographs. Not really. I mean, you learned about that frog for the first time this second without a photograph, and you didn't question me on it at all. It's the scientific system that the creature becomes a part of. That's where the credibility lies. Science recognizes the existence of microscopic organisms and invisible forces and planets billions of miles away— yet it can't find enough evidence to even discuss dead floaty things."

"But there's still a butt-ton of assumption in all of what you just said. Scientific bias against the paranormal, for instance, that either stops the construction of a scientific system for the paranormal or the inclusion of the paranormal in the current system." This is where Thomas really exceled in an argument, using words that end in -ion. And words like butt-ton. "And it could be as simple as we haven't yet developed the right instruments to detect the paranormal. It took a while to invent the ones that helped us find microscopic organisms and planets billion of miles away." I tried to jump in to say something, but Thomas cut me off. "But let's get to your second reason. You don't care about M&M frogs."

"No, I don't. Science also tells me that I should exercise and eat a balanced diet, and I obviously disagree with it there. But it's the personal reasons that I can't get past. And that includes my past. Which is, you know, basically the same as yours."

"Plus the white privilege."

"Plus that."

Thomas and I went to the same Independent Baptist church back when we were high school age. It's how we met. One Sunday morning before the sermon started, I was sitting by myself in one of the pews. It had red padding that matched the red carpet and the red drapes in front of the baptismal. I was doodling in a notepad that my father made me bring to take notes on the sermon. Thomas, whom I had seen here or there, but didn't know, walked up behind me and said, loud enough that I slammed shut the notebook and hid it under my Bible, "Are those the Sentinel Spheres from *Phantasm*?"

My parents didn't let me watch horror movies. But, sometimes, late at night on Saturdays, I would sneak downstairs to catch one on TV. I never made it through a full movie. Not because I was scared of the movie, but because I was terrified my parents would catch me. I would sit inches away from the screen with the volume turned down so low I could barely hear it. For a long time all of my nightmares were full of monsters with muted growls and women screaming with no sound. The previous night I had caught fifteen minutes of a scene where a silver ball the size of a softball flew through the air and impaled itself into a man's forehead via a pair of knives that extended from the sphere. Once impaled, a drill then slid out from the sphere, boring into the man's forehead and siphoning his blood away, where it spurted out the back of the ball. I didn't even know what the movie was called. Thomas sat down beside me in the pew and excitedly whispered the whole plot of the movie to me. The story didn't make any sense, but I was enthralled. Decades later, we were sharing a haunted house.

But being Fundamentalist, we were both raised to believe in ghosts—plus demons and angels, talking animals, god-stuffed humans, resurrection, the evils of movie theaters and women in pants.

"I still can't believe we believed all that extravagant shit," said Thomas, even though I hadn't listed any of it out loud.

"But you still believe in some of that extravagant shit."

"Yvette's still kind of religious. Not me."

"I'm talking about ghosts, man. That's a hardcore belief, right up there with the Holy Ghost." Thomas shrugged. "I won't argue about it. The point is that you eventually sloughed a lot of those beliefs; I sloughed all of those beliefs. I went from *The Exorcist* to *The Texas Chain Saw Massacre*. But that's the nature of belief. It's sloughable. Yet we go around doing it all day, believing that we're not going to die in a wreck when we jump into the car or that the weight we're gaining in our thirties is only a temporary condition."

"I still weigh the same as in high school."

"And you are a magnificent specimen of humanity. But what I'm getting at is that we can believe something pretty intense one day and then disbelieve it just as intensely the next. On top of that, when our mundane beliefs regularly turn out wrong, our extravagant beliefs don't stand a chance."

"And that brings you to . . . "

"Exactly. The Big One. The only reason that matters in this argument." I shut my flashlight off and waved it in the air like I was remote-controlling a presentation on a screen. "The evidence of one's personal experiences. That's what every single belief comes down to. Whether it's a belief in a Holy Ghost or the Canterville Ghost, the basic goodness of humanity or the basic jerkiness of humanity, capitalism or socialism, string theory versus whatever the opposite of that is, we measure it against our own personal experiences, and if it doesn't match up, we say 'go fish.' Even though we fully know that our senses suck, that memory is wiggly, that experiences are limited in every possible way, that what we're not misinterpreting, we're deliberately fooling ourselves about.

"But there's a personal screw-turn on this for me, and that's the intersection of my experience and this topic. I've stayed overnight in a decommissioned nineteenth-century prison, slept at a murder scene, visited haunted castles, hung out in cemeteries at midnight—hell, I've spent more time in cemeteries than in my own guest bedroom. I've tiptoed my way through abandoned asylums. I've participated in séances, had readings done, browsed multiple haunted-artifact collections, entered haunted caves, haunted factories, haunted hospitals, haunted hotels, haunted restaurants. I've been in classic ghost scenarios in my life as often as I've had weekends. And I've done all that not as a debunker but as a dude who likes creepy stuff. And I've never had anything close to a paranormal experience. Not so much as a 'boo.' Not even something I could make sound cool with a little bit of exaggeration."

"I've always told you, man," said Thomas. "You're just one experience away."

"That's great. I accept that. Although if it ever happens, I'm going to be really pissed at Casper for taking so long to say 'hi' to me." I took a swig of my drink and realized that it had mysteriously disappeared. I turned my flashlight back on and started making another drink. "Are you sure you don't want a drink?" I cringed waiting for his response. It came after about ten seconds.

"Okay. Just one."

Night
Five

Chapter 12

I twisted between bleary, burning wakefulness and dank, heavy nightmare. In the one, I was coiled sweaty around my sleeping sack, my eyes burning from the light leaking through the windows and my head pounding. In the other, I was stuck in an old-fashioned diver suit at the black, black bottom of the ocean, no light other than bioluminescent creatures that flitted in the distance. My limbs were weighted down, my heart beat painfully against the pressure. Something unseen beside me clanged against my brass helmet. I was the furthest person away from the rest of the world.

Eventually, I awoke fully, but it was only to a slightly lesser fate. My head pulsed. My mouth was dry, my stomach nauseous, my eye lids thick and stuck to my irises, and all I could smell was gin. I reached across the bed to grab Elsa's hand. No matter what Gordian knot of arms and legs we entangled ourselves in when we fell asleep together, we always ended up at opposite edges of the bed. "Our corners," we called them.

It doesn't matter the quality of your martinis, perfectly made or sloshed together. You still end up here the next morning— hurting and in a limbo of bedsheets. Elsa might be able to sleep hers off, but I needed two extra-strength Tylenol and a glass of grapefruit juice before I had any chance at it. I gave Elsa's hand a quick squeeze, heaved myself out of the bed, and then realized I was in the Murder-Suicide Room.

I didn't want to turn around, didn't want to confirm what I had just grabbed in the bed beside me, the bed that I had just slept the night in. I stared instead at the antique couch, examining it intently. I saw the years as scuffs and scratches and frays on its surface. I examined the wallpaper and saw the years as faded spots and rips and stains. I stared at the single window on my side of the bed, covered with a rotted blanket that leaked light through its rents and holes. I looked down at the doll Thomas had thrown on the ground the night before. It had landed facedown, arms and legs at awkward angles. It looked like a suicide jumper.

Please be Thomas. Please be Thomas. Please be Thomas. I tried to take control of the universe, to will the events of the night previous to conform retroactively into a narrative that ended with both of us in the same bed. Maybe he had spooked himself again. Maybe we had both passed out drunk on the first bed we saw. *Please be Thomas. Please be Thomas. Please be Thomas.*

I waited until I didn't care what happened, until I was ready to take my last breath in the ocean before drowning, until the final second before the fatal collision. And then, I turned around.

Thomas wasn't in my bed.

There was nothing in my bed.

Just my sleeping bag, tussled along with the rest of the bedding from a fitful few hours of sleep.

I headed toward the door like I was walking through four feet of water, reached steadily for the knob, opened the door slowly, soundlessly, carefully. And then, I ran downstairs.

I'm still drunk. I'm still drunk. I'm still drunk. If that hand, that solid hand that I had held and that had disappeared hadn't been Thomas's, if that mantra hadn't worked, then this was my follow-up hope. *I'm still drunk. I'm still drunk. I'm still drunk.*

By the time I skidded into the kitchen, I felt like I was in a different house—not the haunted house that I had stayed in for the past four nights. Had it already been four nights? Why did this place feel so strange? What had changed about Rotter House?

Daytime. That's what it was. Of course, what passed for day-light in a place so boarded up and stuffy was a murky haze, but it was still the first time I could really take in the guts of Rotter House.

To this point, I had viewed the place in flashlight-beam chunks that disappeared from existence when the beam moved. But here, in the massive kitchen, in the daylight hours, I saw everything at once—the counters, the sink, the pantry, the doorways into rooms that gave me peeks of both sheet-covered forms and ancient furniture, the table and those stupid Rotterdam chairs, the antique couch where I had spent the first night in the house, the dumb-waiter—which had shut again. I flicked it open, just in case. No severed head on a silver serving platter.

It felt like Rotter House had finally crawled out from under its rock. Or that I had. Somehow, though, it still looked black and white to me. Or at least the colors had faded to barely discernable hues, like old postcards in gift shop windows.

A light blinked at me, and I remembered the trail cam. The one in the kitchen was recording me hungover and breathing hard, staring around the house as if I were a recently awakened coma victim. I walked over to where I had affixed it to a wooden paper towel holder and turned it off.

One of my bags was on the counter, so I rifled through it until I found the first aid kit. I opened it and my hand skittered over a white plastic bottle. I rattled three Tylenols into my palm and flipped them down my throat. I wondered how Thomas was doing up there in the Spontaneous Combustion Room. He'd only had one lazy martini to my three, and he didn't even finish that, so he was probably just having a great night's—day's—sleep. Since I didn't have any grapefruit juice on hand, I settled for a drink from the sink faucet, the shaking and moaning of the old plumbing almost quaint in light of my recent experiences. The water tasted awful, swampy.

So far in my stay, I'd encountered an unexplained series of noises and whatever had just happened upstairs. Is this it now? Do I believe in ghosts? Has this book become a conversion story? I imagined the first line of the back cover copy: *He entered a smug skeptic and, thirteen nights later, exited a terrified believer.* Is this how it happens? A couple of weird events, some jolts of adrenaline, and your entire conception of the fundamental makeup of the universe does a backflip?

I've always considered myself relatively open-minded about things. Everybody does, I guess. But specifically, in this case, the case against ghosts, I always figured—like Thomas had said, like I've told two dozen ghost-hunter groups, like I've told myself over and over again—that I was merely one experience away from believing. But I'd always thought that experience would be more . . . convincing. Something that I would believe in my soul's soul, regardless of how I felt the next day and regardless of anybody else's doubts about my story.

Five minutes ago, I had been disconcerted enough to bolt from my room. Now, I was hanging casually in the kitchen as if I were trying to decide between pancakes or waffles for breakfast. Maybe it was the daylight. Maybe it was the hangover. Maybe I'd reset myself by coming downstairs. But, right now, the sounds from the previous night and the hand from a few minutes ago were philosophical constructs to me, more conceptual than supernatural, easy to dismiss.

Surprisingly easy to dismiss.

Now that I thought about it, I didn't even know if I was awake when I felt that hand. Certainly I still kind of felt the after-touch of cold flesh on my palm, but I've had nightmares like that before. A giant Pringles can with pincers grabs my ankle and I bolt awake with a cold, tingling sensation encircling the area. The Pringles monster was scarier than it sounds.

And that's kind of what this was. Scary when it was happening, not so scary afterward.

And the sound, well, that was still fundamentally suspicious to me.

Again, even if these occurrences were paranormal, they felt like paranormal pranks—silly and juvenile. But I could see how someone who already believed in the supernatural or wanted to have an experience very, very badly could weave these minor incidents into a major personal ghost story.

And that made me believe in ghosts even less.

I noticed that the bandage on my thumb had loosened again, so I took it the rest of the way off. The wound was scabby and ugly, but it would someday be a nice scar and a great story. "How'd you get that?" readers would ask me at a signing. "A haunted house," I'd say, giving them a wink that they'd probably interpret as creepy, but it's the only way I know how to wink.

I started wandering the first floor, examining it like I was sizing it up for purchase, like I hadn't spent the past four nights here. What seemed spooky at night seemed vaguely romantic in the daylight. Each rotted floorboard the footprint of a previous owner, every shred of falling wallpaper the equal and opposite reaction of some excited husband and wife decorating their nest together (or, more likely, having the hired help do it), every piece of sheeted furniture carefully chosen to fill the spaces of someone's life.

And now it was just a haunted house, ready to be turned into a haunted attraction.

This would be a perfect opportunity to take some interior photos of the place. The daylight would make it a lot easier on the cheap point-and-shoot I had brought. No way would my equally cheap publisher spring for a professional photographer to document the place for the book later. I yawned. I was too tired to go through this giant house and take photos. I rationalized that they would seem more authentic and in-the-moment if I took them at night, even if they were all pixelated and blurry. Plus people might spot ghosts in those kinds of photos.

I stumbled over to the antique couch and laid down. I wasn't so much afraid anymore of what had happened upstairs, but I didn't want to ascend those steps by myself either. Whatever it was could have the bed. I wondered if, in my drunken state last night, I had forgotten to turn off the trail cam in my bedroom before I got into bed. If not, I might have some interesting footage . . . that would have to wait another eight nights.

I then wondered why I ran from it, that phantom sleeper in my bed. What's the worst that a ghost could do to a person? Give them a heart attack? Make their hair turn white? A sound and a touch, that was it.

Exhausted from too much booze and not enough sleep, I dropped hard back into the deep.

Chapter 13

I had almost gotten used to waking up in full darkness, but this time, the feeling of surfacing was horrible—claustrophobic, suffocating, depressing. I wasn't sure why at first, until I slowly realized that I was on the couch in the drawing room instead of in the bed in the Murder-Suicide Room, and then I remembered why I was there: because I had held hands with a ghost. Maybe. I guess the subsequent walking around the house during the day had thrown me off. Once this project was over and I was back home, I would seriously consider giving up my night-owl tendencies for the rest of my life.

I listened to hear if Thomas was up but only heard faint creaks here and there in the upper floors. Must be still asleep. I do make a great awful lazy martini.

It took me a few seconds of clumsily searching the couch and table without getting up before I realized that I had neglected to bring a flashlight down, so I got up and put both my hands out in front of me like a zombie and walked slowly into the kitchen. I felt my way along the coffin-sized cabinets until I found the one with the food. I grabbed a pack of peanut butter crackers and leaned against the counter to eat them. Another new resolution would be to start eating well after this stunt. Write during the day, eat right, regale friends with my new firsthand ghost stories. I was coming home a new man. I hoped Elsa would recognize me.

I felt my way over to the kitchen cam and turned it on. It felt weird standing there in the darkness. Not unnerving, really. Just weird. I stopped rattling the cellophane around the crackers and placed it on the counter without eating the last two in the pack. Other than while I was sleeping, this was something I hadn't done yet—risked Rotter House in the true dark, without flashlight or lantern or company. My eyes had adjusted enough so that I could make out some vague forms in the dark: corners and doorways and humps of furniture. And the musty smell of Rotter House seemed to intensify with my eyesight moot. My ears hurt slightly, like they were straining in the solid silence. I could almost hear a faint hiss. Every so often, some part of the house creaked, and it sounded overly loud.

I felt on the edge of something, like I couldn't exist in this stasis for long. Something had to change and was about to any second—either in the house or in me. The silence, the stillness, my movements, maybe Thomas rumbling down the stairs. Do haunted houses abhor a vacuum?

Then unwittingly, my mind turned to the cracking sound and the phantom hand, and I realized how close I was to the dumb-waiter . . . which was closed again. I decided to get out of there before Thomas found me screaming in a corner.

I stuck my arms out in front of me and made my way to the foyer, crossing it almost by memory. A small pinprick of light from the foyer trail cam blinked at me, and I gave it the thumbs up. At the stairs, my hand slid lightly on the smooth banister as if it were kindly leading me upward.

The Hall of Death was a depth of blackness that halted me like a wall. I shut my eyes to grant myself a more preferred darkness and headed down its length to my room. As I walked, I trailed my fingers across the doors on the right side, rustling the white signs still taped to the doors.

I reached out to the door of the Murder-Suicide Room. It was ajar, just as I'd left it during the day. The darkness in there was as unrelieved as in the hallway. I suddenly didn't think I could go in there, even to find my flashlight. Was the sleeper back? Was it lying in the bed? Was it sitting up waiting for me to return? Was it looking at me right now in the dark?

The door behind me opened, and I almost threw myself onto the floor. A beam of light flashed through the opening, followed by Thomas.

"You scared the shit out of me," he said.

"*I* scared the shit out of *you*?"

"What are you doing standing in the hallway in the dark?"

"I'm going into my room."

Thomas shined his light below my eyes and scrutinized me. "Okay. I'm going to ask you this sincerely, and I want an honest answer: are you losing it? In haunted house stories, somebody always loses it."

"No. I won't be losing it for a good three or four more days."

"Yeah, well, the signs always start much earlier than that."

"I think I touched a ghost, Thomas."

"You are losing it."

"I think I touched one in my bed."

Thomas slowly backed away from me and then retreated into his room and shut the door.

It took about sixty seconds for me to realize he had no clue how to get out of that joke, so I turned the knob on his door and walked in. He was sitting on his bed, grinning awkwardly at me. "Where's your flashlight?" he asked.

"In my room somewhere." I sat down in a nearby chair—which sagged deep enough that I almost jumped out of it—and watched his beam trail around the room, which was mostly bare, with white walls and only a section of wallpaper here or there that had stubbornly remained at its post. The beam settled on a sooty black stain on the wall about the size of a person.

I told him the whole story.

"You drank a lot last night," he said.

"Only three martinis. Business as usual for me."

"Three martinis in plastic cups three times the size of a normal martini glass. You know, you rapped to me last night."

"Holy shit. No way. What song?" I asked, steeling myself for it.

"Whodini. 'Haunted House of Rock.'"

"Of course it was. Man, I was drunk."

"Yes. Yes, you were."

"Well, that doesn't matter anyway because I didn't experience it until hours after I went to bed. After I'd sobered up, I think. I mean, I had a headache like my pillow was spiked with nails, so that usually means I'm in the hangover phase of drunk."

"Do you really think it was a ghost?"

I thought about it all again. The moment, the physical sensation, my feelings, my reaction, my thoughts. It all added up to nothing much. "No. It could've easily been a dream. My mind playing tricks on me. Hell, you playing tricks on me."

"Loud crashes, handholding with a ghost. You're getting what you need for the book, for sure." Thomas shined his light again on the dark stain. "What's next, hide here in this room for a few days? Because that definitely feels like the right decision."

"First we need to go back into my room, kick out any one-night stands, get my flashlight, the lanterns, my camera, and take some photos for the book. I need something to pad out the size so that people think that they're getting their money's worth."

"That sounds like a beautifully boring activity," said Thomas. "Let's do it."

He led the way back into the hallway and shined his light through the half-open doorway of the Murder-Suicide Room. I looked over his shoulder. The bed looked like somebody had jumped on it for two days and rolled around in it for another three. My sleeping bag and the sheets were wadded and twisted, and the bed itself had shifted on the floor.

Thomas walked slowly into the room, aiming his flashlight at the bed like he was investigating a fresh crime scene. He riffled through the sheets for a second before yanking his arm back.

"What is it?" I asked.

He didn't answer right away, instead concentrating on what was illuminated at the end of his flashlight beam. "Looks like you did hold hands with the dead."

I rushed to his side. In the glow of the flashlight, laid out on the choppy bedsheets like a holy relic, was the intricately made wood and metal arm.

"That's not what I felt," I said.

"I don't know. This seems like a mystery solved," said Thomas. "How'd the vibrator feature work out for you?"

He had to be right. The evidence was right there. "How did I become the gullible one and you the voice of reason?" Still, I wasn't satisfied with this obvious of an answer. I hadn't held hands with a piece of wood and metal. It was a hand. A cold, fleshy hand. I think. Either way, I felt extremely stupid. The only thing to do was to get past the moment . . . fast.

I grabbed my flashlight from under my pillow and then shined it into my bags until I'd found the lanterns and my camera. I packed them together in one bag and slung it over my shoulder. "Let's go find the creepiest angles on this house."

My publisher would let me put ten photos in the book, tops, and if past books were any indication, those would be badly printed so that you could barely tell what was in them. Usually, ten photos were far too few for the projects I was doing. This time, it seemed about right. After all, how many photos of dark and spooky rooms did the book need? I led the way downstairs and paused in front of the cellar door. "Let's start down there. We're definitely getting a photo of the monster cellar into the book. Can you grab that tripod there? I'll need it to stabilize the camera in the dark."

After Thomas removed the trail cam and collapsed the tripod, we descended the cellar steps. I gave a creepy wink to the creepy Dr. Freudstein and then shined my light around to figure out how to maximize the monsters in the shot. It wouldn't be hard. It was an impressive collection. The trail cam blinked its light at us from its perch atop the cistern. "We're going to look like real jerks in this footage," said Thomas, setting down the tripod.

"Don't worry. It'll all eventually be deleted in case it contradicts with however I spin the story of our stay here."

"How are we going to do this?"

"Let me figure out the angle and set up the camera, and while I'm doing that, you can start putting out the lanterns. We can use the flashlights too. Maybe we'll get enough light to make it look atmospheric instead of badly lit."

I quickly found an angle that got some of the dirt floor, a patch of the rough wall, and a good cross section of monsters. Thomas went to work on the lighting, and I set up the camera and attached it to the top of the tripod.

I looked at our handiwork. Not too bad. Although, now that the place was lighted, something seemed off about the room—or the monsters. I couldn't tell which. I looked down at the zombie rising from the dirt. "Is he higher out of the floor? I don't remember seeing his belly button before." It had a rubber worm dangling from it.

"Yeah, he's higher up, and every other creature is a step closer to us."

"I'm serious. There's something different down here."

Thomas looked around and shrugged his shoulders. "It's the light and the circumstances. The last time we were down here, it was a couple of guys with flashlights who were fresh off being terrified of a sound."

"Yeah, maybe." I found the low-light setting on the camera and took a test photo. It came out yellow, but there wasn't much

I could do about that now. I didn't know enough about photography. Maybe I could fix the coloring later in Photoshop, which I also didn't know much about. I took half a dozen more and then messed with the settings again. I hit a button and a countdown started on the screen. "Come on," I said to Thomas. "Let's get a photo together. Maybe we'll use it for the back cover or something." We both jumped on either side of a sack-headed scarecrow. Thomas gave it bunny ears. The automatic timer went off with an anticlimactic click.

Figuring that I had enough monsters on the SD card, I picked up the tripod without removing the camera. I was about to ask Thomas to grab the lanterns when I saw him staring into the black eyeholes of the burlap face of the scarecrow like he was trying to figure out what the face looked like underneath. It suddenly struck me that the first horror movie we'd watched together after he'd explained *Phantasm* to me was *Dark Night of the Scarecrow*. It was a made-for-TV movie from the early 1980s starring Charles Durning. Thomas had found a bootlegged DVD ripped from a homemade VHS. It was a great find, and we'd savored it like secret wine. The lanterns illuminated a cross section of monsters surrounding Thomas like he was in the middle of a horror movie finale. Behind the scarecrow was a vampire. That made me think of *Fright Night*, which we'd watched at the end of my bachelor party. We'd watched the sequel to the movie at the end of his. Beside the vampire was a hockey-masked killer, generic enough to avoid any trademark infringements on the *Friday the 13th* series. One drunken night during college, we'd almost gotten matching tattoos of Jason Voorhees's hockey mask—*The Final Chapter* version—but we'd chickened out. We'd almost gotten it again on three different sober nights over the years. A nearby mummy reminded me of my costume for that Halloween party in college where I'd lost my virginity, thanks to some fighter-pilot-grade wingmanship from Thomas. She'd stuffed her bra with toilet paper, and I'd been wrapped in it. I could measure mine and Thomas's life together with monsters. Such strange hash marks on our timeline. "Felix Allsey, this is your life," I muttered to myself.

"What?" asked Thomas, his attention finally diverted from the scarecrow enough to realize it was time to start gathering the lanterns.

"Nothing. One room down, forty-four to go."

We made our way back to the first floor. I made sure to get shots of the couch that had been my bed for one and a half nights now and the dumbwaiter in the kitchen that was certainly going to have a body stuffed in it at some point. The stupid Rotterdam chairs around the large dining room table were a must. I took a few photos of the library, but I was pretty sure none of them were going to make it into the book.

The more photos we took, the more we got into a groove. Thomas manned the lighting while I decided on angles, set up the tripod, and pushed buttons on the camera. Every once in a while, one of us would jump in the shot. "Stand up there," I said to Thomas while we were photographing the foyer.

"Up where?"

"On the landing there at the top of the steps."

He walked up and stood behind the railing. "Like this?"

"Yeah, but cross your arms. Kind of like Ken Foree in *Dawn of the Dead* when he's standing on the upper floor of the mall in front of the J.C. Penney.

"I didn't bring my fur coat."

"Just do it."

Thomas headed up the stairs, crossed his arms, and intoned: "When there is no more room in hell, the dead will walk the earth."

"Perfect."

We moved to the Hall of Death next and set up a shot to get as many paper signs into it as we could. That would also make it into the book—as long as I didn't screw up the shot.

"Are you going to have to take photos in every single bedroom?"

"Why not? We've got all night." I let the joke sit for a few seconds. "Nah. Just mine, I think. Unless you want one in your bedroom for the memories."

"So much masturbation in there."

"Nice, man."

"Defense mechanism. One hundred percent guaranteed to cure a scary situation."

In my bedroom, I made sure to get the bed in the frame. I already knew the caption for this one: bed where author held hands with an antique prosthetic . . . or a ghost.

Upstairs in the game room, I couldn't decide on the best angle. All those dead animals were so photogenic. "Let's set up a bunch of shots here."

So we went about turning the game room into a studio. Thomas set up lights to gleam off glass eyes and shellacked teeth while I tried to find angles that made them look the most ferocious. At one point, we gathered a small herd of elk-like things around the pool table and tried to make it look as if they were playing a round. They were heavier than they looked. Thomas grabbed an eight ball with the "8" worn off, which somehow made the ball look blind, and rolled it across the bumpy felt. "So you've never had an unexplainable experience. Not once in all of your spooky shenanigans across the country were you like, 'There is no earthly explanation for what just happened.'"

"There's always an earthly explanation for what happens. Nothing ghosts are supposed to do is miraculous."

"I don't understand."

"I meant that all the paranormal phenomena we have in the category of ghosts is easy to write off as naturally occurring: sounds, voices, words, moving shadows, cold spots—all that stuff exists in nature. Every single phenomenon ever put in the ghost category could technically be reproduced with natural effects or could be chalked up to a trick of the mind, which is also a natural phenomenon. The truest evidence will never be video or audio. It'll be a good old ghost trap."

"Like *Ghostbusters*?"

"Exactly like *Ghostbusters*. Once you're able to contain and show a spirit, that's the only way paranormalism will ever be able to make science take it seriously. Controlled, repeatable conditions. Open the box, here's the ghost. Open it again, there it is again." I moved the tripod over and leaned against the table. "But I know what you're asking. There was one time."

"Back when you were a Christian?"

"No. During my heathen college years. Let's get this rhino on a memory card while I tell you." As Thomas helped me set up the next shot, I recounted the closest thing to a ghost tale I'd ever had in my arsenal, at least before my stay at Rotter House.

"It was summer break after my sophomore year in college. I was at my parents' house, the one they moved to right after I started school. At the time, they lived in this brand new development, in a lot cut out of a cornfield."

"I remember that place."

"Yeah. We were bordered by corn as far as you could see on two sides, while the other two sides butted against the most suburban neighborhood you could find. *The 'Burbs* on one side, *Children of the Corn* on the other."

"Courtney Gains is in both of those movies," said Thomas.

"My room was in the attic. The folks hated yelling up two floors to tell me that it was dinnertime, so they installed a doorbell in my room. A cheap one, not hardwired. It was a button taped to the wall in the kitchen and a chime plugged into a socket in my bedroom. One weekend, my folks were gone and so was my brother. I was the only one in the house. Of course, I watched a horror movie."

"Which one?"

"I'm not sure. I want to say it was *Ghost Story*. The one with Fred Astaire. I watched it downstairs in the living room, which was right beside the kitchen where that bell was. At about two in the morning, I went upstairs to the attic to go to bed. As soon as I passed the speaker in my room . . . the chime went off."

"Someone was in the house."

"Yes. My mind went right there. And worse than that, it meant someone had been in the house while I was watching the movie, hiding, watching me watch a horror movie."

Thomas looked around at all the eyes that seemed to be suddenly focused on us. "That's Courtney Gains-level creepy."

"I froze, but my mind reeled at light speed. I thought it was a serial killer. I thought maybe it was a ghost. Sounds trivial, but ghosts do trivial things in movies, right?"

"The red ball in *The Changeling*."

"The stacked chairs in *Poltergeist*. Keep in mind that I'm alone in this house at midnight, looking out a window over fields of dark corn. And I was imagining that whatever it was that pushed the button was on its way up to get me."

"Why would it warn you?"

"That's the thing. There was no reason for it, and that made it worse. So I stood there. I couldn't move, although inside I was panicking. It was an impossibility. I didn't really believe in the paranormal. I didn't believe someone was in the house. And then, about five minutes later, while I was still standing there, it chimed again."

"Fuck."

"No, not fuck. Not this time. That's what helped me. One spooky chime froze my blood. The second one made a parody of the whole situation. Like is there really some sadistic killer down there pushing the button every five minutes? Or is some ghost doing it because eternity is that boring? Felt dumb. And that was enough for my rational brain to kick back in."

"What was it?"

"The batteries were dying in the button downstairs. It was chiming as an alert. Like a smoke detector."

"That's the dumbest story."

"All ghost stories are dumb when you break them down to their individual parts. Here, set the lanterns on the floor by the fireplace." It was polished white marble, chipped and cracked as if it had been exposed to desert heat. "Now take a picture of me." I handed the camera to Thomas, walked over to the fireplace, and fiddled with the mantel.

"What are you doing?" Thomas asked as he snapped a few photos.

"Pretending that I'm looking for a secret passageway."

"Does this place have them?"

"Doubtful. I've examined the plans from different time periods, read renovation reports. I haven't seen anything."

"How else are the girls sneaking around scaring us, then?"

"Do me a favor and pull out any random book or press on any knot of wood you see over the rest of our stay, just in case." I turned around and wiped the dust from the fireplace off my hands. "You started believing in ghosts when you were a kid, right? Your grandmother's house?"

Thomas leaned against the pool table and cycled through the photos on the camera. "Yeah, my grandma's house was haunted."

"That factual? Grandma's house had wood paneling, smelled like untrained cats, and was haunted."

"Pretty much. She always insisted that Granddad was still around."

"And you'd see weird stuff happen yourself?"

"Oh yeah. Bottles would unscrew by themselves on the counter when no one was looking at them. You could see carpet moving like someone was walking across it. Every once in a while you could hear Granddad calling out for Grandma. One time, I think I even saw him. Walked by the doorway as if he had never died and was just heading to the bathroom. I ran out after him, but he was gone."

"How old were you when all this was happening?"

"I was a kid. Like eight or nine," Thomas started reattaching the camera to the tripod. "I was never there as an adult. Grandma died and the house sold, and that was the end of it. These days, it's more of a belief than an experience for me. I can't say 'no' to the possibility. I also think that some people are, like, color-blind to the paranormal. Can't tell red from green, can't interpret a phenomenon as anything but natural. It's an issue of the senses. I always thought that was your issue." He collapsed the three legs of the tripod until they were a single shaft with a camera on one end and then extended it to me.

"It wouldn't be my biggest flaw," I said, taking the tripod.

"The tower room's the last thing we need, right? Or can we use the Ouija board photo?"

"I could probably use a shot of the spiral staircase. I can take care of it by myself though, if you're tired of moving lights around. Definitely appreciate the help."

"Even if I was tired, no way are we splitting up. Not in a haunted house. I barely like us staying in separate rooms."

"That's real sweet, man . . . but I've got bad news for you." Thomas just looked at me, knowing full well that he was going to hate what I was about to say. "I need us to split up at some point, ideally if we have more of those sound shenanigans."

"Why?" Thomas seemed legitimately concerned at what I was suggesting.

"We need to play with the tropes."

J. W. Ocker

"*Ten Rules for Not Surviving a Haunted House* by Felix Allsey," said Thomas. He started pushing pools balls around the obstacle course that was the pool table.

I sat down in a large chair with orange cushions that looked like it belonged on the set of a children's show and laid my elbow on the head of a nearby okapi. "I'd originally planned for us to do it randomly as something to break up the monotony of nothing happening every night. But since that sound the other night . . . I don't know. If it happens again, that's when we should try it, I think."

"Any other tropes you have to play with?" Thomas wasn't looking at me. He kept pushing the balls around.

"You don't know them? We've actually already done some. The Ouija board, the trail cams, darkness."

"Darkness?"

"Any time you're caught in the dark, you're vulnerable to the boogeyman. Only staying in the light protects you. That's why flashlights randomly lose power and lights flicker. Hell, every monster movie from *Dracula* to *Gremlins* plays with that trope."

"And we've basically been in the dark this whole time," Thomas stopped rolling pool balls around and looked up at me, more interested. "What else?"

"Acting like nothing happened when something did. Every character sees something, doubts what he or she sees, and doesn't tell the rest of the group."

"We've basically been doing that, too."

"Right. I mean, there's no hiding things from the group in our situation, but we're still here hanging out, acting like nothing weird has happened in the past few days."

"We're past the point in the movie where the audience is yelling at us that we need to leave now before it's too late." Thomas paused. "Possession is another haunted house trope. Somebody inevitably gets possessed and does the house's dirty work for it."

"That one in particular shows how toothless the haunted house is as a scary story device."

"What do you mean?"

"The haunted house movie is basically a monster movie. But that monster has no claws, no fangs, can't move. If you get out the front door, you win. It can only trap you and then hope somebody in your group is susceptible to picking up an ax and taking everybody out."

"Seems scary to me."

"Possession is scary, but that's a whole different monster than a haunted house. It's like watching a vampire movie, but the victims only die when the vampire sics a werewolf on them. But that also brings us to another trope. Because the house itself can't harm us, it has to use our own fears and past trauma against us."

"Haunted houses are always mind readers."

"Right. And that's because it can only scare us with a sheet ghost so many times. It has to make us scare ourselves. It's also a story trope in general because it makes characters seem more complex. Trauma in the past can be dredged up in the present. You're never supposed to write a story about somebody who's lived a charmed life."

I almost dropped the last sentence as I realized what we were getting close to talking about. Things in our past were being brought up. I sunk deeper into the orange chair. Is this when we finally talk about it? Will Thomas bring it up? Do I have to? Things had been going so well, like life before that night. We sat in silence, wondering who was going to say something. Finally, Thomas made the decision for both of us.

"What about the trope where one of the characters is actually a ghost?"

Chapter 14

"Oh, that one is a great trope," I said, although my enthusiasm was less due to the trope itself and more to the relief I felt in avoiding the unspoken topic. "We should solve it right now." It took me two times, but I finally pulled myself out of the depths of the chair and walked over to him with my hand raised in the air, "High-five, man!"

"Stop being cheesy."

"What? You're embarrassed to give me a high five? Nobody's watching. Let's pretend it's 1985 and you just saw me jump out of a candy-apple-red Camaro in a Members Only jacket." He still didn't raise his hand. "Or are you a ghost?"

"Can I punch you in the nuts? That would prove it, right?"

"High-five me, man." I suddenly felt tension between us. Thomas didn't raise his hand. He snorted and looked over at the opposite side of the room. I repeated myself. "High-five me, man."

Thomas snorted again, but then he raised his hand just enough for me to hit it. I made contact extra hard, and the slap of flesh on flesh reverberated about the room. "There, neither of us is a ghost," I said.

"Yay," said Thomas. "You know, there's nothing wrong with doing all the smart things while staying in a haunted house—not leaving your room, not chasing mysterious sounds." He was still worried about splitting up.

"Where's the fun in that?"

We went up to the tower room and started carefully arranging lights to illuminate the staircase without blasting light out the

136

window. Outside, the fog still lingered, although it was thinner now. More lights and shapes shined through. Maybe the rainstorm from the night before had cleared some of it. Maybe the picture window needed rebooting. I should try to come up here during the day, maybe the next time a ghostly hand drives me from my room. My boots crunched on tiny splinters of glow-in-the-dark plastic planchette that we had missed. I took the shot, but the staircase came out boring and flat in the photo. I promised myself for the tenth time in my life that before my next book I'd take a photography class and pick up a decent camera.

"Man, I wish we could get up to that widow's walk. That'd be a cool photo," I said.

"Let's get it done."

"You think we can?"

"Sure. Do we have anything we can use for a crowbar?"

I thought about it a bit. "How about a crowbar?"

"Might work."

"I saw one down in the library."

"That's . . . a long way away."

He was right. Sure, it was only two floors, but crossing this house was crossing a chasm. Not that it was so big, although it was, but because there was something about the way it was laid out that made traversing it exhausting, especially between floors. Time seemed to slow, darkness seemed to thicken. You almost had to take a moment to decompress yourself at the stairs, like a diver returning from the depths. But I really wanted to get up to that widow's walk. Otherwise, that sealed door would be a dangling plotline in the book: "*Two stars. Never investigated the widow's walk.*"

"You're getting old, man. Let's go get it. What else are we going to do tonight?" I said.

We made the trek down the flight of stairs to the game room, down the flight of stairs to the Hall of Death, down the flight of stairs to the first floor, across the foyer, and finally into the abandoned construction project that was so sadly called a library. Looking around, I actually noticed quite a few tools—a saw, a hammer, a screwdriver—all stuff that, I suddenly realized, would make great murder weapons.

"Where in the Dewey Decimal System do they keep crowbars?" asked Thomas. I heard it as "Wendy, give me the bat."

"Uh . . ." I waved my flashlight beam around the room. Finally, I saw the black bar on top of a pile of shelving board. "There it is." I walked over to it, picked it up, and slapped it into Thomas's hand.

"Ow, man. Take it easy. You're just trying to break my hand tonight."

"Sorry. Kind of hard to judge in the darkness."

"I hope that's not a racist comment. Because now I have a crowbar." Thomas hefted it for a bit and then continued, "Let's go stick our heads out of this submarine and get some air."

And so we made our return trek, across the wastelands of the foyer, up the craggy mountains of the first staircase, through the valley of the Hall of Death. We hacked our way through the jungles of the game room. And, finally, exhausted and bleary, we arrived at the summit of the tower room, ready to pry open the sky. Thomas handed me his flashlight and ascended again to the trapdoor. He tried to wedge the curved end of the crowbar into the tiny crevices outlining the door. The thick metal end skittered across the wood a few times, scratching the surface until it looked like someone had tried to claw their way out of the tower.

"How much damage am I allowed to do to this thing before you lose your security deposit?" he asked.

"Just be careful."

"I don't know, man. I think we should have grabbed the saw instead. This thing might be sealed."

"Here. Come down. Let me give it a try."

Thomas changed places with me. After a few tries and twice as many curses on my part, Thomas spoke up. "Eh, valiant try. On the bright side, the widow's walk could just be another Al Capone's vault."

"No, I can make this work. Hold on." It really felt like this was going to work—if I could just get the leverage right. The door bent up a fraction of an inch. I stuck my fingers in, pinching them painfully, and then forced the door slightly open. I pushed on the door with all the weight I could throw behind my shoulder, and it popped open with a loud crack that froze me in place. I held the crowbar in the air like I was trying to block the sound.

Below, Thomas didn't say anything. We were waiting. Waiting for another crack. Another sourceless sound. Another reality-upending moment. But nothing replied to the sound of rusty hinges and swollen wood.

"Open Sesame, I guess," I said.

I stuck my head through the hole and inhaled the moist, cool air. The widow's walk was not really a walk. It felt more like one of the platforms at the end of a high-wire act or atop a masted ship. It was about five feet across and square, with a good portion of the center taken up by the door. Around the edge was a short wrought-iron fence, about three feet tall, the top of which was lined with spear-like points. Above was the cloudy, moonless sky. I pulled myself up and onto the top, looking over the edge, which dropped some four stories to the cold grass below. Thomas followed.

"I don't think this was meant to be functional," I said, feeling myself teeter a bit and holding onto one of the metal spikes.

A thin, sharp breeze blew across the walk. I could see for miles, even if those miles were dark and obscure, the lights of civilization twinkling through the rents in the fog. I raised the camera and took a couple of photos. Being surrounded by so much space after being trapped inside the house felt weird. Out here, it was as dark as the house, but it was an open darkness. The darkness inside Rotter House was claustrophobic, unsanitary. Both were hiding things, but Rotter House was hiding them only inches away from you.

"So this is where sailor wives would watch the ocean and wait in vain for their husbands' return," said Thomas, looking around. "I don't see the ocean."

"Widow's walks were always just architectural flourishes. I think they're actually inspired by Italian architecture. Nobody waited for far-off sea captains up here. Sea widows hung out in front of their TVs like everybody else."

"Great name for a roof, though."

"Yeah, that's for—wait. Shhh." I turned my head into the breeze. I thought I heard something. Yes, there it went again. Voices from somewhere down below. "Do you hear that?" I whispered.

"Yeah, somebody's talking somewhere down there." Thomas lowered his voice, too.

"Back inside, quick!" I jumped back into the stairwell, and Thomas followed, pulling the trapdoor shut behind him with a muffled thud.

"What's the matter?" Thomas asked.

"Somebody was out there."

"So? There's probably a lot of people out there. The voices didn't sound like they were on the property."

"Doesn't matter. I can't have anybody knowing we're here, remember?"

"We're just two dudes hanging out on a widow's walk of a haunted house in the middle of the night. They'd probably be more inclined to turn us into an urban legend than call the police. In another generation, all the local kids will talk about the two ghosts atop Rotter House, forever reenacting some previous argument, probably over a girl, over and over again, until one of them is pushed to their death."

"Hey, I'm the storyteller here."

I found it ridiculously easy to go to bed that morning. I should have been terrified or at least trepidatious of the ghost hand, I guess, but I really wasn't. By this time, I was definitely more than willing to chalk it up to confusing myself about Rotterdam's prosthetic while under the influence of salty gin and the heavy atmosphere of a haunted house. It was almost dumb. That was a good word for it: dumb. Returning to this same bed was me challenging this house to do better.

As for the noise, if that wasn't paranormal, then it was also dumb. If it was paranormal, it was even more dumb. If my beliefs about reality are going to get turned inside-out, then it better happen in a way that's awe-inspiring. None of this "sounds in the night" business. If you're going to convert me, convert me.

I mean, for goodness' sake, I'm in a bed where two people died next to a drawer full of spooky dolls, and I won't even need a martini to get to sleep tonight. I'm getting real pissed at ghosts.

Thomas, on the other hand, has turned out to be the best thing about this project. We're a team again. Instead of setting up a photo shoot, we should have spent the night hacking together a script for a short film and then filming it. Cast of two, set at a haunted house with a cellar full of props and surrounded by amazing production value. Man, that would be a cool marketing device. Upload that to YouTube. I wish I'd brought a video camera.

But should I feel that way? That's not really fair that he can waltz into my haunted house and my book project like nothing ever happened, like everything has been forgiven. I should be more angry about that than about ghosts being furtive.

Eventually, my mind drifted back to the couple who had died in this room.

Every account I'd read about the mystery focused almost entirely on the question of what actually happened over the course of that one week. For me, the mystery was elsewhere. How had their lives led up to that week? What had happened to put them in that situation and make them so susceptible to whatever it was they were susceptible to? What was that first, innocent step they took that eventually led them to inflict such horror on each other?

I reached into the drawer beside the bed and pulled out a doll at random. She was dressed for a picnic with a red and white checkered dress and a basket in her hand. Otherwise, the same black hair, the same black eyes, the same pale skin. I put her on the pillow beside me.

Another challenge for the house to do better.

Night
Six

Chapter 15

I awoke to the sound of a man screaming.

My first feeling was animal instinct. I wanted to shrink and flatten and slip under my pillow to avoid whatever was making that noise—or whatever was inflicting it.

My first thought, though, was *Thomas!*

I opened my eyes in the darkness and stared at the dim ceiling above me. Then I grabbed the flashlight from under my pillow, leaped from the bed, and ran to the door, throwing it open like a hatch on a ship pitching in a storm. The Hall of Death was empty, the signs on the black doors not stirring at all, as if the hallway hadn't just reverberated a scream down its large throat.

The door to the Spontaneous Combustion Room flew open. It startled me, and out of reflex, I quickly shut my door. Then I realized what had happened, so I threw my door open again, but the door to the Spontaneous Combustion Room was shut. A few seconds later, it opened, and I looked at Thomas, "Was that you screaming?"

"No," he said, looking dazed from sleep, "I thought it was you."

We paused, listening in the silence, waiting to see if the scream was going to repeat, fearing that it would repeat, that it would physically come rumbling down the hallway and attack. But nothing happened.

"There's somebody else here, man," I said.

"No," said Thomas, who kept looking down the hallway like he would meet his doom at the other end. "Some*thing*."

"Either way, we gotta find out." Thomas didn't argue. That would come after my next statement. "This might be that moment you're going to hate me for," I said, "but we really don't have time to discuss it."

Thomas stood there awkwardly, flashlight in hand like he'd been caught stealing it.

"We need to split up."

"Nope. Nope. Nope."

"For the book, man. You take the third floor. I'll take downstairs."

"Goddamn your book."

I took off running to the other end of the hall, relying on the childishness of the act to keep him from following me.

"If I hear that scream again, I'm going out the front door. I don't care if it's you I hear screaming," Thomas yelled after me.

I gave him a big thumbs up like he'd said something encouraging and heartfelt and turned the corner.

The stairs to the first floor were maddening. Part of me wanted to run down them at full speed, like a child on chocolate, but the other part wanted to creep down them like an old person with a bad hip. Stairs are a weird space between floors, a purgatorial region, a place of transition. As I came down, my inner ear had to adjust to a new world. If Thomas had indeed followed my instruction to go in the opposite direction, he was a mere two floors above me, but he might as well have been in another house.

Eventually, I made it to the first floor. It amazed me how comfortable this part of the house was to me. It had been my first experience with the mansion, my first bedroom. My only time alone in the house had been spent here. Even with the panic attack, I felt kind of at ease here—or as at ease as I could in a haunted house.

But it could also be because all the exits were on this floor.

I shined my flashlight around the foyer. It was empty. No body on the floor, no wailing apparition. I shook my head to stop myself from doing that: imaging what could be there—or at least what could be there that would scare the shit out of me. I'd save it for when I'm writing the book in my underwear in the safety of my own house, Elsa asleep in the next room and Scott Walker playing on the speaker.

By this time, I'd started to doubt my decision to split up. It had been fueled by Thomas's obvious fear. I couldn't help pushing him a little bit sometimes. But it had always been part of the plan—just not part of chasing a scream. We should have split up when nothing was going on in the house, when we were bored. I could get half a chapter out of that, I thought.

I continued to philosophize about the concept of splitting up in dangerous situations as I patrolled my end of the house. The reason splitting up has become a cliché in scary stories is because it's a way to do something scary without upending the balance of the characters or pushing the story to a conclusion too early. Maybe not all of the characters believe in the monster. So you pick off a character to show the audience that there is indeed a monster and do it in a way that the rest of the characters can continue in ignorance for a while. That's it. Splitting up is a plot device, not usually a danger in itself.

At least, that's what I told myself as I walked through the dark foyer, shining my light into various rooms, looking for I don't know what. Without really thinking about it, I walked over to the foyer trail cam, although it couldn't show me what it had seen. The box sat there dumbly, blinking its "all is well" light. It suddenly seemed more important than ever to have these cams actively documenting the house. Although so far this haunting had only been auditory—possibly tactile—like the haunted house was whatever the blind equivalent of handicap accessible is. That's not a bad concept: a story about a group of blind people trapped in a haunted house. Had that been done before? I'd been waiting for a long time for my first fiction idea. That's where the real money was, anyway. Out of habit and without regard for my circumstances, I reached into my back pocket for the notebook to jot down the idea but discovered that I had left it back in my room.

I walked back across the foyer and entered the drawing room, my light playing across the walls and furniture. I approached the couch slowly from behind, like a deliberate camera push in the movies. I could imagine that's where the screaming man was lying, his face a rictus of horror, his eyes staring blindly up in terror, whatever it was that caused that scream apparently gone— but really creeping up behind me.

But all the flashlight revealed was cushions.

The kitchen was next. Nothing. That dumb dumbwaiter was shut again. Did the door keep falling, or was Thomas shutting it? I gingerly placed my fingers beneath its handle and lifted, half-squinting my eyes. Empty, except for the circular beam of my flashlight haunting the interior.

In the dining room the stupid chairs were all empty of ghosts. No dinner for the dead was being hosted, no feast for phantoms, no person trussed up in the middle for a cannibal course.

Then I felt something. It was like the air thickened, like the hair on my ears had been tickled. I was still facing the table. My beam was frozen in the middle of its dark surface. I turned around.

A figure walked past the doorway, too quickly for my flashlight to fully catch it. Just walked like it was going to another room, just walked from the nowhere on one side of the doorway to the nowhere on the other side of the doorway. All it did was walk . . . and it was horrible.

Chapter 16

"Thomas?" I whispered, the pit of my stomach telling me emphatically that it wasn't Thomas. I didn't move. Didn't scream. It had walked past. Just . . . *walked* . . . past.

I stood there in the darkness waiting for it to happen again, knowing it would happen again—not wanting it to happen again but knowing it would.

Nothing happened.

Finally, I swallowed—or tried to, my throat and mouth were suddenly dry and thick—hefted my flashlight, and walked toward the darkness of the doorway. Part of me was screaming to go the other way, through the kitchen, away from where I saw the figure. But it had been walking in that direction. I was trapped in a corner of this massive house. I felt like I was about to vomit. I was cold. My skin felt as if it were about to slither off my bones into a sloppy pile on the floor.

I had to see it again.

The closer I got, the more menacing the doorway became. A single finger extending slowly around the doorframe would have dropped me to the ground.

I finally gathered my courage and jumped out into the foyer, pointing the light in the direction the figure had walked. Only an empty foyer and the closed front door. I turned around, squeezing my eyes shut because I knew it would be right behind me. I opened them. Nothing. The blink of the trail cam. More emptiness. The figure had vanished. My decision-point was clear: either keep searching the rooms on the first floor to see if it had dived into one of them or run pell-mell to Thomas in a panic.

"Thomas!" I ran up the steps.

I raced down the hallway, still yelling his name, the signs fluttering in my wake. I rounded the turn to the stairs, and there was Thomas running at me, rushing down the stairs like all the taxidermy on the floor above was in pursuit. Our flashlight beams blinded each other momentarily. He looked as terrified as I felt.

"What is it? What happened?" he asked, breathlessly.

I doubled over to catch my own breath, half gone from running and half gone from fright.

"I saw . . . somebody."

"Who?"

"I don't know. They crossed the doorway to the dining room and disappeared."

"What did they look like?"

That was a good question. What did they look like? I had been no more than a dozen feet from the figure, but I didn't have an impression of it in my mind. I thought hard, trying to remember the nightmare. "It was dark, and I only caught part of her with the flashlight."

"Her?"

Was it a her? Why did I say that? "I guess it was a woman. I think. The way she moved." I struggled a little more with the afterimage. "I think I saw long hair. That's all I got. It happened so fast."

"But she was all there?"

"What do you mean?"

"Did she have legs and arms? Could you see through her? Was she naked?"

"I don't know, man. Like I said, it was more an impression than actually seeing her."

Thomas leaned back against the wall and looked at me in concern. "I'm going to have to ask you this next question. Is this a stunt for your book? Like making us do the Ouija? Like making us split up?"

"No, no, not at all." I realized that if Thomas didn't believe me this whole experience would feel twice as horrific. "I saw . . . something, man."

He continued to scrutinize my face. Finally, his features relaxed. "I'm almost glad we split up now. Nothing upstairs but dead animals. What happened to her?"

"I don't know. She was headed toward the front door, but when I walked into the foyer, she was gone." I tried to phrase it like I had been calm and collected and completely analytical for the entire experience.

"Did she go out the front door?"

"No, I would have heard that. She was . . . gone. Wait. Naked? What kind of a perv are you?"

"Shut up, man. I wonder if the trail cam in the foyer got it," he said.

"It should have."

"So weird."

"What?"

"Well, everything about this, but mostly the fact that I heard a man's scream, and you saw a woman's ghost."

"So you didn't see anything upstairs?"

"No. Not at all. I guess the splitting up thing really works. Still, we should look around down there—together. Make sure somebody isn't hiding under one of the furniture sheets or something. Do you think she had time to make it up the stairs before you did?"

"It's possible."

"We should check these rooms too, then, while we're up here. Keep the search area contained." He scratched his head. "A woman, huh? Weird."

We started searching the rooms in the hallway, opening closets and checking under beds. It was strange work looking for a ghost this way, like playing hide-and-seek. We even started tugging at sconces and pushing panels in case there really was a secret entrance somewhere. Once we were done with the Hall of Death, we went through all the rooms on the first floor, this time checking under furniture and ripping off sheet covers and poking our flashlight beams everywhere. We went down into the basement, but there were no ghosts hiding there either, just the usual monsters.

Finally, dusty and with knees aching from kneeling to look under things, we headed back up to the first floor. I was absolutely itching to watch the footage of this stay from the trail cams. The one in the foyer stood there smugly blinking, concealing its secret knowledge.

In the kitchen, I immediately made myself a lazy martini. Thomas raised his eyebrows. "I need this, man," I said as I took a pull of the lukewarm drink. "Want one?"

"No. Do you think it could have been the woman from the Murder-Suicide Room?"

"Monica Wynder? That's not a bad idea. Could explain the whole man-screaming-woman-appearing thing. Chris and Monica's ghosts would come as a combo pack. I have pictures of her upstairs in my research box in the bedroom. Let's go play mug shots."

We went upstairs and into my room. I grabbed the box from off the dresser and we both sat on the couch to dig through it. I had a few pictures of the Wynders, all of them badly printed from low-res internet images. One was a wedding photo, the two of them posed on a beach in full formal wear sans shoes. In another, they were in a driveway of sorts, both wearing stonewashed jeans and shirts that looked like they'd been designed by a surfboard company. The final image was a candid shot in a living room with a Christmas tree and more stonewash and neon, tousled hair, and bad carpet. They looked young and happy. She had blonde, curly locks. His hair was dark, in almost a military cut. They looked like Midwesterners, like there wasn't an episode of *Cheers* that they didn't love, like there should be a dog between them in every one of those photos. I scrutinized the three images, holding the flashlight at my ear.

"Well?" asked Thomas.

"I don't know, man." I reached for my plastic cup of gin and realized with deep and sincere disappointment that I'd left it downstairs. Still, the few gulps seemed to have settled me. Now I was feeling more curious than anything else. "Could have been her. I don't really remember much about the hair, just that it was long. And I didn't get any look at her face. And, honestly, not much of a look at her clothes, either. Could have been stonewashed, I guess. The Lady in Stonewash."

"A man screaming and a female ghost, and the Wynders died horribly here in this house."

"In this very room. Look at this." I lit up a photo with my flashlight.

It was a crime-scene photo. In it, they were both laid out face-down on the bed, inches from where we were sitting. They were naked, the dark line of their ass cracks like exposed seams from slipshod tailoring. They had angry-looking cuts and bruises all over their skin. They shared a large, dried stain of blood that had been a pool at one time. The bedspread and the carpet were different, but that made it feel creepier, like the room was concealing its tragedy.

"Shit. Don't show me that," said Thomas. There was an edge to his voice. He wasn't joking. "Tell me about the ghost stories for this house."

"Like I said, they're all pretty predictable as far as ghost stories go. You could start making them up on the spot and be predominantly right about them." Still, I searched through the boxes for the stories that I'd printed out. I found a sheaf of papers from various ghost forums, paranormal wikis, and local blog posts. They were in a manila file folder on which I'd drawn a Pac-Man ghost in black ink.

"Old school," Thomas said, nodding at the folder. I didn't know whether he meant the Pac-Man ghost or the paper file.

"All righty, so we've got noises. Mostly of the usual kind: footsteps, moans, knocks in the night, babies crying, whispers, animal sounds—from the taxidermy, I assume. Here's a good one." I read from one of the papers, a blog post by someone with ".blogspot" at the end of their URL who had only posted three times in four years." 'The sounds of a ghostly orgy sometimes bounce around the upper floors.' Not every haunted house has that one."

"No cracking sounds?"

I dug through the papers. "None that I can see."

"Screams?"

"Yeah, screams."

"Male? Female?"

"Doesn't say. Lots of smells, though. Sometimes rank like sewer water. Other times flowery like perfume. One time . . . grilled meat. Don't investigate hauntings on an empty stomach, I guess. Looks like people have tasted blood in the tower room. Did you taste any blood up there?" Thomas shook his head. "Me either. The dumbwaiter moves up and down on its own. The piano plays by itself. Lots of furniture moving here, actually, especially the dining room chairs. Once or twice people have claimed to find a couple of them on the front lawn. No 'free' sign taped to them, so that's how they knew the activity was spectral."

"What about—and don't you dare make fun of me for saying this—full-body apparitions?"

I didn't make fun. But I arched an eyebrow at him. "Yeah, a good bit of them, actually. This place is apparently connected to the other side by a revolving door. Definitely shadow figures. A. L. Rotterdam himself, of course. He's usually the one moving the chairs around and starting the ghostly orgies. You can also catch him staring out the window if you walk past the house at the right moment.

"As far as ghosts with specific backstories go, almost every-body killed in one of the bedrooms has been seen here or there. Asa Horton—he's the one from the Head Trauma Room—he's been seen walking down the stairs leaving a trail of blood behind him on the bannister. Ellen Markson, Strangulation Room, she walks down halls with the same beatific smile on her face that they found on her corpse. Joseph Dunlevy, Suicide Room, he's been seen hanging from both the chandelier in his room and the one in the foyer, although which Joseph Dunlevy, I have no clue. The kids from the Familicide Room are sometimes seen cavort-ing in the game room. Makes sense. And, of course, there's the guy from your room. He doesn't have a name. They call him Mr. Crispy. I'm surprised he hasn't tucked you in yet." Thomas snorted. "Some of the figures are anonymous: a man in a tuxedo, a woman in a white wedding dress, another woman in a black mourning dress. So, you know, typical lady in white, lady in black stories. Probably looking for lost lovers and lost children." I stopped flipping through pages and glanced up at Thomas. "There are about a dozen more, all along the same lines. You want me to keep going?"

"What about the Wynders? Any ghost stories about them?"

I flipped directly to a section that I had marked with a yellow sticky note. "A few. It's been said that the windows in their room sometimes look like somebody splashed blood across them. A lot of times the moans and the screams are attributed to them. A pool of blood has been known to appear on the bed. All phenomenon that I haven't come across in a week of sleeping in here, by the way. Psychics have detected them as presences in the home. Obviously, they're the easiest of the Rotter House stories to research in advance before a visit."

"Any of the ghosts in the stories match up to the figure that you saw?"

"Hmm." I rubbed my forehead and squeezed my eyelids shut. I tried to imagine myself back in the dining room, just me and that table and those stupid chairs. I tried to recapture that feeling of suddenly knowing with certainty right before it happened that my neat little rational worldview was about to be punctured. I tried to remember the form crossing the doorway. Despite it being less than an hour since I had witnessed it, my memory of it was already hazy, like a dream thirty minutes after you wake up.

One thing that seemed strange was that the figure had become more feminine in my memory, even though I hadn't been certain of its gender right away. It's like my mind had officially decided on its own after some subconscious processing that the figure was likely a woman, yet I couldn't remember a single detail about her—not her face or her clothes or the way she moved. She seemed . . . flowy. I couldn't even really remember long hair, despite what I had said. Just a general flowiness. Finally, I gave up and admitted, "I don't know. I saw so little of it. I mean, any number of these ghost women could be her, including Monica Wynder." I stopped and thought for another minute. "And then, of course, there are our wives to think about." I somehow managed a laugh. "I can't wait to tell Elsa and Yvette that we considered them suspects."

And then Thomas's mood changed like it had walked over a cliff. "This is getting stupid. This whole thing. Stupid. We've had three different paranormal incidents, and they're escalating. From a noise to a scream to an apparition. Who knows where that goes next. We should get out of here. Now."

"But why?" I asked.

"What do you mean, 'But why?'" He looked at me like I was the dumbest person on the planet.

"Who cares if weird stuff has happened?"

"Who cares?"

"Right, who cares? We've heard some noises. I saw something . . ."—I paused, searching for the appropriate word—"surprising. But nothing actually bad has happened to us. Even if these incidents are escalating in some way, they're all still just a show. Nothing has menaced us. Nothing has harmed us, not so much as a scratch. You're reacting like we've learned there's a gas leak in the house."

"This is something potentially as dangerous as a gas leak."

"Ghosts? Ghosts are as dangerous as a gas leak? You're getting ridiculous. When have ghosts ever hurt anybody?"

"You're being a jerk again."

This time, the comment made me double down. "I know there are cases on the books of people getting scratched or bruised in strange situations. There are urban legends of people having heart attacks. But no death certificate in the entire history of the human race has ever read 'death by ghost.' It's the difference between fiction and life. In the movies, the books, ghosts will mess you up, sure. In real life, they don't even hurt your real-estate value."

"What we've experienced so far? These are warnings." Thomas was showing an obvious frustration with me, the way he'd get when our drunken arguments in the past went too far—or when I was winning them.

"That's my point. Warnings against what? Something that will eventually jump out and scream "boo" or levitate a frying pan to throw at our head? Look at the most famous cases of real-life hauntings, the Enfield Poltergeist, the Amityville Horror, the Perron Haunting. Those people lived with ghosts for a long period of time. They were fine. They all got movie deals."

Thomas exhaled loudly through his nose and shook his head. "Good point. Real good point. Seems to me that makes this little book project of yours really stupid then, right?"

"What do you mean?"

"I mean that you're all hyped up for what you're calling a book that nobody's done before, but by your own admission, these people have already done exactly what you're doing here—and over a longer period of time: months, years. Makes this whole two-week thing trivial."

I stared at him in shock. He'd never ripped on any of my projects like that before. He'd made fun of them, of course, in the way you can only do with your closest friends, but he'd never truly belittled them. He knew very well how much they meant to me, how much they defined me.

I fought back. "This is completely different. What they did, if you believe the accounts—and I don't—but narratively speaking, all they did is go about their lives plus ghosts. They went to work, went shopping, celebrated Christmas. This, what I'm doing here, what me and you are doing here is total immersion, sensory deprivation, a standoff. Us versus the paranormal. They spent their whole time in a haunted house trying to minimize paranormal phenomenon. We're trying to maximize it. But, that said,"—I shook my flashlight at him—"I'd agree with you that all of this makes the paranormal trivial. Because it is. Every single ghost story is nothing but a bad roommate story. You put up with them for a little while. Then you leave or they do. And if that's the way every single real-life haunting story goes, why are you so terrified of ghosts? You'd have to be an idiot to be scared of ghosts. Your grandmother wasn't scared of ghosts."

"Not terrified, you jerk. Cautious. The unknown is exactly that . . ."

But I wasn't done. "And you haven't even seen a single ghost in this house. You heard something breaking, and days later, you heard a scream. That's it. I'm the one possibly holding spectral hands and definitely seeing apparitions. So a couple of sounds and some secondhand stories from me after however many nights you've been here are enough to send you running out of here? Especially when you know that I can't leave? When this project is so important to me? Nice, man. Real nice."

"You can totally leave. And I'm telling you that you should. We should leave."

"Cowardly, man."

Thomas's eyes opened wide and his nostrils flared. "Stop acting like this book project gives you an excuse to do whatever you want. Leave your wife for two weeks, subject me to this, put yourself in danger. And, yes, you're the one seeing things here—things you've never seen before. You should be more worried than I am. Remember that 'one experience away'? You've had it. Three, maybe four times. Stop pretending that the paranormal is silly. Stop pretending that you're better than this project, better than everybody who's ever believed in ghosts, better than me. We need to leave. Think up another idea for a book. Call this one *Six Nights at Rotter House*. Fill it out with research. Every night we've been here, it has become more obvious that we shouldn't be."

"That's horror movie plots bringing you down. That's not how real life works. Real life works like this: we'll spend two uncomfortable weeks here, leave with great relief because we're exhausted and dirty and haven't had sex in two weeks, and then we'll talk about it for years, looking back on it as a great adventure, and wondering exactly what we experienced here. This book project is important."

"No. No it's not. You've written half a dozen books. This one ain't worth it—any of it. Every writer has at least one bad idea that they pursue for too long. This one is yours."

That hurt. Thomas was good with insults. And he knew exactly the ones that would spear me. "It is important. And I need this book."

"Man, no you don't . . . "

"This is my last chance at my life."

Chapter 17

"What are you talking about?" asked Thomas.

I turned my flashlight off, pushed his away from me, and stared at the bed, right where two people had died mysteriously. In the gloom, I could see the vague shape of one of the dolls lying there on the bed. Another lay on the floor near us. "I do need this book, man. Financially, I need this book. Personally, I need this book. You know my books don't sell well."

"You've got an audience."

"A niche one. A niche of a niche one. But that doesn't sell a lot of books. I basically make ends meet with Elsa's salary, and that's not a large one. You don't know what it's like, man. You and Yvette are rich."

"We're not . . . "

"You basically are. You're not one-percenters, but you're doing really well. Me and Elsa? We're scraping by. We've talked a lot about it over the years. Every book, I tell her, 'This is the big one. The one that sets me up, that brings in the money, that opens all the opportunities.' I make huge promises to her. But it never happens. And this time, I promised her one more book. I had to. If this book doesn't do well, doesn't bring in some solid money or some solid opportunities, my writing career is over. I'd have to go after a steadier job, become a copywriter or an English teacher. It's either that or lose Elsa. She won't stay by me if I stick to this, if I put my odd little books above our life together. It was always kind of inevitable that way, I think."

"Why now? Why not five books ago?"

"We had the fight five books ago. And four books ago. And three books ago." I ran a hand through my hair and sighed. "I think she wants a baby. And the way our life is right now, we can't afford one. So this book has to work or else I have to completely change who I am."

Thomas aimed his light at the bed and stared at it for a few moments. "Maybe she's right."

"What the hell do you mean?"

"Maybe quitting on the book career might be a good thing."

"Man, don't."

"What? You've had a good run. You have a bibliography. You're in the Library of Congress catalog. Nobody can take that away from you. And you'll always write. You might not dedicate every waking minute to it anymore or publish any of it, but you'll write here and there. It'll be a hobby. And you'll make Elsa happy. That's more important than your books, right?"

I hated what he was saying. Absolutely hated it. I have the same problem with Elsa. They don't get how important having these experiences and writing about them is to me, how cellular it is for me. But also, they both might be right. Maybe giving up on being a writer might free me. People always claim you should stick to your dreams; they also claim you should sacrifice yourself for those you love. They never talk about how you can't do both or how everything is pretty selfish in the end. I wanted to write books, to see and experience things more interesting than my boring, inconsequential everyday life. It made me, me. No, it made me a better me. But Thomas wasn't done.

"On the other hand, maybe you're right. Maybe these projects you jump into are that integral to who you are. And if that's true, then maybe—and I don't say this lightly—maybe you and Elsa are ready for different paths. Maybe she needs somebody with more stability. Maybe you need somebody who can support your writing better. It's not unusual. It happens to almost everybody at some point."

The suggestion appalled me. I couldn't live without Elsa. I wanted her *and* my books. Why couldn't I have both? I ignored his suggestion. "All I know is that if this is going to be my last shot, I want to give it a legitimate try."

"I don't think writing a hit book will solve your situation."

"Let me find out for myself—including staying here and figuring out Rotter House." I shined my light at the doll on the bed. The shadows from the bedding made it look like it had a dark circle around it.

"You should start believing what you've experienced with your senses, and we should both pack up and leave. Or skip the packing up. Just leave. Come back in the daytime in another week or so and get our stuff then."

"Six more nights, man. That's all I need."

"Idiot." Thomas stood up, stomped on the doll lying on the floor, and slammed the door as he left.

Later, after I'd shut off the trail cam and written down my notes for the day, I lay on the bed and stared at the ceiling. I thought about our argument. On the one hand, conflict is great for a story. More like absolutely necessary. So some friction between Thomas and me wasn't necessarily a bad thing. But it sure does suck.

Besides, he has no right to get mad at me. Like, ever. He lost that luxury a year ago. And he certainly has no place giving me relationship advice. I was mortified by what I had told him, about the book, and Elsa. Man, I told him that she wanted a baby. I can't believe I told him that. I shouldn't have had to do that. But I did. For the book.

As for that apparition, I don't know what to make of what I saw. Nothing about the situation was trustworthy. Darkness and fear and the scream and the aloneness. It's not exactly the most trustworthy context for one's senses. But even accounting for that, I don't know. It seemed like a figure, a woman. But it was so fast, it could have been me interpreting the darkness according to the demands of an exhausted and hyperextended imagination. And my imagination certainly couldn't be trusted. Not even under the best of circumstances.

I did learn one thing tonight, although it's of zero value other than color commentary. There's something especially awful about the sound of a man screaming. I'm not sure why. Maybe it's sexist. Maybe I'm more used to hearing women scream from all the horror movies I've saturated myself in over the years. Hell, I could hear a woman scream back at the house at any point in time just by jumping around a corner at Elsa. More philosophically, maybe it's that there is a musicality to a woman's scream. A definite talent inherent in it. A man's scream is talentless, desperate, rarely used. Maybe I identified with it more.

Yeah, maybe it was just sexist.

Anyway, there is no way I'm leaving Rotter House. Sure, for the sake the book—it was the whole point of the book, actually. But now I had two more reasons: to piss off Thomas and to get at the core of these strange phenomena.

The one good thing about being angry at Thomas right now, though, was that it sure made it easier to sleep in a haunted house, even after seeing a ghost. It's hard to be scared when you're mad.

Night
Seven

Chapter 18

I awoke to the sound of a woman screaming.

My reaction to the sound was different this time. I still tried to squeeze myself under the pillow—but not out of terror, out of abject laziness and anger, like a kid being shaken awake for school. I didn't want to deal with this. Not again. Running around the house, running into phantoms, fighting with Thomas over it. I still hated that he wanted me to leave Rotter House, hated even more that he knew about the direness of my life, hated that we were hiding under ghosts and books and were really fighting about something else.

A few more seconds of collecting myself finally dispelled that sleepy mishmash of thoughts that were just a continuation of my near-sleep thoughts. No way was I not going to follow that scream. Even if it was Garza herself out there making it. For the book, for the book, for the book—always for the book. Maybe Thomas was right about my priorities.

I grabbed my flashlight from under the pillow and shined it around the room. My eyes must have been adjusting to the dark because I was starting to see color in those circles of light. I had gradually noticed it yesterday while we were searching all the rooms for the apparition. I was seeing each room in color instead of in variations of dark and light. My room wasn't pale anymore; it was pink, obviously pink. If I stayed on this reverse schedule too much longer, I'd go owl-eyed. I imagined myself walking into the full daylight of the outside world on day fourteen and then writhing around in agony on the lawn like a mole rat turned from the dirt with a shovel.

A knock on my door startled me out of the bed and onto my feet, followed quickly by a whisper. "Hey. Hey, Felix. You awake? Did you hear that? The scream? A woman this time."

I crossed the room and opened the door. Thomas was there, flashlight in hand. "I heard it." I said. "You ready to chase another mysterious noise through the dark?"

"If I have to, but we're not splitting up this time."

"You just want to see the ghost for yourself."

"At least you're calling the ghost what it is now."

"Where do you think it came from?" I asked.

"I don't know. Far away."

"It probably doesn't matter which way we go to start looking, right?"

"Probably not," said Thomas.

"Let's go upstairs, then."

We hit up the few bedrooms on the third floor and found nothing capable of turning us into gibbering maniacs—only emptiness, furniture, and darkness. What I at one point had thought would be the entire content of the book, actually. Next, we headed to the game room. Flashing my light around, I could see that Thomas was right about the color of the room. It really was deep red. I liked the color, honestly. Maybe it was time to repaint my study. I'd have to see if Sherwin-Williams carried *The Masque of the Red Death* red. After a few minutes of intense searching, it became obvious that although there were a lot of mouths in this room, nothing here had screamed for a very long time.

The tower room was still bare, the fog still wrapped in ever-thinning tendrils around the world outside. Thomas even popped his head up through the trapdoor of the widow's walk to make sure nobody was hiding there. Standing at the base of the stairs below him, the ridiculous image occurred to me of Thomas's head sticking out of the top of Rotter House like the mansion was his body.

"What are you chuckling about down there?" asked Thomas.

"You've got a fat ass."

Next came the Hall of Death, a nickname that I had really liked at first but now seemed to have devolved into parody with overuse. We opened door after door, checked room after room. The sign on the Familicide Room had fallen down, so I reaffixed it to the door, pressing on the weakened adhesive extra hard. It only had to hold out for six more nights.

Downstairs, I followed my path almost exactly as the night before, with Thomas at my heels, even to the point of opening the dumbwaiter. "Do you keep closing this?" I asked Thomas.

"Of course I do. Why would I want to stare into an open dumbwaiter. That's spooky."

Eventually, we found ourselves in the dining room with those stupid Rotterdam chairs. "That's where it happened, man. She walked by right there." I turned my body to face the doorway into the foyer, a rectangle of blackness perforated here and there by our badly guided flashlight beams.

Nothing crossed that threshold, but we still waited for it like it had been promised.

As we stared into the stillness of the doorway, I asked Thomas a simple question. "Are our actions believable?"

"I don't understand the question," he replied.

"I mean, are we responding to what's happening in this house in a way that somebody hearing this story would believe?"

"You mean reading this story," he said.

"Yeah."

"I think this is one of those situations where I don't think anybody really knows how they'd respond. I mean, if you had asked me a month ago if I would have stuck it out in a haunted house after hearing screams in the night, I'd have said 'no way.' But here I am, standing in the dark, waiting for a ghost woman to walk by."

"But you wanted—want to leave."

"I do. But I haven't."

Both of us seemed to be aiming our flashlights away from each other, like we were more comfortable not being able to read each other's faces. I decided not to push too hard. "But a lot of people would have taken off, right? Would have gone directly out the front door after that first series of noises."

"I think the kind of people who would have left by this point wouldn't have been here in the first place. You know . . . the intelligent ones."

I laughed. "I've always wanted to write a scene where a bunch of people are sitting in a theater watching a horror movie. Somebody in the audience yells at the screen because he thinks that the character is doing something extremely stupid and dangerous and contrived. The character on screen immediately stops the movie, looks directly at the audience member, and reams him. Says, 'You're going to tell me how I should act in this insanely high-pressure situation? I just learned twenty minutes ago that monsters exist and that my life is in imminent danger. I'm not in my right mind. You, on the other hand, have no excuse for the dumb decisions you make every day. That's probably why you're here alone in this theater at 11 a.m. on a Wednesday, a hundred pounds overweight and in an ugly T-shirt. Now shut your moron mouth and watch the movie.'"

It was Thomas's turn to laugh. "And then the movie character looks at the mutant killer in the background who is standing with his head down, embarrassed at the exchange and holding his machete uncertainly, before saying, 'All right, sorry about that. Let's keep going.' Then he screams like a seven-year-old girl and runs offscreen."

Finally, after coming to the conclusion that the ghostly figure I'd seen yesterday didn't encore on demand, we walked through the rest of the rooms on the first floor. We found even less than we found on the third floor. All we had left was the cellar.

"What if the scream came from outside the house?" Thomas asked as we stood in the foyer, equidistant from the cellar door and the front door, our flashlight beams chasing each other across the foyer walls and the chandelier, before resting on the long, balustraded landing at the top of the stairs. "Are you allowed to go outside and check everything out in that situation? Does that break your rules for the book?"

"Actually, in this case, I think it's—"

And then she walked across the landing, right through the twin beams of our flashlights, disappearing into the darkness on the other side. The ghost of Monica Wynder.

Chapter 19

"There she is!" I shouted.

"I saw her," said Thomas. "I goddamned saw her."

I took off up the stairs, Thomas not too far behind me. I don't know why I was chasing her. Or why Thomas was. She should be chasing us, right? With her arms raised and screaming. This whole thing felt weird. I hit the top of the stairs, crossed the landing, and ran down the Hall of Death, the only direction she could have gone. My flashlight beam caught the hem of her robe floating around the corner at the far end. It was silky and teal and seemed to have a flower pattern on it, kind of a silly outfit for a ghost.

I picked up speed down the straightaway of the hallway, the paper signs flapping here and there like they were cheering me on, and then I turned the corner . . . and put my face into hers. Directly inside. Her face was split open, the interior skin pink and wet and throbbing. A thin strip of skull bone lined up with the tip of my nose. My face was inside hers, and then I was halfway through her. I could see the walls and doors behind her. But then she backed up, extricating herself from my body, reaching her hands out for me.

I ran in the other direction past Thomas.

Down the Hall of Death.

Down the stairs.

I threw myself into the corner of the foyer by the front door and covered my head with my hands. I could still smell the rich, sour moistness inside her face, felt the bone chill of being inside of her and her inside of me, the fire of her hands reaching out to me. The ghost of Monica Wynder.

"Get up. We gotta get out of here!" I looked up to see Thomas standing over me, his hands shaking a little, his head shaking a lot. He was shouting at me. "Let's go, man. Let's go. Get up!" I heard him from far away.

A woman's scream reverberated through the house again.

"She's coming," Thomas said. He reached for the knob on the front door, but I grabbed his wrist and pulled him down beside me. He was about to leave without me, to leave me alone with her.

Thomas crouched beside me, facing the stairs. He didn't even try to pull his wrist out of my hand. We both froze and trained our flashlights on the landing above us. The circles of light shook from our trembling hands, the spotlight on the curtain ready to ripple open for the next guest on the late-night talk show.

But she didn't come. We waited longer, and still nothing.

"You walked right through her," said Thomas.

"You saw that, right?"

"Yes."

"Did you see her face?"

"It was messed up, right? It didn't look like a face." He cast another glance up at the landing.

"It was split apart. Right down the middle." I shivered at the memory of being inside of that face.

And then I laughed—hard.

"Here it is, man. You're broken," said Thomas, still staring up at the landing. "This story is ending with you in a padded room listening to Syd Barrett over and over again."

"Did you see what she was wearing? A teal silk robe with red roses on it. And I swear she had on red leather heels. What self-respecting haint would wander through the afterlife in a haunted house scaring visitors . . . while wearing an outfit from

173

Victoria's Secret." I couldn't stop myself from laughing again. This time, Thomas joined me, although more quietly, like he was more humoring me than actually finding humor in my observation.

"She definitely wasn't no model with that face."

"You're telling me—" And then it hit me. "Wait. Wait, wait, wait. Holy shit."

"What's wrong?"

I had been imagining how ridiculous the book would look with a split-faced Victoria's Secret model on the cover, like it was one of those throwaway horror paperback novels from the '80s, the lurid ones that only cared if you bought the book, not what you thought of it after you read it. I had just gotten to the image of me sitting, lonely, at a small table in the corner of a tiny bookstore, a large poster of the book cover on an easel behind me. And then it hit me.

"I know that ghost. Come on." I got up and ran the few steps to the cellar door, Thomas following me but not before throwing furtive glances both upstairs at the landing and then back toward the front door. I threw open the cellar door and rushed down the stairs, hardly taking time to use my flashlight and blowing past Dr. Freudstein at the bottom of the stairs. I saw the trail cam light blinking faithfully at its post atop the cistern.

"All right, where is it?" I started shining my light at every monster's face like I was interrogating each one: vampire, were-wolf, killer clown, witch, scarecrow.

"Where is what?"

"The Split-Faced Woman." I frantically shined my light in the faces of more monsters: zombie, mummy, *Creature from the Black Lagoon* rip-off, skeleton.

"She's somewhere upstairs, waiting for us to round a corner again," said Thomas.

"No, that's not what I meant." I was still checking monster after monster but paused after examining the facial deformities of a beast that looked like Sloth from *The Goonies*. I looked at Thomas, or at least I looked at the space in the dark a few feet above his flashlight. "This is where I saw her the first time."

"The first time, what are you talking about? You said that you saw her in the foyer."

"I didn't realize it then, but that was the second time. I saw her the first time down here, the first time we came down to the cellar. That Split-Faced Woman in the lingerie was here, one of the monsters. Standing there like she was made of polyresin. Remember? *Sexy* was what you called her, I think."

"What the fuck. I do remember that," said Thomas, more to himself than to me.

I whipped out a notebook that I had made sure to put in my back pocket this time and wrote, *The first time I saw the ghost, I didn't know I was seeing the ghost.* "I think I've got the first line in the book." I stuck the notebook back in my pocket and returned to the urgent task of spotlighting monsters. Eventually, I had checked every monster in that cellar—every single mutated, ghoulish, toothy, scowling face. The Split-Faced Woman wasn't there. I did find where I think she had stood, though. A blank patch of hardened dirt in the darkness, not even a set of high heel prints to belie that she had been down here.

"Are you saying that the ghost of Monica Wynder was camouflaging herself down here that first night? Like E.T. in a closet full of stuffed animals?" Thomas looked around and then approached an insect-headed humanoid, shining his light into its multifaceted eyes. "I wonder which one of these is her husband's ghost then."

I was still looking at the section of dirt floor where I had first seen her. "I don't think it's Monica Wynder's ghost."

"Let's not argue about that again. You walked right through her."

"I'm talking about the crime-scene reports. There's nothing about her face being messed up that way." The crime-scene photo had shown her facedown and nude, but none of the reports, neither the official autopsy nor the media stories, had mentioned anything about a hatchet wound to the face or anything that would seem to make her ghost wander eternity gashed open. I also didn't remember anything about the clothes she was found with.

"Okay, okay, whatever. But you do think it's a ghost."

"I don't know what to think, man. And I definitely don't want to have that argument right now." I stopped and swung my light around, watching it glint off glass eyes as it passed. "But I do know that I walked right through her."

"I can't believe your 'one experience away' was literally walking through a ghost. Some jerks have all the luck. Although I don't begrudge you all that much. Must suck to lose fifteen years' worth of arguments. Winner." Thomas high-fived a nearby skeleton. The plastic bones clacked in return. Thomas's celebration was short-lived, though. He turned around and looked at me. "I think this book is over, man."

"Are you kidding?" I couldn't believe he was going there again. Especially now. "This book is just getting good. I came in a skeptic, and Rotter House terrified me into becoming a believer. I mean, I have a lot of shit to sort through and think about before I go all ghost crazy, but that will all be part of the story. This book is going to be great."

"You've seen the movies, man. We're to that point in the story where everybody has seen the ghost or the monster or the killer and knows that they are in imminent peril. We're officially in danger. There's no narrative reason for us to survive any longer. Rotter House's owner will walk into this house six nights from tonight and find us dead in our beds from mysterious causes. We'll be the latest ghosts of Rotter House. That's how this goes."

"Ghosts can't hurt us."

"How do you even know what ghosts can or can't do? You didn't even believe in them until ten minutes ago. And now you know things about them? So dumb."

"I walked right through one, you know. I'm fine. And I've seen her twice now. And the noise didn't hurt us, and the screams didn't hurt us. Ghosts can't hurt us."

"This is stupid."

"You can leave by yourself if you want."

"And ruin your book?"

"Oh, my book can't be ruined now. I've got a real, live ghost—and goddamned footage." I pointed at the blinking light above the cistern. "Hell, you leaving now might even be a good plot point for the story, raise the stakes even higher, make the situation even scarier, put the spotlight back on me again." Thomas shook his head and stared at the zombie rising out of the floor. I continued, "Even better, none of the ghost legends I've ever read about this place say anything about what we've experienced in this house. I might be able to invent a new ghost legend. Monica Wynder could be up there with Bloody Mary and every single lady in black in the country."

"I thought you said the ghost wasn't Monica Wynder?"

"I'm saying that it doesn't matter. Call her Monica Wynder. Call her the Split-Faced Woman. Hell, call her the Victoria's Secret Ghost."

"You don't need me at all, huh?"

"Not anymore. And I certainly don't need you putting pressure on me to go home or stop this book project or split up with Elsa. I told you. I need this thing to work. And now, I've got what I need to make it work."

"I never meant that you should split up with Elsa. I was just . . ." Thomas took a few steps backward, increasing the space between us. "You're starting to worry me. There's nothing wrong with ending this book with us fleeing in terror right now. Think of it this way: it might even make it better. It leaves it open for a sequel: *Return to Rotter House*. If one book about this place sets you up to bring in the cash you need to make Elsa happy, think about what two books about it could do for you."

"Shut up about Elsa. And I'm sticking to the original plan. If you want to help me, stay. If you don't want to, then leave. You know how to leave me behind, right? You've got that move?"

"That's where we're going with this?"

"Why not? That's why you're really here, right? To figure that shit out? That's what we're really arguing about. Not ghosts. Not a book."

"Is that why *you* are okay with me leaving? You asked me here, after all."

"I don't know what I wanted when I asked you to come. I don't think I want you here right now, though. The booze is upstairs. Why don't you go get drunk until you can't remember anything."

Thomas stopped and looked around the cellar at all the frozen fiends, at the dirt floor, at the blinking light, at the darkness. "Fuck you." He stomped up the cellar stairs and slammed the door, leaving me alone with the monsters.

Night
Eight

Chapter 20

For the second night in a row, I was in the cellar alone. This time, instead of pacing around, fuming at Thomas while giving the monsters a hairy earful, I was doing routine maintenance, changing out the memory card and batteries in the trail cam perched on the cistern lip. Behind me, in the darkness, monsters of every strain of nightmare lifted their clawed hands into the air. Their presence was starting to comfort to me. I might need to take one home as a souvenir when I left. It would look good in my study against *The Masque of the Red Death*-colored walls.

I had been replacing batteries and memory cards in all the trail cams since I awoke that evening. Over the course of my stay at Rotter House, recording its innards had gone from a vague possibility to a decent gimmick to an extremely important part of the experiment. I really needed the footage—not only to back up my story but for my own clarity. I needed to hear if the house had screamed, if a woman with a split face had walked across its foyer and its landing and its hallway. I needed to see if there were any strings. Basically, I needed something to help me deal with the strange events in this house, strange events that occurred for only an audience of two and a bunch of secondhand trail cams.

But even if nothing paranormal showed up, if I just looked like an asshole running down the Hall of Death, skidding to a stop in horror and turning around for no apparent reason, it wouldn't be the end of the project. The way I see it, if people thought it was a hoax as a result of the ghostless footage—and who could blame them in that case—the controversy might still be beneficial to book sales. Another possibility is that I could pretend that I never set up cameras in the house and just leave that part out as an overcomplication that could obstruct the narrative. Only Thomas would know otherwise.

But I was getting ahead of myself. First, I finish my stay, then I check the footage, and then I do whatever it is that I need to do after that, even if it includes using phrases like "obstructs the narrative."

The entire time that I'd been losing the tiny screws on the battery compartments and confusing full SD cards with empty SD cards, my thoughts were only for that ghost—the ghost of Monica Wynder. Or whoever. Or whatever. My "one experience away." Actually, I tried to force myself to think of it as an apparition instead of a ghost. It was a much more comfortable term for me. If it was the soul residue of some dead person, then it was an accurate term. If it was a complete joke on me by Garza and a few high-tech projectors, it was still an accurate term. The word "ghost," though, put me directly on a team, gave me a philosophical bias. But it was such an easy word to use, and it didn't help that the only person I could talk about it with for the next few days would only use that term.

Speaking of Thomas, after he and I parted ways yesternight, I spent most of my time in the Murder-Suicide Room. I was partially avoiding him, of course. I didn't want to be around the guy. Things were getting ugly and teetering in the wrong direction. Some of that was my fault. But some of it was his. Most of it was his. It was his move, had been his move since he showed up in that foyer. But he hadn't made one, wouldn't even drink with me more than half a martini's worth.

But I also spent the rest of the night in that room hoping that I would see the Split-Faced Woman again. I'd seen her in the foyer, on the landing, in the Hall of Death. It seemed inevitable that she was making her way to the master bedroom—especially if she was Monica Wynder.

And I was excited about the prospect.

I probably should have been on the couch in the drawing room, all my flashlights and electric lanterns and candles powering the darkness away, singing the theme from *Mister Rogers' Neighborhood* as loudly as I possibly could, anything to render the terror of a ghostly encounter in a haunted house ridiculous and safe.

But even as I lay in bed, disappointed that she had not reappeared, I maintained a hope that the apparition would return, that she would awaken me by bursting through the door screaming, by creeping slowly out of the corner where there always seems to be a shadow, or with a cold hand around my neck. All the things a normal person would never want to happen in a haunted house.

Listen to how I sound—like I totally believe in ghosts. I mean, I didn't totally believe that Garza was playing a trick on us. I'd been inches from the pulsing pink membrane, been inside of it. It was real. Whatever "real" meant, that was it. But I also didn't totally believe that she *wasn't* playing a trick on us, either. Who and what sort of trick, I had no idea. As far as I knew, projection technology wasn't advanced enough to create what Thomas and I had seen, even if Garza was rich enough to afford technology that was basically science fiction to the rest of us. Screens and headgear were still needed to augment reality. But who knows? Maybe the trick could be pulled off with couple of good old-fashioned mirrors. Regardless of whether it was a trick or a legitimate unexplained phenomenon, my course of action was still the same: document and discover.

And not at all flee in terror.

I kept playing the moment over in my mind. Seeing her on the balcony. Chasing her. Being inside of her. And then running away from her. For all my bluster about ghosts not being able to hurt anybody, I had taken off, terrified, like she had an AK-47 pointed at me. I played it totally wrong.

I should have stayed there, in front of her, inside her, behind her, didn't matter. But I should have stared her down, face to split face, to see what would happen after the jump scare. That's where they always cut away or end the chapter.

A light blinked at me as I finished with the trail cam. I wended my way through the monsters to the stairs, tripping slightly over the zombie rising from the floor. I swung the light around one more time to make sure the ghost in the ridiculous Victoria's Secret robe wasn't trying to camouflage herself again among the polyresin terrors and then headed upstairs, still hoping for an encounter.

I just needed to see if I really believed it all. Because, honestly, even after all that had happened in this house, I couldn't say I believed in ghosts yet.

When I lost my religion, my belief in invisible presences both angelic and demonic, my belief in an afterlife, my belief in the resurrected dead, it was a gradual process. Almost a glacial one. Doubt of this minor element and then doubt of that minor element and then practical life experience upon practical life experience and eventually, one day, I realized I hadn't believed for a while. It had happened without me realizing it.

That's kind of how I thought it would go with the paranormal. I'd write about it and write about it and write about it, and then suddenly, I'd look back and realize I believed it in some way. Not in like a Whitley Strieber kind of way, just softly acknowledging—what's the phrase?—more things in heaven and earth than are in your philosophy. Actually, that might be a literary reference. Arthur Conan Doyle or something. I liked him a lot, felt a kinship with him. I mean, here I was, writing about the supernatural while believing in the rational, and there he was writing about the rational while the whole time believing in the supernatural. He even made the Baskerville Hound a little bitch.

Monica Wynder never came to my room. She was too much a lady, I guess. I eventually figured that tomorrow night I'd convince myself that the apparition wasn't real—or whatever Ebenezer Scrooge had said, "an undigested bit of beef, a blot of mustard." But that guy got to have a whole conversation with his first ghost, and then he hung out with ghosts all night, what I should have found a way to do with the Split-Faced Woman. If only I hadn't run. If only I'd waited until she disappeared or until the science fiction projector that Garza had brought back from the future with her expensive time machine was turned off or until things got so awkward that it sucked all the haunt out of Rotter House.

Speaking of beef and mustard, I realized that I was hungry and hurried up the cellar stairs to the kitchen. Hopefully I had some Tabasco-flavored Slim Jims left.

I had to admit, my excitement over the experience had abated somewhat as I robotically exchanged batteries and memory cards. In fact, I'd surfaced on this night bleary, slowly putting pieces together from the evening like I drank too much, although I didn't remember drinking anything.

I figured that once I was back home, done with this phase of the project, I could delve into my feelings about the existence of ghosts in a more objective way, with some time and this haunted house far behind me. The possibilities were terrifying, though. Where else was I wrong? It was the same question I had asked myself when I'd finally sloughed off Christianity. Where else was I fundamentally wrong about life and the universe and how everything worked? When would the next shattering evidence against my beliefs happen? Does it ever stop, or is life a cycle of us realizing how stupid we are over and over again until we die?

But all those conflicted feelings were somewhat paper-weighted by the fact that it was totally making this book a better book. Hell, a book at all. A book I needed to be great—a book I needed to sell well, more accurately. A career starter after a career of books. So pathetic. As I swung my flashlight around tattered wallpaper and old wood and snatches of carpet, the house seemed less murky for some reason. I could name each color almost down to the shade, like I was an interior designer. I seriously wondered if my eyes were not merely adjusting but permanently altering. I pulled out my notepad and made a note to look through the science journals when I was back in the Internet world, see if there were any studies on the effects of prolonged darkness on human eyes. That would make a great aside in the book. It would give me a foundation to doubt the evidence of my eyes—at least as far as figuring things out in the book went—to keep judgmental readers from wondering how I couldn't immediately believe the evidence right before my own eyes. It made me think of the theater scene that Thomas and I had joked about.

But I could handle the sudden world shift, the process of changing sides to the crazy team, the *mea culpas* I would need to pass out for some of the sentences in my previous books, the actual terror I might start feeling of the world when ghosts became real to me. The one thing I was having troubles with at the moment was that Thomas would have been right all these years—paranormal is reality. I really am starting to hate having him around. Everything he does reminds me of what he did. I don't think I can ever get over it. For a while, I thought I could. That's why I invited him on this project. But I can't. At least I tried. I can go home to Elsa, tell her I did my best, but Thomas is no longer a part of our life. I'm barely sad about it.

I'd rather have ghosts anyway.

Thomas hadn't bothered to come out of his room tonight. It seemed strange to have both seen this full-bodied apparition thingy in Rotter House with our own eyes and then to have split up and stayed split up. How could we be by ourselves in this massive house of horror? If the stories were true, we would immediately make ourselves vulnerable targets.

But it was the anger, man, the anger.

Anger, I was learning, is the most powerful antidote to fear. You can't be afraid of a ghost if you're pissed off. You can't be afraid of anything if you're pissed off. I remember once, when me and Elsa were dating, we got into a massive fight one night about an old boyfriend of hers. I immediately left, walked to the park, and ran seven miles. Barefoot. I'd never run more than three miles in one go in my entire life. Anger, man. Never go to bed angry—unless you're in a haunted house. And, tonight, our mutual anger was keeping us from needing each other.

As I followed my faithful circle of light into the kitchen, I heard rumbling noises from somewhere deep upstairs. I immediately whipped out my notebook and jotted the phrase down. *Deep upstairs.* I wanted to remember that one. It fit the situation well. I could do a whole page on its paradox.

The circle of light landed on one of the cabinets, and I opened its door. I was delighted to find one last Tabasco Slim Jim lying there at the bottom of the cabinet, all sad and alone like a downed tree limb. *Look at me,* I thought, *not investigating a weird noise in the middle of the night in a haunted house.* I must be jaded now that I've had a close encounter of the ghostly kind. Really, though, it was because I knew exactly what that noise was: old pool balls knocking around on an uneven table. Thomas—I was sure of it—keeping his distance. Maybe waiting until he hears me return to my room so he can take a crack at the cabinets. Hopefully he's not looking forward to a Slim Jim.

It was that thought that kept me in the kitchen, just to be an annoyance to Thomas. Every once in a while, I'd bang a cabinet door shut or unleash the earthquake of the kitchen faucet to let him know I was still down there so that he kept his distance.

One thing among many in this experience that I couldn't quite put together was hearing male and female screams but only seeing a female ghost. Again, it was tempting to resolve it by saying it was the Wynders and that we hadn't come across Chris yet. But then there were the autopsy and injury reports that didn't at all match up to the Split-Faced Woman's eponymous mutilation. I'd have to do more research to see if I could find any pictures of her face postmortem. The image of her lying on a stainless steel autopsy table with her arms at her side made me think of the hand I had grabbed in bed. Even the explanation of Rotterdam's prosthetic combined with my own anger wasn't enough to chill the horrifying idea of her split face lying inches away from mine.

And then there was Thomas, up there shooting pool by himself, surrounded by dead animals in a haunted house. Why was he so intent on me leaving the house? Was he really that scared? As much as I wasn't too keen on him right now, I was glad he'd come. I was definitely indebted to him just for making the book better. But the real reason he'd come, he hadn't done anything about. He hadn't tried to explain it to me. Hell, he hadn't even apologized. He was just here, ignoring everything as if it had never happened, like we'd been hanging out every day for the past year. I leaned against the counter, chewing on the straw of greasy meat and thinking for the thousandth time that the recipe needed a lot more Tabasco.

Technically, Thomas had five more nights to fix everything. Or we both did, I guess. Maybe I needed to take the lead. After all, now that the book had a direction, now that we had a real purpose for being here, now that there was an apparition, maybe I could concentrate a little bit more on us. That's what I'd do. Tonight we'd give each other space, let the anger dissipate. It wasn't the first time we'd been mad at each other. Wasn't even the hundredth time. I'd write some more notes, explore the house, look for secret passages—because there was still that chance that somebody was running a great con on us. If Thomas didn't bring it up tomorrow, I would.

I opened the dumbwaiter. Inside was a severed arm.

Chapter 21

Whatever was left of my anger at Thomas was replaced by simple, icy fear. Discover and document, my ass. I yelled for him and kept yelling until those pool table sounds subsided and were replaced by the thudding of feet on stairs.

As grotesque as it was, I didn't want to pull my eyes away from the arm, didn't want it to disappear before Thomas got there. He had to see it. I couldn't bring myself to touch it, though. The thing looked so real. White-gray bone protruded from the end as if it had been snapped badly from the shoulder. Blood welled all around it, like it had been thrown in the dumbwaiter as soon as it was severed.

"Oh my god," said Thomas behind me.

"You see it, right?"

"Oh, I see it. That can't be a real arm. Or is it? It looks . . . fresh."

"Body farm to table. Do me a favor and shine your light on it." Thomas complied. "Now don't take your eyes off it." I then moved my beam away from the arm and slid it around the floor and the surrounding counters and cabinets. "I don't see any blood anywhere but in the dumbwaiter."

"You're going to have to do more than that to figure out if it's real."

"I don't want to touch it," I said.

"We need to see if it's one of Garza's props," he returned.

"How would I even know? I've never touched a severed arm before—or a silicone arm. For all I know, they feel the same."

190

"Flesh knows flesh, man. And it's your book. Do you really want to write that you chickened out at a key moment in the narrative?"

That was a good point. I flipped my flashlight around and, using Thomas's beam to guide me, slowly and shakily extended the butt end. It made contact with the forearm, about three inches above the wrist. After letting it sit lightly on the skin for a few seconds, I summoned the nerve and poked at it . . . a little harder than I intended. The flashlight pushed the skin toward the wrist, pulling it back at the severed end and ripping it softly like it was the fat on a rib eye. I almost wretched. My gag reflex believed it was real. "I can't do this."

"You can't even fish dead skunks out of your pool."

Elsa and I had a crappy little in-ground pool in our backyard that spent the offseason attracting and killing animals. It was usually small creatures like mice and birds, but every once in a while, something larger, like a skunk, drowned in it. And I never could bring myself to fish them out with the pool net. I literally couldn't touch those things with a ten-foot pole. Elsa could, though. She grew up in Alabama shooting groundhogs in her backyard. She hates when I bring that up. Maybe I'll put it in the book and not tell her to see if she really reads my stuff.

Thomas moved closer to the arm and stared at it intently. "Man, I'm pretty sure that's real." He reached into the dumbwaiter, touched the arm in a few places, and pulled his hand back. There was blood on his fingertips. He grabbed a rag off the counter and wiped his hand off.

"What do you think?" I asked him.

"I think it's gross. And I think we should get out of here. The same thing I've said every night since the night I first stepped inside this stupid house. And now we should call the cops on top of everything else. Although, I think that we've successfully contaminated this crime scene." He started picking at the blood beneath his fingernails.

"Real, then."

"I'd guess it's real."

"What about the other thing?"

Thomas threw the rag back on the counter and looked at me, puzzled. "What other thing?"

"You know, the other thing about the arm."

"Still not getting it."

My flashlight beam already illuminated the arm, so I shook the flashlight, wobbling the beam for emphasis. "The color of its skin."

"I'm sorry, what?"

"That's a black man's arm," I said, still staring at it, waiting for it to disappear.

"That's . . . pretty racist."

"How am I being racist about a severed arm? It's a black man's arm. I didn't cut it off."

I could feel Thomas staring at me, as if I were more appalling than a dead arm in a dumbwaiter. "You're saying more than that."

"I'm saying what are the chances of that? That's not racist. I can't be racist against an arm."

"Just because it's black, you think it's a message to me? Or a reference to me?"

"Yeah," I said, confused.

"Look, if it were a white man's arm lying in that wooden box, you'd just think of it as a severed arm, not a white man's arm. Just an arm. No statement. Nothing to read into except the obvious things. Just a severed arm. Jerk."

"Yeah, maybe," I admitted sheepishly. "But how can I be racist? My . . . best . . . friend . . . is . . . "

"Shut up."

I risked taking my eyes off the severed arm to flash the light at Thomas's torso to make sure he had both of his arms.

Thomas lifted his hands in the air, palms out in my flashlight beam. "Don't shoot, officer," he said. "Speaking of that, are we going to call the cops or keep staring at it?"

I had already turned back to the arm and aimed my flashlight on it like it was a leash keeping the arm in place. "Honestly? I want to keep staring at it. Because if this were a movie, it would disappear. A careful edit, a simple special effect and . . . gone."

"You still think this is a ghost arm? I have blood underneath my fingernails from touching it. This arm is real, man."

"Or a really good special effect. I don't know how long this arm has been bodiless, but I feel like it should probably be somewhat rotten, right? At least a little smelly and possibly discolored?"

"You already think it's discolored," Thomas whispered.

I ignored him. "Look, if this is a product of the haunting, it'll need to disappear into the ether. If this whole haunted house thing is a setup, whoever's behind it needs to get rid of it. The arm is evidence, either way. It's got to go. And it can't as long as I'm looking at it."

"And if it's a real arm?"

"Then I don't know what's going on with this story."

The arm lay in its pool of blood.

"What color was Rotterdam?" asked Thomas.

"The whitest. Prussian, remember? Had he lived a generation or so later, he'd have been a Nazi."

"Are you sure? Are there any images of him?"

"Yeah, a few. I have a couple of them in the box. But Rotterdam was a total whitey. And so was his severed arm."

"I'm just saying. This is exactly the type of twist entire horror stories are based on. Black person gets successful and wealthy, fear of a black planet sets in, he gets lynched, and the story and the person are both whitewashed. His ghost then haunts his mansion until the secret is finally revealed and his soul is set free. Maybe we aren't dealing with the Wynders or any other boarders with bad ends. Maybe we're dealing with the man himself. A lingerie ghost would really fit his style. And he probably doesn't like that you're holding hands with his prosthetic in bed."

"I like where you're going with it. I do. Merits some paragraphs in the book. I just don't think it's true. Now help me stare at this arm."

The more I stared at it, the more disconcerting it became. I started noticing fine details like wrinkles and hairs and blemishes in the roving beams of our lights. It felt too intimate.

We waited, but nothing happened.

The dumbwaiter slammed shut. Inside, the slow, creaky sound of an old, stiff pulley started up. I dived at the dumbwaiter door, wedging my fingers underneath the edge of the handle and yanking up as hard as I could while holding the flashlight in my hand. It wouldn't budge at first, but then finally, as if somebody on the other side had gotten tired of holding the door, it slammed open with a thud that reverberated throughout the house. Our flashlights revealed thick, dangling ropes, twisting and writhing like strings on a giant puppet.

"Holy shit, where does this go?" asked Thomas.

"Um . . . up, man." We both took off for the stairs and took them two at a time. We landed at the end of the Hall of Death and stopped.

"I meant where upstairs, asshole," said Thomas.

"I'm not sure," I said, trying to figure out in my head how the geometry of the downstairs fit the geometry of the upstairs. "The dumbwaiter is not on the architectural plans."

"It has to be the master bedroom, right?" said Thomas.

"Right." We sped down the hallway and burst through the door to the Murder-Suicide Room, looking around at all the pink walls and white lace and the few dolls that were still scattered around on the bed and the floor.

"Where would it be?" asked Thomas.

"Shhh!" I said, listening. I could hear the creak of the pulley. The noise came from the corner by the dresser. I ran over and started trying to shove the dresser out of the way. It was a big, heavy antique piece of walnut furniture, the sort the town had been proud of at one time. And it was barely budging. "Help me." Thomas got on the other side, and we manage to angle it away from the wall, freeing up enough space where we could see another wooden dumbwaiter door painted white. I threw it open only to see more of the thick, dangling ropes. I looked up the shaft, and dust sifted onto my face. I wiped it away with my sleeve and ran for the door. "It's passed this floor already. Game room."

We dashed up the stairs and to the game room. I could hear the high-pitched squeak of the pulley again, but in a room that size, it was hard to tell where it was coming from. I flashed my light around in a panic.

Thomas figured it out first. "Rhino!" he yelled.

We had learned during the photo session that the rhino was unmovable, so we both squeezed behind it, where we quickly found the door. I slammed it open.

There was the dumbwaiter car. Empty.

No arm. No pool of blood. Not even a stain.

"You were right," said Thomas. "Just gone. And I guess that means . . . we still don't know what it means: haunt, hoax, or. . ."

"Homicide," I said, trying to surreptitiously pull the notebook from my back pocket to steal the line. It was too hard to do squeezed there behind the rhinoceros.

And that made me realize what a ridiculous position we were both in, squeezed together in a few feet of space, our backs to the rough hide of a dead monster, a few inches away from an open dumbwaiter. I led the way out of there, around the wicked-looking horned head of the beast.

"Weird. This, more than anything else we've experienced so far, feels like a magic trick," I said. "Like a trick cabinet with a false floor or something. I don't know how Garza could have faked the apparition last night, but this dumbwaiter trick definitely seems fishy. And, still, even though you hate the question, I need to ask it: why a black man's arm?"

"I'm telling you. Rotterdam was black. Or maybe these ghosts are just big into diversity."

"It's really the same question as why the apparition has a split face. Monica Wynder's face wasn't split as far as I know. She and Chris were white, and neither one's arms were severed. The last two, at least, are pretty clear from the crime-scene photo. These experiences aren't fitting the story I want them to fit, dammit."

"Rotter House is supposed to have a lot of ghosts. That's why you picked this place, right?"

"Yeah, I guess so. I mean, it has a lot of ghost *stories*. But they're all so vague and unsatisfying and will be hard to use as the core of this story," I said.

"Still, looks like you might be sleeping in the wrong room," said Thomas. He threw a glance in the direction of the dumb-waiter. "Speaking of which, I'm sleeping with you in your wrong room tonight."

Night
Nine

Chapter 22

When I found Thomas, he was drinking. The plastic cup in front of him was large and smelled of rum. That he was boozing made me happy, but it also made me sick.

He was in the den, sitting in that same chair where I'd filled him in on the house that first night he was here. Again, he had neglected to remove the sheet. My electric lantern was on and doing its best to hold back the darkness, although it mostly gave the darkness nuance.

"You're getting started early," I said, setting Rotterdam's arm on the coffee table. I had started using it like a talisman, wanting it to be no more than an arm's length away anytime I sat down.

"Are you kidding me? It's nine o'clock at night."

"Did I even bring rum?"

"You sure did. You have a fine booze selection in there. Your food choices, though . . . I'm getting tired of eating off 7-Eleven shelves. Didn't you bring any real food?"

"It is real food."

"It's snacks. Like we're in a haunted elementary school."

"You were looking forward to sitting down to meals with me? Maybe holding hands, saying a little grace before we ate?"

"Can we order a pizza? Does that break your rules?"

"Your phone still charged?"

"No."

"Doesn't matter. We can't call for delivery any more than we can turn the tower into a lighthouse."

"I just want real food."

"How long have you been up?"

"Got up before dark. I needed to see this house in the daylight, needed to banish some of the nightmares, to figure out why I'm still here."

"Any progress?"

"Ask me when I get a little deeper into this." Thomas held up his cup with one hand. As I sat down on the couch, he said, "Have you had any nightmares here?"

I thought back. I had a lot of nightmare imagery in my head, thanks to this house, but all of it occurred while I was awake. "I haven't. But that's kind of normal for me."

"I don't' think it's normal for anybody under these circumstances. But I haven't had any nightmares either. Seems strange for two people living in a haunted house, right? Does that mean our brains are refusing to process what we've been experiencing?"

"Or maybe that this place hates haunted house tropes?"

Thomas laughed. "That's a horror trope in general. Nothing interesting going on yet? Throw in a nightmare."

If I was going to have a nightmare, yesterday would have been a good opportunity. Without meaning to, I had spent some serious hours in bed during my previous sleep. Not only was REM achieved, it was possibly lapped. Maybe the reversed days and nights and the strain of the experiences were getting to me. Maybe it was the comfort of knowing Thomas was on the couch a few feet away. Most likely, it was my suicide pills.

Thomas and I had spent the rest of the previous night searching through the many Rotter House ghost stories in my box, looking for anything that would make the severed arm of a black man and the bisected face of a woman make sense—make sense in ghost-story terms at least. The most obvious leads were the stories from the third-floor bedrooms. The woman who was possibly dismembered and put into a suitcase was the closest contender for the apparition. The other dismemberment, the man whose separated parts had been arranged into a swastika, could fit the appearance of the arm, although there was no information about his race in the story. That was the problem in general. There wasn't that much information about any of these stories. On top of that, we knew there must have been crimes committed within this house over the years that were never recorded. It was possible that we didn't even have a template story for our ghost, which would be a big bummer once it came to writing the book. By the end of the night, we were both in pretty rough shape, so I introduced Thomas to my suicide pill stash.

I had pulled a small translucent orange bottle out of my bag, simultaneously squeezing and twisting its white cap until it popped off. The sound of cascading pills against plastic was familiar and pleasant—and a bit loud in the silence of the house—as I dumped a pair of oblong yellow pills into the palm of my hand. The Percocet was Elsa's. She gets bad menstrual cramps sometimes. Every once in a while, I'd sneak one of her pills for kicks. It made me feel four feet above myself and full of goodwill, and then it ended with a pleasurable tumble down a long, dark hole into sleep. I had brought them in case I had trouble reversing my sleep schedule, but I was fine using them for this purpose, too. Thomas took one without hesitation and made a Heaven's Gate crack. We'd fallen asleep pretty quickly after that.

"Play a game of Film Fight with me?" I asked Thomas, as he continued to stare at his plastic cup of rum.

"What are the stakes? Leaving the house?"

"Just for practice."

Thomas looked around the room. "Horror movies with the word 'house' in them. Same rules as last time, but only horror movies. *Only You*, my ass. Go."

"*House*," I said, getting it out of the way.

"*House on Haunted Hill*," Thomas said, probably for the same reason.

"*The Last House on the Left*."

"*Hell House* . . . I mean, *The Legend of Hell House*."

"*House of 1000 Corpses*," I said.

Thomas took a swig of his drink, a stalling mechanism that I'd have to call him out for if he took it too far. "*House of Wax*."

"*Housebound*."

"*The Funhouse*."

"*The Funhouse Massacre*."

"*Madhouse*."

"What's that one about again?" I asked.

"Does it matter?"

"Yes, because I want to make sure you're not just throwing out something that sounds like it would probably be a movie title."

"It's the Vincent Price movie from the '70s. The one where he's an actor in a television series called *Dr. Death*. You've seen the poster. His face is painted into a skull and he wears a black fedora."

"Isn't that *Theatre of Blood*?" I asked.

"No, *Theatre of Blood* is the one where he plays a theater actor who kills his critics. Totally different."

"I need to watch them again. I should be up for a horror movie marathon in about . . . oh, I don't know, seven years after leaving this haunted house. Whose turn?"

"Yours."

"Right. Have we said *House of the Dead* yet?"

"No. *The House of the Devil*."

"*House of Usher*. I've got your Vincent Price."

Thomas paused, took a long sip of his drink, and then, right before I was about to call him out on it, threw the empty cup across the room, where it hit the sheeted piano and fell to the floor with a pathetic little plastic sound. "*House Party*. Fuck."

"You made the rules," I said. "*I Am the Pretty Thing that Lives in the House.*"

"You win again, I guess."

"And I didn't even practice in advance for that one. Also, I just decided what the stakes were."

"No way."

"I get to interview you." I pulled out a small battery-powered audio recorder and placed it with a loud clink beside Rotterdam's arm.

"I didn't know you brought one of those. Why aren't we using it for EVPs?"

"EVPs are dumb," I said. "Worse than orbs. And I don't care if I come off as a jerk about that. Electronic voice phenomena make no sense. There are a dozen really obvious explanations for wonky electronic recordings, not even counting the human need to create patterns where there are none. This recorder," I gave it a shove with my boot heel, "is solely for classic *Kolchak: The Night Stalker*-type journalism—to interview you while we are in this house."

"I think I need another drink first," said Thomas, looking wistfully in the direction of the sheeted piano.

"Of course. More rum?"

"Nah. How about one of your lazy martinis? Still have plenty of those blue-cheese-stuffed olives left?"

I smiled. "Of course. I brought two jars."

I wandered into the kitchen like I was already buzzed. We were about to get into it. I could feel it. I turned on my flashlight, set it on the counter top, and started tossing ingredients into two disposable cups. They turned into quadruples pretty fast. As I dropped those magnificent olives into the liquor with a splash like bombs from a plane, I noticed that the dumbwaiter door was shut again. I didn't bother to open it. I wasn't going to let severed body parts interrupt this conversation.

Back in the drawing room, I handed Thomas the drink, which he took clumsily, sloshing a little over the side, which is exactly the proper etiquette for drinking a lazy martini. I sat back down on the couch, took a swig of my cocktail, and then hit a button on the recorder. The tiny red light on the device looked expectant.

"So . . . what do you think about old Rotter House?" I asked Thomas.

"I think it's spooky as shit."

"And you believe it's haunted?"

"Yup. So do you, I think."

"Let's leave me out of this. I'm just Anderson Cooper right now. So you believe that Rotter House is definitely haunted, but you're still here. On your eighth night here, in fact."

Thomas paused for a moment, eyeing the rim of his glass with one eye closed like he was using it to measure distance. "Feels weird to me, too."

"Are you scared of what this house can do to you?"

"So far, I guess, the house hasn't done anything to us, really. But that's always the last words of the guy who keeps a lion for a pet. I think it's highly possible we've got bad things in our future as long as we're here. But right now, it feels like, not as immediate or something. I don't know. Like texting while driving. It feels dangerous while you're doing it. You know bad stuff could easily happen, but you still do it and are pretty sure nothing's going to happen." He looked around, as if he were waiting for something to jump out from behind a piece of furniture and belie his statements.

"Yet, even though it hasn't done anything to us, we've still experienced all the classic phenomena. Strange sounds, apparitions, phantom touches—I'm not sure what category that severed arm falls under—and yet here we are, the two of us, in the dark, surrounded by sheeted furniture . . . "

"Above a cellar of monsters, below floors of horrific stories of violence and murder . . . "

"Chugging bad cocktails and talking about Rotter House like it's a conceptual thing a million miles away."

"This is the part of the story where everybody has become used to the situation—the characters, the audience. It's the calm before the chaos at the climax," said Thomas.

"I've always thought haunted house stories are anticlimactic by nature. They end one or all of three ways: the characters leave the house, one or more of the characters die, or the house is destroyed—departure, death, destruction."

"That's how every story in the history of stories ends."

I laughed. "Probably right. But haunted house stories are different because most of the story is contained within a few thousand square feet. Three floors, a cellar, a tower. That makes them more effective as literary devices than as real-world stories. They're great as metaphors for, well, anything—isolation, entrapment, parochialism, self-obsession, everything. But as real-world stories—I mean, any peril where you can just walk out the front door or yell 'help' to the mailman isn't much peril. We could have done that at any point in our stay."

"You suck at being Anderson Cooper."

"Thanks."

"It ain't that easy. The house becomes a trap. Maybe supernatural forces seal doors or discombobulate the characters. Or maybe it's simple things like underwater mortgages and general denial of the danger. It's almost like hearing you wonder why somebody doesn't leave an abusive relationship. There are adamant interior forces at play."

"A haunted house as the abuser in a bad relationship. There may be something to that." I looked into my cup. The booze level was lowering faster than I liked.

"Yeah, of course there is. Because you trust your house, right? It's your house. It protects you from the world and, even more important, all the people out there. It sees you naked every day. It knows your sins. It's the only place where you are your true self. Most of your cash goes into it. So when that gets corrupted, when that becomes haunted, that's terrifying."

"But it still constrains the story. Everything's happening inside a small volume of space. While outside, to passersby, it's just a house. A monster hiding in plain view."

"Like a serial killer," said Thomas.

"Sure, except even less slippery than that because it's always in the same place, on its foundation between numbers 1311 and 1315 on Mockingbird Lane. The cops don't have to track it down. It's cemented in place."

"That makes it worse to me. Knowing that we were trapped inside while people go about their lives just a lawn away."

I pondered my next question on my own for a little bit, like I was at the Ouija board and unsure how the spirits would react. "What's the difference between a haunted house and a house?"

"One has ghosts, dummy."

"No, I guess I mean, how does a house become haunted?"

"You probably know as well as I do. Who builds it is important, I guess. A monster. A madman. Where, too. On a Native American burial ground, old execution grounds. Lovecraft had a giant slumbering god buried beneath his in *The Shunned House*." Thomas looked off into the darkness. "Mostly, I guess, it's what happens after the house is built."

"Violence, death."

"If people can make a house a home, they can make a house a hell."

"Holy fuck, hold on. I need to write that down . . . and attribute it to myself." I reached back into my pocket to retrieve my notebook.

"You're recording this, man."

"I'm an idiot." I pushed the notebook back into my pocket and checked to make sure the recorder was still going, although the red record light made it obvious. "Shirley Jackson said that some houses are born bad. But thinking of a shell of stone and wood as inherently evil has always struck me as unsatisfying. I mean, I love Shirley Jackson, but, if anything, it makes more sense that the houses are the victims of what goes on inside them."

"Maybe. My two favorite haunted house books have houses that are born bad—*The Haunting*, of course, and *The House Next Door*. You ever read that one?"

"Sounds vaguely familiar—also vague."

"The one by Anne Rivers Siddons."

"Oh, that one. Yeah, I did read it, although it took me years to get to it. I always thought it was a romance novel pretending to be a haunted house story because of her bibliography."

Thomas laughed. "Yeah, the cover of the version I read had a *Better Homes & Gardens* feel to it. But it's one of the best haunted house stories out there."

"I remember it had a pretty good ending, too, which is rare."

"How's yours going to end?" Thomas asked.

"Oh man, I already know." I reached back for the notebook again and flipped through it until I found the right page. I cleared my throat for about three seconds too long. "I laid down beside my wife, in my own bed, in my own unhaunted house, wondering for the first day of the rest of my life if I believed in ghosts."

"Needs editing."

"I'll get there. How do you think it'll end?"

Thomas looked up at the ceiling for a bit. "I think I can come up with two different endings. One, more of the same until we leave. We catch a glimpse of a ghost here, some more sounds there. Maybe we'll finally see the ghost of Christopher Wynder wandering around here. Then we leave, with no answers. Maybe we come back when Garza opens it as a Halloween attraction. That would be the epilogue."

"Oh man, you're brilliant. That really should be the epilogue." I scrawled some notes.

Thomas took a sip of his martini, the thin plastic cup popping in his hand, and continued. "The other, well, that's the bad scenario. Like I said, the events seem to be escalating. First sounds, then apparitions, then actual contact. Next could be some serious ghost-on-the-living violence."

"You don't sound very scared."

"I'm pretty medicated right now. Or Lubricated. Whatever the word is."

I laughed. "I'm catching up." I looked around at the sheeted furniture, which seemed more crowded than usual, like they were pressing in, listening to our conversation. "Ghost stories are hard to end."

"That's why most ghost stories are actually mystery stories, gives the story something to solve without really having to deal with the ghost. 'Oh, the ghost wanted somebody to find his treasure? Done.' 'Oh, all those jump-scares were the little girl trying to tell you who her murderer was? Got it.' They never really have to deal with the existence of the ghost itself."

I sighed. "We almost had one here, you know? A mystery, I mean."

"The Wynders?"

"Yeah, it really seemed that it was all connected and pointed directly at finding out what happened to them."

Thomas squeezed the cup in his hand tighter, making it pop again, and then laughed. "If you're trying to make sense of things in your book, you might already be going awry."

"What do you mean?"

"Maybe everything that's happened to us in this house doesn't fit into a single story. Maybe it's a mishmash of Rotter House stories. An element from this one, an element from that one. Hell, maybe it doesn't even fit across stories. In the books, the movies, that stuff, hauntings always make some kind of sense because they have to. They need a storyline. A ghost with a noose around its neck needs to be a person who committed suicide on the property. The house needs to be built on a graveyard because that makes the dead angry. A violent crime yields violent ghosts. Even ghost-hunters try to make sense of hauntings. Soldiers haunt battlefields because they don't know the war's over. A lady in white sticks around because she lost her child and is still searching for it. But it's paranormal. It, by definition, doesn't make sense as we know sense. Maybe that arm in the dumbwaiter has nothing to do with the Split-Faced Woman or the screams or the history of the house. Maybe it's just something that appeared and disappeared at random. A mystery of the universe, confusing and surreal."

"But I'm writing a book. I need a story. It can't be, *The Random, Inexplicable Hauntings of Rotter House*."

"That would certainly be your new kind of haunted house book."

Both of us fell as silent as the sheeted furniture. What could have been a pat little story about a pair of dead lovers or a possible hoax based on the history of the house had turned into manifestations of an unknowable phenomenon, like something out of weird fiction. It was unsettling.

"At least something's happening here," I finally said. "I don't know what I would have done with this book if nothing had happened. I somehow honestly thought that us wandering around this spooky place would be enough. I mean, that'd be a unique haunted house book, I guess. But it would also have been boring. I can't afford that."

We sat in silence for a minute or two, until Thomas finally asked, "Are you serious about all that? Is Elsa really putting pressure on you to get a different job?"

I knew he was going to ask that. "Yeah, she is. But she has help. I feel the same way. Every time I travel for a book project, bankrolled more by her paycheck than my advance, it feels icky. When she comes home after an hour commute and I'm still in my slippers typing away, it feels wrong. Honestly, if I didn't think she was right, I'd probably fight it more. But she is right." I stared again into the black depths of the room. "I wonder why that piano hasn't played itself."

Thomas laughed a little too hard at the joke and then turned his plastic cup upside down. I looked into mine and saw a couple of humps of olive above a shallow pool of cloudy gin. The room definitely felt a little wavery. I imagined it filling with gin, staining the walls like the Suicide Room upstairs, here and there an olive floating past.

I decided to say it. "It's been a long time since we've gotten drunk together."

"I know."

"Do you drink much anymore?"

"Why would I have stopped?"

"No reason, I guess. I'm glad you came. I really needed you for this project."

"You know why I came."

"I know why you came." I reached over and turned the recorder off, paused for a moment, and then turned the electric lantern off. I spoke into that blackness like I was talking to myself. It made it easier. "After everything, what I want to know most, I think, is what happened that night."

Chapter 23

I had finally done it. I didn't want to be the first one to bring it up, but I had. That's all there is to it. I sat in the darkness, waiting for the answer.

Eventually, one came. "I don't know . . . "

"You do know!" My shout felt strange. It's the last thing you want to do in a haunted house, call attention to yourself. Screaming in reaction to something is encouraged—but shouting, that was disrespecting the horrors of the house. Again, anger took out fear without breaking a sweat. Although, maybe I couldn't call this anger. Maybe this cry was more frustration, more pleading, more pathetic.

"It was like any other night, right?" said Thomas.

"I thought so."

"Me too. Just the four of us. Watching stupid horror movies. Drinking 'til we knew our tomorrows were ruined. But not in the way we thought." I could hear Thomas struggling with the confession. "You were supposed to go up with us. We'd joked about it before. Remember the time Elsa brought out Twister?"

"We never played it."

"It was always a joke, that's why. Always a joke. That night the joke went . . . too far. We went upstairs, and that's all I remember. The three of us. To the bedroom. I said, 'Where's Felix?' And then I blacked out. Yvette doesn't remember anything either. We hit the alcohol really hard that night—too hard. Asteroid hitting the earth hard. We were too comfortable with each other, had gotten drunk together too many times. We thought we were all in a safe place."

"The last thing I remember is seeing the three of you go upstairs to your . . . bedroom." The memory of the moment sickened me even sitting here, a year later, surrounded by ghosts. I could feel the carpet burning into my cheek, see the Roomba that had been stuck under the couch for two weeks, smell the leather on Thomas's ratty shoes that laid nearby. I was so drunk that I was happy to see them all go upstairs. Excited for them, rooting for them. Meanwhile, I was unable to even sit up from the floor, easing instead into a blackout.

"What does . . . Elsa say?" asked Thomas.

"The same thing as you. That she doesn't remember. But something happened. We all know that. And it's all I can think about." Hot tears starting rolling down my cheeks, and I was glad that we were sitting in blackness. "I can see it. The three of you, in your bedroom, together, while I was downstairs face-first in a pool of slobber on the floor."

"We don't know what happened. The next morning, we woke up. You and Elsa were gone. And that was it."

"You were all naked." I didn't know that. Didn't know that at all. I'd awoken in the car, groggy and hurting. Elsa was driving. But I noticed she had missed buttons on her blouse. And she wasn't wearing a bra.

"I don't think so. Not totally. Not like we'd . . . been together. Like we'd all gotten ready for bed. You know me, man. I can drink anybody under the table as long as my feet are on the ground, but the second I go horizontal, I'm gone. I didn't even have birthday sex on my thirtieth because of that."

"How could all three of you not remember anything?"

"I don't know. But, man, I wish it had never happened," I could hear Thomas's voice catching, as if he were silently crying, too, and then another pop of the plastic cup, as if he were trying to hide it by taking a drink from his empty cup.

"*You* wish it never happened? I asked Elsa if she felt different the next day. You know, physically. Sore or something,"

"I don't want to hear this."

"She said 'no.'"

"I don't think anything happened, man."

"But you don't know for sure. Say it. Something might have happened."

The silence was as thick as the darkness. Finally, Thomas spoke. "You're right. In the end, I don't know what happened, so anything could have. But that doesn't mean the worst happened. We were silly drunk. We could have played rock-paper-scissors until we passed out. I wish we would have all woken up in that bed together, including you. As awkward as it would have been, as strange as it would have been, we all could have survived that together." He paused for a long time. "We can survive this, too, right?"

"It's easy for you to say. Or Yvette. Or even Elsa. I was the one on the floor alone. Nobody needs to survive what I did."

We sat there for a while, both of us softly crying, neither of us knowing which way to go, the room swimming around me in the dark, the Split-Face Woman, I assume, tromping around on the floors upstairs, screaming her cloven face off, trying to get our attention. The worst thing for me about the whole situation these days, after a series of worst things that seemed to change every week, wasn't that my wife had possibly drunkenly cheated on me with my best friend, it wasn't that she'd possibly had a threesome without me, wasn't that she might have been treated as a sex toy by Thomas and Yvette. It wasn't even that I wanted to be involved that night. It was that I was suspicious that at least one of them remembered. Just one was enough. This talk of blacking out was just that: talk. Maybe they all remembered. That would actually be the worst for me. Maybe they all made a pact that night or the

J. W. Ocker

next morning to tell me they'd forgotten it. Just the possibility of it hurt bad.

On the other hand, I had definitely blacked out. I couldn't even get off the floor, much less climb the stairs. So how could I dismiss the idea that they had blacked out, too? That last memory. That last memory before the sick darkness. The three of them, Elsa in front, holding Thomas's hand, Yvette behind him with her hands on his shoulders, all of them giddily going up the stairs as if it had been something they'd wanted to do for years. And not a single one of them looked down at me. Not a single look. It was like I didn't exist.

Thomas's voice broke the solid silence. "The past year has been the worst year of my life. If there was anything I could do to make it right, anything at all, I'd do it without even hesitating."

Like staying at a haunted house with me. It was a hypothetical I'd thought of many times in the past year. Was there anything that any of them could do to fix it? Or anything I could do? Why couldn't I get over it? My fantasies about it always disturbed me. I often thought maybe a revenge threesome would fix it. Maybe I still think that. But there's no way I could suggest it. No way it would work. It would be perverse and sad to push Elsa and Yvette into doing that, especially if they were all telling the truth about not remembering that night. But I still thought about it. Sometimes I even thought about fucking Thomas. It wouldn't get my dignity back, but I always thought it would take some of his—at least the way I would do it. I wish that was my ugliest thought about the whole situation.

"Yvette and I haven't slept together since that night."

"What?" That jolted me right out of my dark fantasies.

I could hear his hand sliding roughly across his face, like he regretted telling me. "Sex, I mean. We haven't had sex since that night. We don't even touch each other."

214

"I didn't know that."

"Why would you?"

"But why not? I don't get it."

"We were all traumatized by that night, not just you. Zero memory. Ruined friendships. Hurting you. Our marriage tarnished. Possibly doing things we would never even think about doing under any other circumstances. And not knowing was the worst of it. One night in ten years of friendship. Even longer if you don't count the girls." He paused again. "How have you and . . . Elsa . . . been?" That was the second time he had paused around her name. Like it was hard to say. Like merely saying her name was crossing me.

I wasn't sure what to tell him. Obviously the money pressures were affecting our relationship. But we'd kind of gotten through the worst part of the fallout from that night. We were still together. That was a big win. And our sex was the best it had ever been. I always suspected she was making up for that night. But I couldn't tell him that. "Okay, I guess. I think we're close to getting over it. As much as we can, anyway."

"I never will."

"How come you waited until I brought it up to talk about it?"

"Man, I didn't feel like I had the right to bring it up. I could only talk about it if you gave me permission. I was waiting for that. And I didn't want to mess up your book. I was hoping you would do it sooner, though. It hurts being around you."

I turned the electric lantern back on. Thomas looked like a wreck, his face puffy and his eyes and nostrils glistening. "I could use another drink. You want one?"

He looked away but held his cup out to me. "Yes, please."

I took it and walked into the kitchen, making my way using the light leaking in from the lantern in the drawing room. This was it. The moment I had been waiting for all this time. It felt . . . I don't know. I felt some relief, sure. There was some anticlimax, sure. A lot of uncertainty, though. Like the morning after a surgery, like seeing a ghost.

It sounded as if we had both been living in haunted houses of our own for the past year. No wonder Rotter House hadn't been able to chase us away. I'd take screams in the night over anger and guilt and suspicion any day. As I poured the drinks, mostly on the counters, I heard a discordant twang. And then another. And then another. Thomas was attempting to play something ominous on the piano.

I walked back in, and he was still leaning over the instrument, the sheet half thrown back, the keys bared. Some were missing, others rotted. Dust was swirling around him in the nimbus of the electric lantern.

"Here you go." I handed him the drink. He sat down on the piano bench, his back to the piano. He threw an elbow onto the keys with a harsh collision of notes.

"Do you think we can survive it? Go back to the way it was? I miss that so much," he said. "I want to do a horror movie marathon with you. I want one of Elsa's cocktails. I want my wife to touch me again. I want our lives back."

"I do too." I actually had the impulse to hug him, which surprised me. I think the only time we had ever hugged in our life was at his mother's funeral. Instead, I went back and sat down on the couch. We talked some more. And laughed. And tried to figure out the book and haunted houses. All seemingly great stuff, but we were so drunk, and I never turned the recorder back on. Neither one of us rapped to the other, but we did invite the Split-Faced Woman to come party with us, yelled for her across the floors, taunted her, asked for her husband. We called for Rotterdam, arm-wrestled with his prosthetic, stuck it in our crotches and turned on its sad vibrator. We dragged a werewolf and a mummy and a vampire and a Frankenstein monster out of the cellar and reenacted scenes from *The Monster Squad* in the foyer. We ripped off sheets from the furniture and wandered around the house, moaning and laughing and stumbling. We stacked those stupid Rotterdam chairs in a bad Jenga formation on the dining room table.

And now I can say that one of the best nights of my life happened in a haunted house.

But the happiness would be short-lived.

Night
Ten

Chapter 24

Some hangovers hit you like death. You wake up in an advanced state of decay, hoping that death itself has a death. Others are like resurrections. You wake up feeling energized and super-powered and ready to tackle the laundry at seven in the morning after a spirited run on the treadmill. Of course, that usually means you're not really hungover—you're still drunk.

Tonight's hangover was of the latter sort for me. I felt giddy as I wandered through the usually depressing dankness of the house. As I did my rounds of the rooms, checking on trail cams and hoping for phantoms, I was euphoric.

Everything seemed different. Even before I turned my flash-light on, I felt like I could see in the dark. The pink and white of the room was brilliant. The green of the foyer less like dying moss and more like a tropical forest. The wood of the bannisters and chairs absolutely shined with hues of cherry and mahogany and oak. I don't know how I ever saw the house as black and white. Probably way too many silver-screen spookies.

Hell, I even loved Rotterdam's stupid chairs, still stacked on the dining room table from our shenanigans the night before.

And Rotter House suddenly seemed like home to me.

I was happy in a haunted house. I don't remember reading this kind of chapter in any of my haunted house stories before. Well, maybe in *The Haunting*. It sounded like something Eleanor Vance would say. And things ended bad for her.

But, unlike Eleanor, who was on the run from her issues, I had faced and fixed mine last night. I had my best friend back, my past back, my life back. No more avoiding each other. No more awkwardness. We'd all throw a party at the end of this project. Maybe we'd even play goddamned Twister. No, that was too far. We would forget that night. Like we'd been through the horrors of war together and would never talk about it ever, ever again. It would be a scar that no one would get to see.

But I hadn't merely fixed my life. I might have improved it, thanks to this book project. Actually, that might be taking things too far, too. It was a night for taking things too far, I guess. My book had the *potential* to improve my life. I was really starting to believe in it. That's a great feeling for an author, but a fleeting one. Even if nothing happened during the rest of my stay, if I found no explanation for the strange phenomena we had witnessed, if it was all just a gendered scream in the night, a vagina face, and a severed arm, I had enough experiences to at least make an intriguing book. And with paranormal nonfiction, that's all it had to be: intriguing. Fodder for debate, a data point in the quest, an object of ridicule, even, was good enough sometimes. The only thing that could make things better were if the trail cams caught anything. I could imagine the press release. It would be the first thing I wrote. Long before the introduction or chapter one, "Author stays at Haunted House, Catches Footage of Terrifying Ghost" or "Skeptic Turns Believer after Thirteen Nights in Infamous Haunted House." Two million YouTube hits later, and the book release becomes an event. On the mere clickbait of that, even if I wrote the book completely in emojis, it would sell enough to help me stay a writer, to make Elsa happy, to pull my weight in the relationship.

The only thing that I wasn't certain of was how I was going to write about my relationship with Thomas in the book. I couldn't tell the truth, just couldn't—a scar no one gets to see. But I couldn't be vague about it, either. The living couldn't be the loose ends in a book about ghosts. I could remove the subplot entirely. But that, too, felt like a mistake. It needed an internal struggle because, on the page, it would be as important to make us real characters as it would be to make the ghosts feel real. Maybe I could substitute a different, less personal, less shameful issue in place of the real one, the way I could change names in my nonfiction books to protect privacy. Maybe Thomas would have an idea of how to approach the subject.

I lost my euphoria in the drawing room. It was shouldered out by stabbing terror.

My flashlight beam traced four shapes looming in front of the couch. They were tall and shapeless, covered in sheets like the furniture throughout the house. They just stood there in a row, patient, as if my fate were inevitable.

A few frozen beats later and I remembered that they were the four monsters we had dredged from the cellar. I guess at some point Thomas and I had thrown sheets over them. So now we had four sheet ghosts in this haunted house.

I walked over to them to pull the sheets off—no way was I going to let something like that loom around in the dark—when I saw movement. Just a twitch of sheet, like a stray breeze had caught a fold. I turned quickly to see if the front door was open.

When I turned around, one of the sheeted forms staggered forward fast, contorting its sheet-covered limbs like it was in tremendous pain. "Get out of my house!" it screamed.

A hand lifted from under the sheet and grabbed my arm.

It was a black man's hand.

I yelled.

For a second, my mind went to the dumbwaiter arm and whatever past victim of Rotter House it must have been connected to. And then I realized the simpler explanation.

"Goddamn it, Thomas."

The sheeted form guffawed like an idiot. "Put that in your book," it said as it sloughed its cover to reveal a grinning jerk who looked as if he'd just won a national award for being an asshole.

"Yeah, well, that was . . . pretty good. Where's the fourth monster?"

"Over there." He pointed to the other side of the room, where the werewolf stood in front of the fully unsheathed piano. "Guess what he's playing?"

"I'm not saying it."

"Come on."

"I'm not saying it."

Thomas started humming a few staccato notes and then abruptly stopped. I made a big show of sighing and dropped my head, before singing, "Werewolves of London."

Thomas let loose a two-note howl. "What's on our agenda for tonight in Rotter House?"

"You sound excited."

"Four more nights. That's all we have to get through. Making the best of it."

"Well, first, we should get these rooms back in order. Take nothing but pictures, leave nothing but footprints."

"It was a good time," said Thomas.

We put the chairs in the dining room back in their places. As I hefted one in my hands, I had to admit that they really were well made. This antique chair could support the upward-trending bulk of the average twenty-first-century American without issue.

I had my camera on me, so I asked Thomas to walk across the doorway between the foyer and the dining room to recreate my first ghostly encounter. I took me a few shots and some well-placed flashlights to get him looking the right kind of blurry and supernatural.

"Let's lug these brutes downstairs, too," I said, pointing at the sheeted monsters in the drawing room. "I don't want to forget they're up here again." Thomas moved over to the werewolf, grabbing it by one of the elbows.

"We can leave Warren Zevon, though," I said, nodding at the monster at the piano. "When we leave, I want to set him up at the front door and hopefully give that Garza bastard the type of welcome she deserves."

Our monster-moving accomplished, the sheets back in place on the furniture, and the plastic cups picked up, the first floor looked again like a rotting set of abandoned rooms instead of a rotting set of lived-in rooms. "Up for a game of Film Fight?" I asked Thomas.

"You know it," he replied. We played two straight games, one on monster movies featuring mammals and another on horror movies with the word "demon" in the title. He beat me in both rounds, so I made the executive decision for us to move on to something else. I chose pool.

We headed up to the game room, where I set an electric lantern on a small table made out of an elephant's foot. "I don't see any pool cues," I said.

"There aren't any," said Thomas.

"What are you talking about? I heard you playing up here by yourself a couple nights ago."

"That . . . wasn't me," said Thomas. I stared at him and he stared back at me. To his credit, he maintained his poker face for a good thirty seconds.

"Kidding. That was me. But there aren't any pool cues. I used this," and he walked over to the wall and pulled off one of two crossed narwhal tusks. He grabbed the second and handed it to me. It was pretty close to standard cue length, about five feet long, twisted, bone white, and tapered to a nasty point at the end. I looked at Thomas, and he had flipped his around, leaned against the rim of the pool table, and aimed the thick end at a yellowing cue ball.

"This is barbarous," I said. "What do you use for chalk?"

Thomas broke. The ball wobbled around rents and holes and divots like it was some game that Dr. Seuss dreamed up. It turned out to be a lot of fun, even if it felt nothing like pool.

"Are we going to do this all day, or do you have something else planned for us?" asked Thomas as he launched the cue ball up a long bump, sending the ball into the air and then straight down on top of another one, squeezing it into a side pocket, where it fell through the rotted net and hit the floor with a thud before rolling over to a stop at the hooves of an ibex. "That was totally on purpose."

"I'd like to canvas the house in a more careful way. Not this frantic searching we've been doing. I've been meaning to do that since the first night, but, you know, something always came up."

"What would we be looking for?"

"I don't know," I said, taking my turn with the inverted narwhal tusk and almost stabbing myself in the gut. "More strange events. The strings and hands behind those strange events."

"You're still not totally on Team Ghost? After everything we've seen? After being inside of a ghost, for God's sake? And don't say, 'I don't know what to believe.'"

"Belief's a more gradual thing than that. It's more like . . . I don't know, grieving. There are stages to it. And I'm at the 'still in the moment and I'll think about it more later' stage. The last thing I want to do is cry ghost."

"Well, let me know when you arrive at the only and inevitable conclusion so that I can send you an 'I told you so' card."

"Between you and me—and the only reason I'm saying this is because I can change this entire conversation when it gets to the book—I feel like that will be the conclusion. How do I escape it? But the thought terrifies me."

"The paranormal can do that to a person. It's not too bad over here, you know. You don't have to wear the T-shirt if you don't want to."

I laughed. "I'm terrified of how it'll change my view of the world. Otherwise, I think I'll be fine with it. I've always been glad that other people believe in ghosts."

"Yeah?"

"I like ghost stories. And if people didn't believe in ghosts, we'd have fewer stories. Our lore would be impoverished, our legends weakened." As I spoke, Thomas poked at a ball with his fish horn, causing it to leap over the wooden rim of the table in a magnificent escape before clacking dumbly to the floor. I retrieved it for him. "I also like those kinds of people better. I much prefer the guy who makes curly fries at Arby's during the day and runs through an abandoned mansion at night with an electrical device of dubitable purpose than the guy who spends his day looking at analytics reports and hits the beach on the weekends."

"You like weirdos."

"I do."

We shot three straight games of crooked pool. It felt like we were back in our dorm rooms spending entire weekends playing board games, our only sustenance coming from the pizza joint whose number one of us had scribbled on the back of his hand so that we could call without stopping play. I wished I had brought other board games besides the Ouija, which was a useless rectangle of cardboard stuffed in a bag in my room without its planchette.

Or was it?

"Do you know how to make a planchette?" I asked Thomas as he tried to angle an impossible shot by wrapping himself around the corner of the table and holding his tusk in one hand.

"Yeah. It's not difficult. You can use an overturned glass or a hoop earring or anything that will slide across the board and isolate a letter, really. The important part is the people touching it. They're the real conduit."

"I was thinking maybe we should try the Ouija board again."

Chapter 25

Thomas's response to my suggestion took me completely by surprise.

"Okay," he said.

"What? Okay?"

"Yeah. Why not?"

"Because the last time I suggested it, I almost had to superglue your fingers to the planchette for you to play it with me."

"And don't think I haven't noticed that everything weird in this house started after our Ouija board session."

It was true. "That sucks for my story," I said.

"I'm feeling pretty good about everything right now. We were extremely irresponsible last night and nothing strange happened. If that's what you need to do, then I'm up for it." Thomas was a real friend.

"Okay. Want to talk to the dead on a dirt floor this time?"

That seemed to push him a little bit too far since he didn't answer immediately. When he did, it was with an, "Okay, I guess."

"You've become the bravest guy ever overnight. I'm proud of you." I ducked out of the way of an arcing narwhal tusk. "It makes sense anyway. Last time we pulled out the Ouija board, the noise led us there and to our first look at the Split-Faced Woman. We might as well start there this time."

We headed downstairs, passing through the spot where I'd come "face in face" with the Victoria's Secret ghost. I wasn't afraid of running into her again—not at all. I was hoping to, in fact. I had gotten used to thinking that "haunted" was a quirk of the house, like noisy pipes and smelly water. I used to doubt haunted stories when the people put up with the haunting for months or years, but I was realizing how faulty that criticism was. They had adapted. Although, it's all fun and games until someone gets possessed, I guess.

From my bedroom, I grabbed the board, Rotterdam's arm, and one of our discarded plastic cups, and then we tramped down to the cellar.

"Let me do a monster check," I said to Thomas, dropping my armload of stuff onto the dirt floor. I pulled out my notebook and flipped over to an inventory of monsters I'd made after realizing that the Split-Faced Woman had been down there. I aimed my flashlight at the page and walked around, checking each one off with my pen.

All monsters were present and accounted for, minus the Split-Faced Woman and the werewolf.

We set up our lights and then sat down on the hard-packed dirt. As I opened the silly glow-in-the-dark board, I wondered: if I now believe in ghosts, does that mean I automatically have to believe in Ouija boards, too? What does believing in the paranormal mean you have to believe? Everything? Alien abductions? Bigfoot? Or was it more like sects of Christianity, where each believes varying things but everybody can at least agree on Jesus. Man, and that doesn't even count the implications of an afterlife that I'd have to sort through . . . again. The warp in the board was pretty bad from where I had stepped on it, but I managed to flatten it out.

"Too big," said Thomas.

I looked down and saw the mouth of the upturned cup swallowing three letters and a number. We would need something a little more precise.

"I could cut the bottom out and use that. It's smaller. You have a pocket knife?" I asked.

"Is this 1957? Who carries around a pocket knife?" asked Thomas.

"All right, shut up." I shined my flashlight around, not sure what I was looking for until the light reflected back to me off the oversized monocle of a mad doctor. "That should do."

The doctor was old and short, with a white coat and black gloves. In one hand was a metal instrument that looked obstetrical, and his face exhibited the type of glee no doctor should ever display. It took no effort at all to pry the monocle off his eye and pop it off its chain. Sitting back down and placing it on the board, I was delighted to discover that it fit nicely over a single letter, and even magnified it slightly. We placed our fingers on it. Something felt different. Not because we were using the eyepiece of a mad doctor instead of a heart-shaped piece of plastic. It was something about Thomas. His intensity was gone. His eyes weren't closed, and he even made a joke as we started, forcing the makeshift planchette to magnify the letters L-O-L.

I started the questions. "Is the ghost—"

"Not the G-word!" Thomas hissed, playfully, like I was a recalcitrant kindergartner. I changed my question.

"Is Monica Wynder here?"

Nothing but thick darkness and the smell of dirt.

"How about Chris Wynder?" asked Thomas, without waiting much time for an answer to my question.

Double nothing.

"Who is the Split-Faced Woman?" I asked into the air, before realizing my word choice might be offensive. The monocle didn't so much as quiver in indignation. "Man, I don't think this is working. Maybe we should draw a pentagram around us in the dirt."

"You didn't think it was working last time, either. Give it some time. It might be taking them longer to get to us, or it could be we haven't asked the right question yet. Unlike last time, we now have some very specific questions to ask."

"Go for it."

Thomas tilted his head and looked at Dr. Freudstein in the dimness. Then he straightened his shoulders, closed his eyes, and said, "What happened to Monica and Chris Wynder?"

Nothing.

It was my turn. "Whose arm was in the dumbwaiter?"

I half expected Rotterdam's arm, lying in the dirt like one of the Halloween props surrounding it, to jump to life at the question. But it didn't. Nothing did.

"Why are there screams in this house at night?" Thomas asked.

Silence and stillness—both from the house and the Ouija board.

"How many of you live in Rotter . . . dam Mansion?" I asked.

The glass piece began to move. Maybe I would have to start believing in Bigfoot.

The letters were in two rows in parallel arcs, like frowning lips. The glass moved slowly, encircling the letters twice like it was warming up before leaving them and heading to the numbers. They were in a straight line from 0 to 9 at the bottom of the board. The glass paused on the one. I looked up at Thomas and saw him staring intently at the numeral.

It started moving again, back to the letters this time, where it stopped on the first letter of the second row, the N. I felt dizzy as I tried to focus on the planchette while keeping my fingers light. I was afraid to move for fear of interrupting the message. From there it rose to the top line, highlighting for a moment the I, then the G, and then the H.

It was then that I wanted to tell Pat Sajak that I had solved the puzzle. Although I had no idea what it meant. I let the planchette continue to the bottom line where it magnified one more letter before moving to the center of the board and resting.

"One night," said Thomas, staring down at the board and our fingers and the makeshift planchette. "What does that mean?"

"I don't know. Is it telling us something is going to happen in one more night?"

And for the third time in our stay in Rotter House, we heard a scream.

Chapter 26

This time, we took off almost ecstatically, although I immediately regretted conducting the session in the cellar. All we could tell about the direction of the scream is that it came from above. We flew through the first floor, ducking our head into the empty library, checking under the table in the dining room, opening the dumbwaiter in the kitchen, looking in on the werewolf at the piano.

By this time in our stay, we'd searched the rooms in this house enough times that we almost had a system for it, and we could make extremely efficient work of the task. Hell, if I ever became a Rotter House ghost myself, I knew exactly what my doom would be: searching from floor to floor for other ghosts. Still, this wasn't the careful search I'd mentioned before. We ransacked the place.

As we ran up the stairs to the second floor, Thomas turned to me and said, "You know that scream was different, right?"

"It was a man screaming."

"Yeah," Thomas said. "But it sounded different. Maybe a different man. That would make two men and a woman. I think we're starting to meet everybody from the Hall of Death."

That was the extent of our conversation as we headed down the Hall of Death, each of us taking a side, the opening and slamming doors playing a percussion duet. I found myself thinking of the rooms more in terms of their color instead of their crime scenes: the Blue Room instead of the Suicide Room, the Green Room instead of the Shotgun Room, the Red Room instead of the Unknown Causes Room.

I was about to bring this up to Thomas, but then we walked into my room, the Pink Room.

"What the fuck, man," I said.

On the bed were three dolls. Their clothes had been removed and their pale ceramic bodies glowed in the flashlight beam. A blonde-haired girl was on all fours, its head turned to the side so that it was looking right at me with its bright blue eyes. A second doll, a boy with dark hair, was behind it, leaning against the smooth curve of her backside. A third one, a girl with dark hair, lay on its back beneath the blonde doll.

I turned to Thomas, shining my light right in his face, my eyes blazing their own light.

His face slackened, and his eyebrows drew down in panic, "Man, I didn't do that. You have to believe I wouldn't do that. Why would I do that?"

"Because you're the asshole who had a threesome with my wife." I went for him, my hands like claws grabbing at the softness of his neck. He parried me away easily with his arm but fell back out the door and across the hall to the far wall. I moved at him again, pounding at him with my balled fist, out of control with anger. He lifted his arm and absorbed the blows. He didn't try to fight back.

"Don't say that, man. Please, God, don't say that," pleaded Thomas. "I would never do something like this. I mean tonight of all nights, man."

I stopped attacking and he reached out a hand and put it on my arm. I shook it off, stormed back into the Pink Room, and swiped the three dolls off the bed and onto the floor. "What do you mean, 'tonight of all nights'?"

Thomas hovered in the doorway. "Last night, man. We fixed things. As much as we can, anyway. If I were going to do something like this," he gestured at the naked dolls on the floor, two face up and one facedown, as if a child had dropped them after growing bored. "Why wouldn't I have done it any other night?"

I was still flush with anger, and most of that anger was still aimed at the only person within arm's reach, but I at least saw the sense. There was no way Thomas did this. I'd been with him all night. "You could have done that on any other night."

"So you believe me?"

I pretended to think a while longer, just to lash out, but finally I said, "I do. But I also no longer believe that the phenomena we've been experiencing in Rotter House has been paranormal."

"What?" Thomas didn't look relieved at all. He just looked sick, the same way I felt. It softened me a little.

"If you didn't do this and I didn't do this, who are we left with?" I asked.

"Monica Wynder?"

"Why would a ghost do this? Actually, that's the wrong question. In stories, ghosts do stupid, silly stuff all the time. The real question is the one that you asked before. Why would a ghost do this tonight of all the nights we've been here? The Split-Faced Woman eavesdropped on us last night from another room and then did this to screw with me? That doesn't sound very ghostly. It sounds like a prank." I raised my voice and shouted at Rotter House, "A perverse, shitty prank." I hardened again. "I think somebody did eavesdrop on us last night, and I think that person was very, very much alive." I bent down and picked up the blonde doll off the floor and threw it across the room. It hit the wall with an almost sickening thud, the ceramic head shattering and an arm coming loose as it fell to the floor. It felt a little like I had just thrown a baby. "And I think that person has been screwing with us this entire time. We need to find this fucker."

We ransacked the house again. I started in the Pink Room, figuring somebody might have used a secret entrance to get into it. With Thomas's help, I flipped over the bed and pulled out the couch and the dresser. Nothing but dust and wood floors and ragged bits of rug that I also picked up and tossed across the room in case they hid anything. I poked at every brick in the fireplace, took down every picture frame, whether it still held a painting or not. I knocked on the walls.

"Hold on. Stay here." And I ran out of the room and toward the third-floor stairs. Thomas followed right on my heels. I didn't stop until I had skidded into the tower room, where we'd left the crowbar when we'd pried open the door to the widow's walk. I hefted it like a baseball bat.

"What for?" asked Thomas, backing away from me.

"Watch me." And then I ran back down to the Pink Room and started waling on the walls with the crowbar. If I couldn't find a secret entrance, I'd make my own. If there was anything hidden behind the walls—a tunnel, a mechanism, anything—I'd find it.

Thomas stood in the middle of the room as I sweated and grunted and gradually broke through the interior wall. Nothing but Thomas's bedroom.

I did the same in every other bedroom on both the second and third floors. In the game room, it was a slaughterhouse. Thomas eventually joined in on the destruction. We toppled and ripped and broke those beasts. I pushed the foosball table over and threw myself at the pool table, feeling it skid across the floor, gouging the wood beneath it. I pulled down the massive dartboard, which snapped a pair of horns from a nearby antelope as it crashed to the ground.

Nothing.

We demolished the first floor in much the same way.

In the cellar, we hit every stone in the wall, in the cistern, the sharp ting of crowbar on rock hurting my back teeth and leaving bright scratch lines across the rocks. We moved the monsters around or pushed them over, breaking a few necks and arms in the process when they hit the hard-packed dirt floor.

Throughout my rampage, Thomas was sincere in his search efforts—even if he wasn't as violent—as if finding the person behind the ghosts in this house was vital to our friendship. Maybe it was. I don't know. This made it even more frustrating when we didn't find a single thing out of the ordinary in the entire house. Not a hidden closet, not a piece of wire, not a projector in a vent, not even anything inexplicable. The Split-Faced Woman, the Victoria's Secret Ghost, Vagina-Head, Monica Wynder, whatever I would eventually call her in my book, she stayed away from us. Not one ominous sound reverberated throughout the old house except our own knocking and dragging and stomping and breaking. Whatever we did was better than any exorcism could have hoped to achieve. Anger, man. It motivates, it destroys . . . and goddamn, does it tire you out.

That plus a hangover finally caught up with me.

We ended up in Thomas's room at the end, with its anthropomorphic burnt section of wall and its new window between his room and mine. I threw myself on the bed without asking his permission.

"Are you okay, man?" he asked, standing in the middle of the room. He had been treating me like fragile cargo throughout the entire search of the house.

"Yeah. I mean, no. I mean, that was just . . . I'd rather have found a severed head or a dead dog or anything else on the bed than what we saw. Stupid, huh. Dolls. And I don't even have anybody to get angry at yet."

"Not stupid, man. I think your reaction is . . . appropriate." Thomas was being careful with his words. Afraid of pushing me in any direction. I almost felt for the guy.

"I think the worst part is that somebody knows about what happened that night beyond us. Somebody who doesn't deserve to have that information." Thomas stayed silent. "And it's humiliating. I hate it."

"Three more nights to go, man. Then things start going great."

"Yeah, I hope so." I leaned on an elbow and shined my light at him. "How do I write about this in the book?"

Thomas's eyes strayed to the holes in the wall and the plaster and wood covering the floor. "I say lie. Do whatever you need to do to keep the emotional heft of the story. But lie. Or tell the truth and tell everyone it was a lie. That's probably the best way to hide it. Lie either way, though."

"Yeah. Lie. Right. I have no idea what could stand in for this subplot in the story. No idea." I pushed myself up from his bed and stood up. "You know what's funny?"

"Nothing?" he answered.

"No gravestones in the walls."

"What?"

"A. L. Rotterdam was supposed to have lined one of his foyer walls with gravestones. It's in the original plans and was well documented by witnesses across the centuries. I figured it had been covered up over the years."

"That wall is Swiss cheese now."

"Yeah, and, like I said, no gravestones. This whole house is bullshit. I think I'm going to bed."

"Do you need help flipping it back over?"

"No, I got it."

I stumbled to my bedroom in the dark, righted the bed with some difficulty, and tumbled into it. I was drained. I needed to sleep. Maybe straight through the next three nights. That'd be a surprising way for the book to end.

I hung over the edge of the bed and grabbed a doll out of the dresser drawer. She was clothed in an ancient brown dress and her hair was done up in two buns, one on either side of her head, like

Princess Leia. I tucked it in close to my body, unzipped my pants and then jerked off on it. When I was done, I threw it on the floor before rolling over and almost immediately falling asleep.

I didn't even turn off the trail cam or care that there was a gaping hole in the wall between me and Thomas.

Three more nights to go.

Night
Eleven

Chapter 27

Something was definitely wrong with my eyes. I awoke like they were on fire, like the full heat of the noon sun was on them. But when I opened them, I stared only into cool, inscrutable blackness. I pulled the flashlight from under my pillow and turned it on. As the beam played across the room, the pink walls seemed almost vivid. The house had gone from a black-and-white Universal Studios movie to a Technicolor Hammer film.

It was true in every room. As I wandered down the Hall of Death, rubbing at my eyes, I peeked inside a few. The Blue Room was very blue. The Green Room was very green. They still looked old and dusty and bedraggled, but it was as if somebody had turned up the saturation. It seemed a strange thing to happen in a haunted house. In stories, rooms got so hot the floor varnish bubbled or so cold the walls frosted. But ghosts tweaking the color palate? That was weird. Actually, the natural explanation was more ominous. Maybe I needed an MRI to make sure I didn't have a tumor pressing my optic nerve or something. I'd have to ask Thomas if he was seeing the same thing. And then go right to the doctor after three more nights.

Three more nights.

More troubling to me than the color of the walls, though, were all the holes that I had bashed in them. I had done far more damage to Rotter House than I remembered. The place looked like somebody had been playing dodgeball with grenades.

I can't say I was in a rage last night. I mean, I was mad, for sure. Those dolls—those stupid, stupid dolls—had parodied my greatest humiliation, violated my private shame. But it wasn't blind anger; it was justified anger. The sort that I knew would feel even more justified when I found the secret passages or hidden machinery that whoever put those dolls on my bed was using to make the house seem haunted. I was in the right, so the damage was right.

But, since we hadn't found so much as a peephole in a bathroom, it was wanton destruction. It seems I had put a foot or a crowbar through almost every wall in the house, pried up floorboards, and pulled down every mirror and picture that had beaten the odds and still clung to those decaying walls. No vent went unpopped and no piece of furniture avoided being overturned or shoved across the room, clean streaks in the dust trailing each leg as if they moved by themselves like those mysterious sailing stones in Death Valley. But that mystery had been solved a few years back through hypothesis, observation, and testing. Unlike ghosts.

Garza would be furious. Worse, Garza was wealthy, so that meant she was capable of serious legal retribution. Rich and raging are not qualities I want in an enemy. I was fucked. To the point that a hit book wouldn't help me one bit.

I went down to the kitchen to grab something to eat, ignoring both the damage and the trail cams I passed. The house seemed more still and empty than usual. In my imagination, that was because Rotter House was afraid of me, afraid I'd poke more holes into it, afraid that I'd rip it down to the ground, piece by piece, until the ghosts had not so much as a frame to haunt. I looked down at the healing wound on my hand. Rotter House might have taken first blood, but I got my revenge last night.

But the stillness and the emptiness really only meant that Thomas hadn't gotten up yet.

I drank some water from a plastic bottle and then nibbled on peanut butter crackers as I walked through the rooms, imagining myself as a bored ghost looking for a living person to liven up my afterlife. Three more nights. The night after tomorrow would be the last night of the project, my last night in Rotter House. Thirteen straight nights in a haunted house. Was I going to miss this place? This experience? The place where I might have had my first experience with a ghost? The one that eventually led me to believe in alien abductions? And then Bigfoot, Hollow Earth theory, and the teachings of Joseph Smith? Or would this be the place where I saw through the ruse and unmasked the bad guy, firmly cementing myself in the role of skeptic, a skeptic with thirteen straight nights of proof, sitting brazenly on the bestsellers table at airport bookstores around the country.

Or would I go my whole life wondering what the hell happened during my stay at Rotter House.

If it weren't for the unsolved mystery of my experience, I think I'd be completely ready to go. No. I was definitely ready to go. Some day in the future, after the book was out, maybe I'd look back on Rotter House as my favorite thing on the planet. The thing that had saved my career, my marriage, my closest friendship. Maybe I'd come back once a year to visit the haunted house, donate enough to its historical fund to give it a fresh mow and hedge trim, replenish all the autographed copies of the book in its gift shop. Maybe one day I'd miss the place, but that one day would be far in the future—if Garza didn't raze it now.

And then there were those dolls. The entire experience was tainted because of them. After this was over, part of me didn't ever want to think about Rotter House again because I'd have to think about those dolls and my humiliation. But I still had to write the book, had to relive Rotter House all over again.

I couldn't wait to talk to Elsa, though. Couldn't wait to let her know that things were patched up with Thomas. That would make her happy. She and I didn't talk about him or Yvette or that night anymore. A couple of times we got drunk enough to fight about it or some other argument would segue into that one, like it was waiting in the corner to be tagged in. But the next morning, appalled, I would apologize, and she would apologize. And I'd viciously renew my claim to her body, and then we'd move on, the thing freshly—but shallowly—buried, waiting to break through the surface again at the slightest provocation.

Where was Thomas? I looked at my watch and saw that it was almost 11 p.m. He should be up by now. Destruction is hard work and takes some time to sleep off, but I couldn't have him missing the home stretch of this project.

Really, though, I needed somebody to talk to.

I went back upstairs. The Hall of Death had suffered its own kind of death. The paper signs littered the floor like a failed chapter in a manuscript, only a couple hanging onto the moldy wood by their thin filaments of tape. A mirror lay facedown on the floor about halfway down, small slivers of shimmering glass spread around it like a bloodstain. The walls were more gouged and scraped than punctured, although here and there a jagged hole interrupted the privacy of a bedroom. I stamped squarely on the mirror and continued to Thomas's door. I knocked lightly on it. In doing so, I had the uneasy feeling that one of the other doors in the Hall of Death would open, freeing something to step out into the hallway. I stared down the dark row of doors for a few seconds until I shook the feeling off and knocked again, louder. "Thomas!" I called through the wood.

No response.

I stuck my ear against the door but didn't hear anything inside. I started to put my hand on the door to test if it was locked when I remembered that our rooms were adjoining now. I headed into the Pink Room and right to the large hole in the wall. I gazed through like it was a porthole in a submarine, my flashlight barely piercing the inky ocean blackness.

The bed was empty.

Thomas wasn't there, just that stain on the wall, even darker against the almost glowing white walls of the room.

I sat down heavily on my bed. Where was he? Was he playing another trick on me, like with the sheet last night? No. Not after what happened. Not after the dolls and the destruction. He wouldn't do that.

I listened for the sound of pool balls knocking erratically upstairs. Nothing. Still, I ran upstairs to the game room. Nothing but dead animals strewn in pieces across the floor. I ascended the steps to check the tower. Empty. Outside, the fog was the thinnest it had been so far, like the town was leaking atmosphere. Or maybe like it wasn't trying to hide anything anymore.

Unlike Rotter House, which was trying to hide my best friend.

If he wasn't up here or in his bedroom or downstairs, that left one of the other bedrooms or the cellar. I dropped to the floor, my back against the rhinoceros. I hadn't been able to tip it over last night, even with Thomas's help, but I'd wounded it pretty bad in its exposed flank.

As I sat there, I decided that I wasn't going to search this house again. I had searched it too many times. I was tired of searching.

Had Thomas fled from the house in terror? Did he finally meet Mr. Crispy? Did he run from Monica Wynder?

And then a horrible thought struck me.

Was he afraid of me? Had he been that disturbed by my violence last night? I shined my flashlight around the room, taking in the devastation. I was responsible for that—and all because of a couple of dolls—a trio of dolls. If that could set me off, maybe I hadn't come to terms with what had happened a year ago. Maybe Thomas realized that. Maybe he figured his best move was to put some distance between us for the time being.

I could see that answer. Sure, I'd told him things were okay between us, but he couldn't be so sure about that. It had only been one night, and I had turned on him so fast after seeing what was on my bed. I don't know if I'd trust me either.

I heaved myself off the floor and waded through decapitated horns, fragments of furry hide, glass eyeballs, and severed hooves until I exited the game room and headed down to the second floor.

What was I to do now? As I walked down the Hall of Death, I ripped a piece of paper off a door—FAMILICIDE ROOM—and let it drop to the ground. Why wouldn't Thomas have left me a note? He had stayed so long, despite all of his instincts telling him that he shouldn't, that we shouldn't. He'd overcome that. Overcame it every night. He wouldn't have left me behind. Not without telling me first.

I was halfway down the stairs to the first floor when an ugly thought darkened my brain. I felt it travel down my neck and shoulders and into my chest. I sat down hard on the steps.

Humiliate me and run away. Had this been his plan all along?

I shined my flashlight on the line of locks on the front door while I tried to reconstruct events in my mind. Over the past year, he had never tried to contact me. Not once. I was the one to finally call him. Maybe he would never have tried to reach me otherwise. Maybe he was done with me, didn't need me in his life anymore. That night had changed things for him. He was satisfied with us going separate ways.

And then I had reached out to him.

Maybe that worried him. Maybe he was afraid that I was never going to get over it. That if he didn't quash it and quash it hard, I might try again. So he came to Rotter House. And he waited for the opportunity. Waited for me to bring up that night. He wasn't going to. He was never going to. And then, once I did, once I was at my most vulnerable, he arranged the dolls on my bed. One last "fuck you" before going back to his life.

I moved the circular beam of the flashlight from the locks on the door to the window beside it that had given me my first obscured look into the house and then to the spot on the floor where I'd had my panic attack and then to the back of the antique couch where I had spent my first night here.

And that's when I remembered the message from the Ouija board.

The dolls, the destruction, Thomas disappearing. It had all pushed the Ouija board out of my mind: one night. That was the message. Had that been Thomas's note that I was looking for? Did he manipulate the planchette? Was he warning me? The message came before the dolls, before I'd taken out my frustration and anger and terror on Rotter House. Was that simple phrase telling me that we had one more night together and then he would be gone and it would all be over between us?

And did that mean the entire haunting was him? Was he setting me up? Was that a "fuck you *and* fuck your career"? Or was that his last gift to me? Sorry I screwed your wife. I don't want to see either one of you again. But here's one last gift: your book will be interesting now.

Did that story make sense? Was it ridiculous? I couldn't even tell anymore.

Where was Thomas? Where did he go? The last thing I needed in this house was one more mystery.

I stood up on the stairs and tried to decide what to do, where to go. I shined my light around the foyer. The beam caught my box of research sitting on the steel and glass coffee table in the drawing room. That decided it for me.

I crossed the foyer and sat down on the couch. I reached into the box and pulled out one of my haunted house books. I read it for a while before switching over to my research on Rotter House. And then I read another haunted house story. I played with the prosthetic arm. I wrote in my journal—mostly listing all of the questions I had been asking myself all night. I ate. I drank. And I drank. And I drank. I didn't look for Thomas anymore, or a ghost, or a hoaxer. I didn't check on the trail cams.

Eventually, I drifted to sleep, my final thought a hope that Thomas would blast through the front door any second and shout "boo!"

Night
Twelve

Chapter 28

I awoke to a feeling like my chest had been scooped out. The house. The project. The dolls. Thomas. It had all eaten away at me in my sleep. It felt like my head had been scooped out, too, but that was because of the booze.

But, then, the sound that had actually woken me repeated itself. It had come from the stairs. A moaning noise. I waited a few seconds to see if it would be followed by the sound of chains rattling, and when it wasn't, I gingerly peeked my aching head around the side of the couch.

The foyer was completely dark. I couldn't see anything. But one more moan had me jumping over the back of the couch with my flashlight flicked on and trained on the direction of the sound—a seated figure on the stairs, its head in its hands.

"Thomas!"

He looked startled and squinted in the beam of light that I was assaulting him with. "What the hell, man," he said. I lowered the beam but kept it trained on him, terrified, I guess, that he'd disappear again. "I thought you were still asleep upstairs," he said.

"Where have you been?" I shouted the question as every theory I put together from last night crashed in on me.

"Asleep. We sleep during the day here, stay up all night. Like the Slaughter song." He looked confused.

"No, you haven't." It was my turn to be confused. "You've been gone for . . . "—I checked my watch—"about twenty-four hours."

"No, I haven't."

"How many more nights are left in our stay here?"

Thomas paused. "Three," he finally said.

"No. Two. Look." I showed him the date on my watch. He tilted his head and he pursed his lips.

"That doesn't tell me anything. I don't know even know what day it was yesterday or the day before that. I'm on Rotter House time."

"There are two more nights left. I spent last night looking all over for you, man, and you were gone. Disappeared. Not in your room. Not in the game room. Not down here. Nowhere."

"You must have been dreaming."

I didn't know what to say. I hadn't been dreaming. Thomas had disappeared. I thought hard. "This is a haunted house trope," I said.

"What do you mean?"

"Missing time. Limbos. Disappearances. Is that really what's happening here?"

"Too bad we weren't marking days with lines of chalk on the walls, like we were in prison," said Thomas, wiping his hand down his face. "I still think you were dreaming hard last night."

I dragged my flashlight beam around the foyer, looking at the house in a whole different way. It would be hard, if not impossible, for somebody to pull off a stunt like that—unless Thomas was in on it, I guess. My light brightened the box in the drawing room. "Wait. I can prove what night it is. Follow me."

I heard Thomas heave himself off the stairs, and I led him into the drawing room. I took him right to the box and pulled out my mint-green journal. I handed it over, and after a couple of confused seconds where I realized he didn't have his flashlight on him, I opened it up myself and trained my light on the last entry, which was headed "Night Eleven" and had my notes from the previous night.

He stared down at the page for about a minute, and I realized too late that it had *all* my notes from the previous night.

"You thought all that about me?" asked Thomas.

"I didn't know what to think, man. You were gone."

"You got confused."

I started flipping violently through the book. "Night Ten, Night Nine, Night Eight . . ." I kept going all the way to Night Two, showing him exactly when he had entered the house.

Thomas scratched his head. "This isn't much proof." Then he seemed to grow agitated. I risked shining the flashlight at the side of his face and scrutinized him closely. He looked like absolute death. Maybe this experiment had worn on him much more than me. Maybe he wasn't used to the drinking we'd done or the crappy food I'd brought. Maybe he just needed sex in his life. No, I shouldn't joke about that, not even to myself, not even if I did take satisfaction in that turn of events. It made things better for me somehow.

"Is this experiment over?" he asked. "I'm ready to go home."

"Almost to the finish line."

"I don't know if I can make it." He leaned his arms on the back of the couch and looked around. "I didn't think this place could look more like an abandoned house than it did when I first arrived."

I shined the light around the room and into the foyer. "Garcia is going to sue and/or kill me, probably both."

"Garcia?

"The owner."

"I thought you said her name was Garza."

I paused. I did mean Garza. "Yeah, Garza. That's her name. I can't even keep the characters in my own story straight."

"As long as you get mine right." Thomas walked past me, and I followed him into the kitchen, passing Rotterdam's arm, where it lay nestled among the papers of my research box on top of the coffee table. The arm hadn't really added to the story. I'm not sure what I was expecting from it, honestly, other than the intrinsic coolness of an antique prosthetic sex aid. Might act as inspiration for some great chapter heading art, though, or maybe some bookmark giveaways.

In the kitchen, I'd apparently ripped off most of the cabinet doors as well as the dumbwaiter door. Thomas walked over to the cabinet where the food was stashed and wrinkled his nose at what he found in there. "Man, you took this place apart."

"Why didn't you stop me?" I asked.

"Wasn't my place. In both senses of the phrase. But certainly not considering the situation. Not considering what set it off."

I guess that was true. "So what am I going to do about this? Short of hiring every handyman in town . . ."

"I don't know. I need to sit down. It feels like I have a hangover. I'm very tired, very achy."

At the mention of achy, I realized my own head was still throbbing from the booze. And at the thought of booze, I got a craving for a sot salad: olives, maraschino cherries, and cocktail onions. Not eaten all together. That would be gross. But eaten in turn from their jars in a drunken haze while standing in the coolness of an open refrigerator. I only had olives and no refrigerator, so I picked up a jar of them from the cabinet, as well as the electronic lantern off the counter, and followed Thomas to the dining room, where we pulled out chairs across from each other. As I sat down, I noted again how well-made they were, sturdy and comfortable. But still not worth making a multimillionaire out of their maker, even if he did make them with one arm tied behind his back.

I set the lantern and the jar on the table in front of me, turning on the one and opening the other. It was a nice setting. We probably should have done the Ouija board here. Thomas put his head in his hands and looked down into the shiny dark wood of the table.

"Want some olives?" I asked.

"Pass." He rubbed his head like he had a headache and then, without looking up, said, "Why don't we tell Garza that you went a little mad, that you were driven to it by the ghosts, *her* ghosts, in fact. She does bear some culpability for you going Jack Torrance on this place."

"Seems like a bad excuse," I said. "Temporary insanity? Is that even a thing anymore?"

"Makes your ghost story more interesting, though, right? And she definitely wants your ghost story to be interesting. Hell, her getting mad in interviews about it when the book comes out would be great press for you both. And, honestly, this damage is probably blue on black for the damage she was already replacing. I don't think you hit a board that wasn't rotten. You probably saved her money on demolition." He stopped and looked at the doorway where I first saw the Split-Faced Woman. "And then there's the bigger issue: we didn't find a damn thing despite you almost making the house see-through."

"I know," I said, downing two salty, cheese-stuffed olives at one time and then wiping my oily fingers on my pants leg. "It would totally have been better if we had found something. All this," I said, motioning to a particularly ugly hole in the wall leading to the kitchen, "would have been self-defense."

"Right, right. But that's not what I mean." He stopped to make sure I was looking him in the eyes. "We didn't find a single piece of evidence for asshole pranksters in this house. That means what we've experienced over the past few nights is paranormal. Especially if what you're saying is true about me vanishing into oblivion for a night."

I shrugged. "That . . . is an interesting angle. I could totally write it that way. Put the burden of belief on the reader. Show them that not only did stuff happen that I couldn't explain, I wrecked the house, and possibly my life, trying to explain them. Allows me to have a picnic on the high ground of the argument."

"I'm not talking about your book."

"I know. I could also use it to convince Garza to be okay with the damage if we treat my actions as proof of her investment being haunted." I laughed. "*The Haunted Investment*."

Thomas jumped up from his Rotterdam chair, which didn't even so much as rock back in response. Well-balanced and solid, that Rotterdam craftsmanship. "Who cares about that, man!" Thomas was yelling at me. "Ghosts. You heard ghosts. You saw a ghost. You walked through a ghost. I . . . . disappeared . . . for an entire night. This is a life-changing experience. Two decades of arguments between us silenced. Nothing you believed is as it seems. Nothing is the same from here on. You've seen ghosts. You've. Seen. Ghosts. Screw Garza and her busted up house." Thomas dropped heavily back into the chair.

I looked up at him, at how earnest he was, how frustrated he was. But I couldn't let it go. "Is it a life-changing experience? Really?"

"Of course it is, you jerk."

"I don't know. I mean, I know lots of paranormal believers. Their lives aren't that much different from mine."

"You're an asshole. I'm not having this argument if you're going to be a wall. If you don't believe in the paranormal after what you've seen and what you failed to uncover last night . . . or two nights ago . . . or whatever, then I'm not wasting breath on you." Thomas jumped from his chair again and stomped off into the foyer.

"Give me time to believe?" I said, too quietly for him to hear. I let him go, though. He'd been grumpy since I found him on the stairs. And I couldn't give him the satisfaction that I might be close to switching sides—not after all these years of arguments. I legit-imately had some weird experiences in this house. And, though I had tried with both hands and a crowbar, I could find no evidence that someone was running a ruse on me.

Sitting there popping olives in my mouth at an antique dining room table, I started to feel guilty. I shouldn't rile Thomas up. He'd come out to help me. He *had* helped me.

It's just that going from Scully to Mulder is really damn hard, it turns out.

And then I got angry.

What right did he have to berate me about fucking ghosts, of all things? Screw him. For all I know, I was right about him being the prankster in the house. Actually, now that I really thought about it, that idea made tons of sense. He would have to be in on the disappearing act. And no wonder I couldn't find the puppeteer at the top of the strings. He was right beside me the whole time. That gave him all the advantage to hide evidence and distract me from it.

Most importantly, he was the only one of four people on this planet who knew what those dolls on my bed meant.

I jumped from the table, upsetting the jar of olives, which seeped thick olive juice all over the expensive antique, and tore into the foyer, my flashlight beam a broad circle ahead, searching for a point on which to focus my anger.

I found Thomas sitting at the base of the stairs in total dark-ness. He looked confused, uncertain, like I must have been last night when I sat in the exact same spot.

"You bastard. It's you, right? You're haunting this place?" I demanded.

"What the fuck are you talking about?"

"You're the one setting up the noises and the apparitions . . . and the dolls. Maybe you're working with somebody, but it's definitely you. Why? To trick me into believing in ghosts? To torment me about that night? Why are you even here?" I wanted to hit him with my flashlight across the bridge of his nose.

He looked at me. His eyes were watery. He looked sick. "I want things to go back to normal," he whimpered. "The way they used to be. That's why I'm here." He stopped and stood up, drawing to his full height and throwing back his shoulders. "But I am not the one haunting this house. You need to believe in ghosts, man. Stop fighting it."

I wanted to look anywhere but at Thomas. I threw my flashlight beam into the foyer behind him, at the holes I'd punched in the walls, at the debris that covered the floor, where there weren't gaps from the boards that I had pried up. A large, ornate mirror with a crack in it leaned against the wall below the spot where it had hung for so many years. Thomas took another step toward me, and I instinctively moved away from him, my back coming up abruptly against the wall beside the front door. My elbow hit something. The ratty chandelier that had, for the past twelve nights, been hanging despondently over the dark foyer, its incandescent bulbs mere glass ornaments, suddenly flared into bright, electric life.

Chapter 29

"Holy hell," shouted Thomas, shielding is eyes with the back of his hand. "I thought you said the electricity wasn't working in this place. What's going on?"

"I don't know, man. I don't know." The light from the chandelier hurt my eyes. Spots of color swam across my vision.

"Did you even try the lights when you first got here?"

I didn't answer his second question. I suddenly didn't care about the light. Instead, I was staring at what I saw around us.

The damage to the walls and the floor looked worse in the light. Much worse.

But it was the dolls I was staring at.

There were dolls everywhere in the foyer—on the floor and on the console table and on the deacons bench and the hall tree, all naked and arranged in obscene triads. Some were covered in dust and debris, others were broken into pieces. Around them, among the splintered studs and chunks of horsehair plaster, were liquor bottles of clear glass and pill bottles of orange plastic, most of them empty.

I hit the light switch again like I was punching another hole in the wall and everything disappeared into darkness, struck out of existence. "I don't want people to know we're here," I said. "I don't want them to come poking around to see why the lights are on at the old, abandoned haunted house. I can't have them interrupting the project." That was right, wasn't it? But I didn't know about the lights, did I? That's why I didn't bring any horror movies to watch. Did Garza lie to me? Things were getting confusing. My head was starting to hurt, one of those pressure headaches like I was fathoms below again, like the house was a wrecked ship at the bottom of the ocean.

"Why did you lie to me?" asked Thomas. "I'm okay with doing the project in the dark if that's the ambiance you need, but you shouldn't have lied to me."

"I didn't lie. I don't think I lied."

"Something ain't right with you, man."

"Not right with me? Not right with *me?*" Tears fled from my eyes and sped down my cheeks as I stared at where Thomas loomed in the darkness. "Why did you have to sleep with her? She's my wife! You were my friend!"

"We're back to this? Now? Man, we're not going to be able to put this behind us, are we? It's impossible." Thomas started pacing back and forth. "I told you, man, I don't remember that night. Yvette doesn't remember that night. Elsa doesn't remember that night. And don't forget you—you don't remember that night. I have to assume the worst because I was the one in the position to wrong you, but it doesn't mean that the worst happened. We. Don't. Know. None of us do."

"I think you do. And I think Elsa does. Why else would you two have gotten together again."

Thomas stopped dead. I was tempted to turn the lights on again, to see his reaction, to have that moment flash-imprinted in my head so that I could always remember it. I settled on throwing my flashlight beam at his face. He hardly squinted. Just stared at me. Empty.

"What?"

"I know you've been sleeping together. It was because of that night, wasn't it?"

Thomas looked at me coolly. Finally, his shoulders sagged, and he dropped back onto the steps. He stared at the floor in front of him. "That's when it started. I mean, we always flirted, like you and Yvette did, but none of us meant anything by it. That's just what we did. It was safe. We were all friends. And then that night happened, just like I said it did. We all got too drunk, decided to go upstairs, and you passed out on the floor."

"And you three kept going. So you *do* remember it."

"Not all of it. It was foggy, weird. A drunken memory."

"What do you remember doing to my wife?"

"I'm not talking about that. Besides, at this point, I barely know. It was hazy the next day. It's hazier a year later."

"But it was enough to keep you thinking about her. When did it start with Elsa?"

"About two months later."

I screamed and grabbed my face, pulling at my cheeks, my lips, my hair like I wanted to dismantle myself. I stepped backwards and hit the wall again.

Thomas jumped up and walked over to me, extending a hand, but didn't say anything.

I moved away from him. "I didn't know it was going on for that long. I thought it had just started. I didn't know." I kept clawing at my face. I didn't know. I didn't know. How do I fix this?

"We've fallen in love."

"I fucking hate you."

That's when I heard a board creak above me, and my head twisted automatically to look upstairs. Another creak followed. And then another. Slowly and slightly, as if someone were trying not to make any noise but was still walking across the floor. I hadn't heard a board creak since, when? Since Thomas first got here. Was that right? Since the second night at Rotter House?

I turned back to look at Thomas, "Do you hear that?"

But Thomas wasn't there.

I flashed my light around the dark foyer. "Thomas? Thomas, where are you?" He was nowhere to be seen. Again. I hadn't heard him run off, but he must have, into one of the rooms off the foyer, maybe, to another one of the outside doors on this floor. He was running away. Back to Elsa. But for some reason, I didn't try to chase him. I stood there in the dark. Like the nothingness around me erased what I had just learned, what had just happened, the whole past year. Gone forever into the depths of Rotter House.

And then a light flickered on the landing. An old hanging lamp in the corner with a yellow and red glass shade and a trailing black chain. It illuminated the landing like a stage in its flickering, sickly light. The colors on the walls stood out brightly, almost too radiant to look at. My eyes were starting to hurt again, the same burning sensation from when I had awoken yesterday. Except this time, instead of staring into cool darkness, all I saw was blazing electric light and neon color. The place seemed too alive, those garish colors pulsed in gaudy hues. Maybe I did have brain cancer. The thought made me feel better.

And then I saw Thomas standing on the landing, his hands on the railing, like when I'd gotten him to act out the scene from *Dawn of the Dead*. One flicker, and he wasn't there. Another flicker and he was. He looked different. Less there or something. I don't know how he had gotten up the steps without me noticing, but he was there, standing and looking down at me, silently, disgusted by me. Disappointed in me.

"Does the room look weird to you?" I asked him. "Is it too bright? Too colorful? Do I have cancer?"

He didn't answer. He just kept staring at me.

Another creaking board. And this time Thomas took his eyes off me and looked in its direction, somewhere around the corner in the Hall of Death.

"What is it?" I hissed up at him. He ignored me, staring uncertainly in the direction of the sound. "Do you see anything?"

And then came another sound. A familiar sound.

The crack. Loud, so loud. I covered my ears and half crouched. It came from the direction of the Hall of Death. It hit again and again and again and again. The sound didn't move this time, just kept exploding from the same point in the house. I looked up at Thomas. He wasn't covering his ears. But his eyes grew wide, and he jumped at each blow, looking around the landing in panic.

"Down here, man! Thomas! Down here!" He didn't listen to me. Instead, he kept running around the landing, looking back at the sound like it was keeping him in place and shouting, "Stop! Stop! Stop! Stop!"

Then the cracking ended. Thomas backed up until he was almost above the stairwell, and then he ran forward, toward where the sound had been.

He stopped. He screamed. His body started jerking as if he were being beaten. I tried to yell for him, tried to move toward the stairs, but it was almost like my first night in Rotter House. I couldn't get up those stairs. I was wedged in the darkness, unable to help him.

Bright red wounds burst open on his chest and arms. Blood flew from the glistening rents in grotesque trails, across the landing, the bannister, down the stairs. A warm, wet line splattered across my face.

And then his right arm started to shake rapidly, like it had tremors. Slowly it pulled down from his body in a ragged, bloody spray. It dropped to the floor.

Thomas collapsed to his knees as if his skeleton had been ripped through his new wounds. I saw the side of his neck depress strangely and then split open, wider and wider, his body shuddering as his head canted more and more. His head separated from his neck like his body had given birth to it. It hit the floor and rolled across the landing, coming to rest against the bannister. Two balusters framed his eyes. They were open, staring down at me, disgusted by me. Disappointed in me.

I was crying, tears streaking through the blood on my face. "Thomas!" I yelled.

I heard another scream. A woman's this time.

She came running in from the Hall of Death, her teal robe with the red roses on it flying behind her like a cape, exposing matching lingerie and beautifully strong lengths of perfect leg and a stomach that made me want to cum on it. It was Monica Wynder. The Victoria's Secret Ghost. Vagina Head. The Split-Faced Woman. Except that she wasn't split-faced. Her face was whole and human and beautiful. And it wasn't Monica Wynder. It was Elsa, my Elsa, in lingerie that I had never seen before. That I didn't buy her. That she hadn't bought for me.

She ran toward Thomas's devastated body but was brought to a terrible stop, her face splitting open messily, and her body stumbling backward from the invisible blow until she hit the wall and dropped to the floor, instantly lifeless and unrecognizable, killed by the same phantom weapon that had dismembered Thomas, that had broken through the door that wasn't there with loud, violent blows, a phantom weapon that, twelve nights ago had been a very real survival hatchet—my hatchet. The one I'd bought to cut firewood and protect myself from racoons and a winged demon in New Jersey. It was black and vicious-looking, and when Elsa first saw me holding it after I bought it, she laughed and called me manly.

Its edge was the last thing she saw, right after I caught her sleeping with Thomas in my bedroom.

This time I screamed. Loud. Screamed at the betrayal. At Thomas. At Elsa. At my life. At the irrevocableness of it all. At the horror, the loss.

The bright colors of the house were still searing my eyes, and as I looked up at the two dead bodies on the landing, the colors started pulsing in lurid red and blue.

And then a new scream. Not a male scream, not a female scream, not my own scream. An inhuman scream, high and piercing.

And then the strangest thing: the most normal voice. A woman's voice.

"We're coming in. Stand back from the door."

Chapter 30

I turned around and looked at the front door, saw the hole in the side pane. I remembered that I had made that hole. With the rock I had found under the rhododendron bush. I looked at the wound on my hand in the flashing blue and red, a wound twelve nights healed from when I had ripped it on the glass reaching through the smashed pane to unlock the door and break into this place. The thick bar of blood streaking down the pane below it was dry and dark now, the beginning of a macabre stained-glass installation.

I had enough time to take a few steps backward, deeper into the foyer, when I heard a loud boom. The door burst open.

People dressed in dark clothing poured through like they were from a nightmare.

"There he is!" Yelled one of them.

Guns were aimed at me, lots of them, one from each officer crowding into the foyer. They said a few more things, all the phrases you hear in movies. I felt like I was watching a movie. It had been so long since I'd watched a movie. I stood there numbly, looking at them, and then looking up at the crumpled teal and red form that was my wife, at the pieces of Thomas. And his eyes. His eyes.

That normal voice again. Comforting, almost.

"Drop what's in your hands, sir. Raise them above your head. Do it now."

I dropped the flashlight to the floor, where it landed with a sharp thud on the old rug. I raised my hands. They all rushed at me.

I was forced to the floor. I crumpled willingly. It felt good. The old rug beneath my cheek. The smell of the cops' boot leather. The men and women behind me roughly moving my limbs and talking to me and each other according to procedure.

"You had a good time here," I heard one of the officers say, surveying the damage.

"This house is haunted," I mumbled into the floor. "Do you see them up there? The ghosts? You see them, right? On the floor. That's my wife and my best friend. They're dead." I saw one of the cops glance up at the landing before returning her gaze to me.

"Sir, you are under arrest for the murder of Thomas Ruth and Elsa Allsey." She pulled my hands into the small of my back and wrapped them in a plastic band with a sharp tug. She heaved me to my feet with the help of another officer.

A passing policeman addressed the one behind me, "Look out. He's packing." I looked down at the swelling in my jeans and then looked away.

All the lights in the house were on, transforming Rotter House into a stranger's house for me. I could see cops moving through all the rooms. I looked up and saw two of them walking across the landing, stepping across the bodies as if they weren't there. They didn't even look at the floor. The cops behind me started pushing me to the front of the foyer.

"No, no, no. What are you doing?" I pleaded, the open door growing closer. "I can't leave! I need to stay here one more night. My book won't work unless I stay for thirteen nights." I struggled to get away from the front door. "Elsa won't let me write anymore if this book doesn't do well. It's my last chance. The book is my last chance."

"Right now I need you to calm down so that I can take you out to the car," said the officer.

"Sir," one yelled down from the landing, his boot an inch behind Thomas's severed head. There are cameras up here, too."

"For the book," I yelled. "For the book. Be careful with that footage. It proves everything. Ghosts, Bigfoot, UFOs."

"Man, this guy reeks," said one of the officers near me.

"I don't think he's changed his clothes in two weeks," said the woman driving me from behind by my bound hands. I looked down and saw that my shirt was covered in old, dark blood. Too much to have come from a gash in my thumb.

As the cops pushed me forward, we all stumbled through the empty bottles of booze and drugs on the floor, interrupting toy threesomes every few steps.

"Sir, you're going to want to come in here." That was a voice from the drawing room.

As they jostled me toward the front door, I stole a look into the drawing room, which was bright with light from the brass sconces on the walls. I saw my research box sitting on the glass table, three police officers gathered around it.

"Be careful with that!" I screamed. "My research, that's my research! It took me six months to gather all of that together. It's critical for my book!"

Two of the men looked up at me, as a third, green rubber gloves freshly flicked onto his wrists, reached in to retrieve something.

He pulled out a severed arm. Even through the decomposition, I could see it was the right arm of a black man.

"Here's that piece we were missing," one of the men said.

I was pushed through the front door of Rotter House. I shouldn't be walking through this doorway for one more night. This was unbearable. There's no way *Twelve Nights in Rotter House* will sell.

Outside, the place was livid with cop cars flashing their red and blue lights. Across the street, in the parking lot shared by the convenience store and the bowling alley, a crowd had formed, staring at the commotion, pointing at the chaos. No, pointing at me.

The whole street was busy. Cops were directing cars around the area. People had gathered on this side of the street as well. It was like a block party had erupted, and I had gotten too drunk, embarrassed myself, and had to be driven home.

They pushed me into the back seat of a car, and I laughed. The officer looked at me as if that was exactly what she had expected to hear from me.

"One night." I said. "I get it. One night changed everything." The officer started walking away. "I've been to the grave of the man who invented the Ouija board," I yelled after her. "There's a Ouija board inscribed on his headstone."

Beside me sat Thomas and on his far side Elsa. Both stared forward, ignoring me. I looked at them. "One night," I said again. They continued to ignore me. For a flash second, Elsa's face split open and Thomas's head dropped onto his lap, and then they were back to normal. I wished Elsa was sitting beside me instead of on the other side of Thomas.

I thought of the monster statues in the cellar. I thought of three more joining them, two mutilated ghosts and a madman with an ax.

Through the closed car window, I looked up at the haunted house, Rotter House, Rotterdam Mansion. The house still towered over me like that first night, but I could see more of it than a mere silhouette. The flashing lights illuminated it clearly. Everything was mostly there. But it wasn't quite as big, not as ornate. It seemed to have lost a story.

I closed my eyes and leaned my forehead against the smooth glass of the backseat passenger window and whispered, "I'm sorry."

Acknowledgments

This grisly tale was the work of my own perverse imagination. But to get these dark thoughts both into shape and into your hands, it took the support and consideration and hard work of a lot of people to whom I owe a large debt of gratitude.

My wife Lindsey, for everything she is and does. My oldest daughter Esme, because who knew a nine-year-old kid could be so supportive of her dad's writing, even when I had to repeatedly tell her that she wouldn't be allowed to read the book. Her five-year-old sister Hazel, for keeping to a minimum her attempts to sabotage this book for kicks by mashing the keyboard and leaning on Delete when I left my desk. My agent, Alex Slater, who never gave up on it despite a lot of good reasons to and without whom this book would be permanently trapped in the haunted house of my hard drive. Stephanie Beard, of Turner Publishing, who decided people should read this book, and the amazing team she assembled to make it happen—Heather Howell, Kathleen Timberlake, Lauren Langston Stewart, and M. S. Corley.

My pre-readers, Brandon Medley, Mary Davis, Brianna Catton, Kevin Lagowski, and my friend from the other side of the world Chris Everson, all members of the OTIS Club, who have supported me in ways far beyond this book.

John Rozum for focusing at my humble manuscript his deadly set of storytelling sensibilities that I've respected ever since reading *Xombi*.

Most important to the story in these pages is Christian Haunton, whose sharp ideas and counsel and attention absolutely improved key elements of the story and whose surname gave me endless enjoyment during his involvement in the project.

About the Author

J.W. Ocker is the Edgar Award-winning author of macabre travel-ogues, spooky kid's books, and horror novels. His books include *Poe-Land: The Hallowed Haunts of Edgar Allan Poe*; *A Season with the Witch: The Magic and Mayhem of Halloween in Salem, Massachusetts*; and *Death and Douglas*. Ocker is from Maryland but has lived in New Hampshire for more than a decade. Visit him at oddthingsiveseen.com.